MW01087889

WRIGHT WITH BENEFITS

WRIGHT WITH BENEFITS

K.A. LINDE

TAKE ME DUET

Take Me for Granted | Take Me with You

STAND ALONE

Following Me

Hold the Forevers

FANTASY ROMANCE

BLOOD TYPE SERIES

Blood Type | Blood Match | Blood Cure

ASCENSION SERIES

The Affiliate | The Bound | The Consort

The Society | The Domina

ROYAL HOUSES

House of Dragons | House of Shadows

ISBN-13: 978-1948427463

PART I

A NO GOOD, VERY BAD DAY

1

ANNIE

A brisk wind whipped around my bare legs, swirling the skirt of my black dress and flipping it upward, Marilyn Monroe–style. I shrieked, batting at the material in a desperate attempt to bring it back down to an acceptable length. The wind didn't seem to hear my string of curses because it just bit into me harder, making me regret forgoing tights.

"Oh my God," I snapped as I clutched the material in my hands.

The wind whistled in response. A cackle if I'd ever heard one.

I glared up at the stupid Lubbock wind. It wasn't enough that the temperatures were in the low thirties already at five thirty on this Friday afternoon right before my last semester of medical school started; the wind had to rub it in.

"Annie, why are you standing out here?" Cézanne asked. She wore a black jumpsuit that highlighted her dark brown skin with her box braids pulled up into a high ponytail. She somehow looked professional and like an imperious, avenging angel. "It's below freezing."

I prayed to the Lord for patience and grinned at my closest friend in my cohort. "The wind attacked me."

She eyed me skeptically. We'd known each other pre–med school, and she still sometimes looked at me like I'd sprung a second head.

I waved her off. "Whatever. I'm not having a good day."

Which was an understatement. My house had *flooded*! Like, straight flooded. My room was a wreck. I'd lost half of my closet, including *all* of my shoes. Like, every pair, except the impossibly high snakeskin heels that I'd scrounged out of a pile of donations I hadn't gotten rid of yet. My room was essentially awash until maintenance showed up. I'd be living on the couch for the foreseeable future.

If that hadn't been bad enough, I'd been nearly run off the road on the way here. Some dipshit had driven straight through a red light, and I'd had to swerve to avoid getting T-boned.

Today was officially over.

I stepped inside the rustic building the medical school had rented for the event, and Cézanne closed the door.

"Well, if you've been having a bad day, I hate to ask, but where's the wine?" Cézanne asked warily.

"What wine?"

"The...wine. You know, the case of commemorative wine for Professor Rodgers and the rest for the retirement party. The entire school is coming, and...there's no wine."

"What the hell? Who was in charge of that?"

Cézanne looked at me blankly.

"No," I told her.

"It has your name next to it."

I shook my head. "I swear I wasn't in charge of the wine."

She passed the list to me, and I saw where my name was scrawled unintelligibly. I groaned.

"Are you sure it was even called in? I didn't do it."

"I'm not sure who called it in, but I have the original order request."

"Let me see it."

I plucked it out of her hand and stared down at it. Phew! It was three thousand dollars' worth of wine. The commemorative case alone was a grand. Well, no wonder Cézanne was wondering where the hell all the wine was.

Unfortunately, it didn't say who had put the order in. But I knew for a fact that it wasn't me.

I took a deep breath and then released it. "How can I help?"

Cézanne grinned. "Can you please call the Wine Boutique and find out what happened?"

"Yeah, I can do that."

"Thank you. Thank you. I knew I could count on you to get shit done."

I sighed. What else could possibly make this day worse? Might as well try to get the wine, so we could all get fucked up today. Professor Rodgers was only retiring once.

Cézanne checked off a slot on her to-do list that rested on an actual clipboard. I loved Cézanne to death, but sometimes, her organizational skills were so extra. There was a reason she was top of our class and in charge of all of our events.

I stepped away from Cézanne to make my phone call. The Wine Boutique's number was on the top of the order, and I dialed it with another sigh. This was what I got for being dependable. The line rang and rang and rang. It felt like an eternity before the voicemail clicked over.

"Thank you for calling the Wine Boutique. Sorry we missed your call..."

I hung up and tried again. And again. And again.

No answer.

Their hours said that they were open until six. I had another thirty minutes. They should have answered their phone.

"Gah!" I growled, wanting to throw my useless phone across the room.

Of course no one was answering. It was just my day. I checked the address on the sheet again. I knew where this place was. It was only a five-minute drive downtown on a good day. Today was not a good day, but I had enough time to still make it.

"Cézanne!" She glanced over at me. "No one is answering. I'm going to head over there and find out what happened."

"You're a goddess, Annie. Truly."

"I still say that I wasn't in charge of this."

"Well, find out who was then, 'kay?"

"Yeah, yeah," I muttered as I headed back outside.

I braced myself against the cold and hustled back to my car. As soon as I shut myself back inside, I blasted the heat. The Spirit Ranch was a wedding venue on the north side of town that we'd gotten at an uber discount since it was the off-season. But Cézanne had somehow still made the space look gorgeous, even going as far as renting an outdoor tent, complete with heaters. But with the sun already going down, I couldn't imagine standing out there. Maybe with enough alcohol in me.

I winced.

Right...alcohol. That thing we didn't have.

With a groan, I peeled away from the building and headed toward downtown. The Wine Boutique was nestled in the heart of the city between an old city hall and a historic hotel, which had recently been renovated into high-end apartments. Downtown was finally—*finally*—beginning to blossom into the Lubbock local scene that everyone had always hoped for. It had a long way to go, but I could see where it was headed.

I parked out front, bracing myself for the cold, and rushed toward the front door. My hand settled on the gilded doorknob, and I yanked on the door. I groaned, feeling my shoulder give as I pulled too hard on a door that wouldn't budge.

"Fuck," I spat.

The hours on the front door said I had another fifteen minutes before they closed—because, of course, it had taken me longer to get here. I peered inside at the darkened interior. A few lights were still on, and a woman sat behind the counter, typing on the computer.

I banged on the front door. "Hello!"

The woman's head popped up in confusion. Then she

dashed across the room, unlocked the door, and threw it open. I nearly fell inside.

"Hey! Sorry about that. I didn't expect any other customers," the woman said. She wore a blue dress with sensible heels. Her brown hair was severely parted down the middle and pulled back into a bun. Her lips were painted a pretty pink, and her dark eyes were lightly lined.

"Not a problem."

"I'm the owner, Sophia. How can I help you?"

"Annie," I said, taking her outstretched hand and shaking it. "I'm actually here from the medical school. We're hosting a retirement party for one of our distinguished faculty up at the Spirit Ranch today. We ordered a few cases of wine from here, but it was never delivered."

I passed over the order form to Sophia, who looked even more surprised when she scanned it over.

"I have this order," she said, "but it's for next weekend."

"No, it's for today. We're all back in rotations next weekend."

"I don't even have to look it up. I know that I have it for next weekend."

Sophia immediately went to the computer. I followed her, standing before the desk. She quickly printed out a similar form and passed it to me.

I glanced down at it. It was nearly identical to the draft form I'd handed her, except that the date was filled in on the completed form and it was in fact for next weekend. What the hell?

"Oh God," I groaned as I looked at the signature.

Who the hell put Bryan Clifford in charge of this?

Bryan was our resident fuckup. He'd only gotten through the last three years of medical school because his mother was on the board and kept bailing him out. I prayed for anyone who had him as a doctor after we finished all of this. Lord, save me from mediocre white men.

I had no idea how it had gone from my name on Cézanne's list to Bryan ordering the wine and putting the wrong date on it.

"You're right. It is for next weekend."

"I'm really sorry," Sophia said.

"Do you have the wine in stock?"

"Sure, I have it, but my drivers are already gone for the day. I don't even have a van here tonight to deliver it myself."

My heart sank. "Can't you call someone?" I asked, teetering toward desperate. "It's, like, a three-thousand-dollar order. You'll lose that if we don't figure this out."

She shot me a pained expression. "I don't know who I could get to come in time. I can text a few drivers, but I'm sorry. It seems like a stretch, and I have a meeting after I close."

"I'd appreciate it. It would be really helpful. I don't know what else we're going to do."

Sophia patted my hand across the desk. "Let me shoot off those texts. Hopefully we can fix this."

"Thanks," I said with a sigh and then pulled out my phone to text Cézanne about the disaster. I had a feeling Bryan was about to get eaten alive by her after she found out.

I waited for news from Sophia when the bell over the door jingled.

I glanced up from my phone, praying to whoever would listen that one of the drivers had come back for some reason or another. Some serendipitous reason that would save my shitty day. We could pack up the van and drive out to the ranch, and I'd look like a hero.

Instead, I turned around and found the last person in Lubbock I wanted to see. The one person who had fractured my trust and left me a little more cynical than I'd been before. A line had been drawn in the sand. No matter that we'd had a one-night stand with the best sex of my life, I wouldn't open myself back up to be shattered by Jordan Wright again.

2

ANNIE

"*A*nnie," Jordan said warily. He still held the door open, letting freezing air into the lovely heat of the boutique, as if he needed an escape route. Just in case. "What are you doing here?"

I crossed my arms over my chest, immediately hitting the defensive wherever Jordan was concerned. "Believe it or not, but some people frequent the same places as you."

"That wasn't what I meant." He clenched his jaw. "I just..."

"I know what you meant," I snapped, turning back toward Sophia.

Her dark eyes were wide and bright when she saw Jordan standing there. He closed the door at her approach. Escape no longer needed.

"Hi, Sophia," he said with an enthusiasm that I hadn't heard from him in years. His normal response to seeing and talking to me was tightly controlled warfare.

"Jordan," Sophia gushed. She brushed past me and swept into his arms. "So good to see you again."

I bit my tongue to keep from gagging. Instead, I clenched my hands into fists in the pockets of my peacoat.

Ah, so when Sophia had mentioned that she had a meeting, she'd meant, *date*. Sophia, the owner of The Wine Boutique, was dating Jordan Wright. My not-quite ex. If you could even call our one passionate night together and subsequent months of anger and deterioration a relationship. Most days, I didn't. Today I did.

Three years ago, Jordan and I had fallen head-over-heels in a matter of hours. It still felt indescribable that he could just be the hot guy at the bar and then, I couldn't get enough of him. Then he'd left for Vancouver, forever in my mind as that perfect one-night stand. Until he'd moved to Lubbock and ruined everything.

"Sorry about this. There was some miscommunication with a client," Sophia said. "I'm going to try to work this out, and then we can have our meeting."

"Sure. No problem. What's going on?" he asked.

Our eyes met across the space, and heat blossomed in my body. I stifled it, ignoring the way he still ignited something hot and needy in my core. It was purely sexual. I couldn't help that he was probably the hottest guy I'd ever met in my life, and who wouldn't want to fuck a guy this attractive?

He was six foot four of pure muscle with wind-tousled dark hair that sometimes swept into his chocolate eyes, which always looked straight through me. He peeled off his overcoat to reveal the black suit underneath that molded to his muscular physique. I could picture the six-pack and V-lines beneath. Somehow, my imagination had only intensified his body in my mind.

With that body and a quick mind that missed nothing, all signs should have pointed to us banging constantly.

Instead, here we were. A chill colder than the January wind against my bare legs settled between us.

"Some idiot at the medical school wrote down the wrong date for our party," I told him. "Sophia doesn't have any drivers tonight and there's no way to get three thousand dollars worth of wine to the event now."

"We'll find a way to make this right," Sophia assured me. "I can stay a little later if Jordan doesn't mind waiting."

"I don't mind. You can't get ahold of any drivers?"

She cringed. "No. Everyone's already left for the weekend."

"Maybe we could get a few cases in my car," I suggested with a shrug. "I'd probably have to make a couple trips, but at least it'd get done."

"We could do that," Sophia said uncertainly.

Jordan interrupted. "I...have a truck."

All of my blood dropped into my toes. I felt woozy. Oh, this was not a good turn of events.

Sophia brightened. "That would be so helpful, but... what about our meeting?"

Definitely, *definitely* a date. But...maybe Jordan didn't know?

"We can reschedule. I don't want you to lose business. We need to keep small businesses around for the sake of our economy."

She laughed softly. "Says the man who is a executive at Wright Construction?"

"Absolutely," he agreed. "We started out as a small business."

Oh God, I could not stay for the business-talk foreplay.

"Well, great," I said, running a hand back through my now-hopelessly-tangled red hair. "That might solve our problem. You're just our knight in shining armor, aren't you?" I said with just enough saccharine sweetness for him to second-guess my sincerity.

Jordan's eyes shot up to mine. Calculating and defensive. I saw all the things he wanted to say like a window to his soul. But then he seemed to remember Sophia standing there—his not-quite date, just like I was his not-quite ex—and he decided to let it go.

He smiled brilliantly. Blindingly. "I'd be happy to help. I'd hate for the whole party to go without wine."

"I'd really appreciate that," Sophia said when I didn't immediately thank him for being the best person this side of the Mississippi. "You can pull your truck around back. I'll get everything together to load up."

"Sure thing. I'll meet you both in the back."

Sophia smiled again, putting her hand on his sleeve. "Thanks, Jordan."

I actually rolled my eyes this time. Unfortunately, Jordan saw it—because of course he did—and he just grinned wider before departing. This day sucked.

Sophia showed me the way through the back of the store and into their warehouse, where cases of wine were stacked nearly to the ceiling. She opened a garage door, which let in a burst of cold air, and Jordan backed into the spot with his heavy-duty F-250. Who the hell knew why he needed a truck like that, but I couldn't deny that it was a fine-ass truck...and he looked hot as fuck, jumping down out of the cab.

I never would have guessed that the guy I'd met in too-nice dress shoes from Vancouver would three years later be driving a lifted F-250. Texas sure owned a person.

"All right, what am I loading?" he asked.

Sophia walked briskly around the warehouse, pointing out how many cases of which wine I needed for the party. Jordan lifted the first load like it weighed nothing and set it into the back of his truck. I tried to pick up a case of wine and my back groaned in protest.

"Jesus," I muttered, dropping it back down the inch I'd managed.

"I'd leave that for Jordan. They're each about fifty pounds," Sophia said.

"Yeah, I guess I'll leave that for Jordan." Not to be outdone, I kicked off my stupid shoes and hopped into the bed of his truck.

"What are you doing?" Jordan asked as he dropped down another case. "You're going to freeze."

"I'll be fine." I shoved against the case of wine and positioned it into place. Maybe I couldn't lift it, but I could make this go faster by shoving them into place. Plus, it kept my blood pumping, so I didn't think about the cold. I just wanted to get this over with and not see Jordan Wright's handsome face again for a very long time.

By the time we finished loading, I could barely feel

my feet. I grabbed the slingback straps of my heels and nodded at Sophia.

"Nice doing business with you."

"I'm so glad that we got this figured out," she said. "Good luck with the person who put in the wrong order."

"Oh, have no fear. He's going to get an earful."

Sophia laughed and held her hand out. "I hope we can work together in the future."

"Likewise."

We shook, and then I found Jordan waiting next to his truck. Right. I still had to deal with him.

"I'll just, uh...follow you?" Jordan asked.

"Just head to Spirit Ranch. I'll meet you there."

He looked at me blankly. Right, he wasn't from here.

"You have no idea what Spirit Ranch is, do you?"

"Should I?"

Fair question. He probably hadn't been to a wedding in town. Or any number of other events that were held there. That wasn't exactly his repertoire.

"Just meet me out front. You can follow me."

"Sounds good." He waved at Sophia. "Sorry about all of this. I'll text you for the reschedule."

She and nodded as he retreated. He hopped in his truck and veered off toward the entrance.

"Thanks again," I told Sophia.

"Enjoy the wine."

"Will do," I told her. I trekked through the warehouse, back through the store, and out to the parking lot.

Which was the moment when I realized that I'd left my headlights on.

3
___

JORDAN

I was going to have to make this up to Sophia. We'd been talking in circles for the last couple weeks to get together to discuss the new winery Julian and I were considering opening. This was the only night she'd had available, and here I was, doing a favor for Annie instead. Not that I particularly minded. Especially with the way Sophia had looked at me back there. I was beginning to think that she'd want dinner to make up for this mishap. And I had no interest in dinner with Sophia Valero. Strictly business for me.

I gritted my teeth and pulled into the parking lot in front of the Wine Boutique. Annie stood out front with her heels in one hand and her hair in the other. She looked like she was about to have a mental breakdown. I'd never seen her like this.

Not that we'd been on the best of terms since I'd moved to Lubbock. But this felt like a tipping point. She hadn't even been able to hold back her eye roll in there. Usually, she was still cheery, bubbly Annie.

Not tonight.

I left the truck rumbling and stepped out onto the pavement. "Everything all right?"

She looked manic, and fuck if it didn't draw me to her more. I remembered the first time I'd seen her in the coffee bar in Daisy Dukes. All wild passion and aggression. Her bright green eyes full of mirth and her body promising seduction. I still saw that Annie when I looked at her sometimes, but she reserved that person for others. Not me. Not anymore.

"I left...my fucking...lights on."

"Oh fuck," I said as she darted for the front seat.

I rushed after her, hoping that she hadn't been here long enough to do any kind of damage. She fumbled with the key a few times before getting it into the slot. Then she pushed it forward with a look of desperate hope on her face.

The engine clicked a few times. It seemed as desperate as Annie to get going, but it never turned over. Just kept trying to force the battery to do its job and failing.

She beat her hands against the steering wheel. A scream erupted out of her chest. I winced at the pure rage seething from her in the car. It was almost something that I shouldn't witness. I'd seen Annie angry, of course, but not like this.

I backed away slowly, giving her a minute alone. I would have gone in search of jumper cables, but I knew that I didn't have them. I'd been driving a Tesla before this. I'd finally caved in the last two weeks and bought the truck. Before moving to Lubbock, I never would have considered getting a huge truck, but I already loved it. My friends back home wouldn't even recognize me.

Annie finally got out of her car and came around the side of my truck, looking defeated.

"I don't have cables in the truck. It's new," I said right off the bat.

Her face deflated further. "Of course. Right. I don't have any either."

"We could ask Sophia," I offered.

She tilted her head to the sky overhead. Anyone else this frustrated might have been close to tears but not Annie. Annie looked like she might murder the entire world for doing this to her.

"That would be great. Do you think you could ask her?"

"Sure. Do you want to wait in the truck? It's warm at least."

I didn't bother mentioning that she probably should be wearing pants and shoes when it was supposed to drop into the teens tonight. She looked miserable enough.

"I guess I have no other choice," she said and then stepped past me to get into the passenger side.

I shook my head. She must have been having some night to actually accept that offer.

When I headed back to the boutique, the front door was still unlocked. Sophia sat, slumped behind the front desk on her phone. She looked up when the bell jingled.

"Hey," I said with my same winning smile. "You don't have jumper cables in here somewhere, do you?"

Sophia's hope died before my eyes. Two girls in one night. Man, I was on a roll.

"I don't," she said.

"Ah. Annie's car died. I guess she left her lights on, and she needs a jump. Anywhere close that would have them?"

She shrugged unhelpfully. "I have no idea. I don't think so."

Yeah. She was pissed.

"All right. Sorry about all of this," I said, gesturing around us. "We'll definitely have to reschedule. My schedule is pretty tight, but I'm sure we can figure something out."

Sophia looked down and then back up, as if steeling herself for what came next. "Maybe we could do this over dinner...and drinks."

Ah. Well, fuck.

"Maybe," I said with that same smile. "Just, uh, text me."

Then I pushed back out into the cold, unforgiving January weather, back to the girl who didn't seem to give two shits about me. I probably should have been interested in the cute wine owner, but instead, I couldn't ignore Annie. Even when she wanted to jump down my throat.

I walked back to the passenger side to find Annie rubbing her long, lean legs. She was trying to get warmth back into them, but fuck, those legs.

I needed to get my shit together. I rapped on the door. She jerked up and met my gaze through the window.

"No luck?" she asked when I opened the door.

"No," I confirmed. "She didn't have anything."

She dropped back against the seat and sighed. "I'm not surprised." She ground her teeth together. "I guess I could call someone to come help."

"What about the wine?"

"Fuck."

She wasn't going to like my idea, but I pushed forward anyway. "How about you just ride with me to take the wine to whatever ranch your party is at? Someone there probably has cables. Then we can come back and jump your car. I know it's not ideal, but it's better than waiting in the cold for someone to show up."

She mulled it over, trying to find a way to get out of riding in my truck with me. It was a sign of her desperation that she was even thinking about it. We hadn't been alone this long in years.

"Fine," she said, crossing her arms and facing forward.

Fine. Huh. I hadn't expected that to work.

Well, I wasn't going to look a gift horse in the mouth. I wanted Annie Donoghue in my truck. Wasn't going to lie —I wanted a lot more than that. I always had with her. If only I wasn't so fucking terrible at relationships. Then I might have been able to see where everything went wrong three years ago. I might have been able to pick us up out of the pieces of it all. But that sure as hell wasn't my specialty. The only thing I'd ever been good at in relationships was ruining them.

If I had a chance to make up for it, I'd take it. And just hope I didn't fuck it all up again.

4

ANNIE

ine.

I'd just said fine.

Here I was, in Jordan's truck, with two ten-minute drives in front of us. Jordan and I had been circling each other for years. It was impossible not to be around him when I was best friends with his cousin, my brother worked with him, and we existed in the same circle in this small West Texas town. Still, I'd managed to keep my distance.

It wasn't like what he'd done was so egregious. I'd had worse done to me by other assholes. Much worse if I was honest. I just hadn't expected it from Jordan, and that made everything so much harder.

I couldn't keep my typical vivacious, extroverted personality in his presence. Which was why my arms were crossed and I looked determinably out the window as we pulled away.

"Where is this place again?" he asked.

"Just go north on 27, like you're going to the airport."

He nodded and took the exit for the interstate. The silence stretched interminably. His hand drifted to the radio as if he was going to switch it on before pulling back. I'd never been good at quiet. I liked to fill space, but I couldn't fill this one. I was too defeated from this brutal day to even consider it.

"So, what's this party about?" he asked, finally breaking.

"You know, I really don't want to talk about anything."

Jordan clenched the steering wheel. "I'm doing you a huge fucking favor, Annie. You could maybe seem a little grateful."

I whipped my head to look at him. "Grateful? Are you fucking serious right now?"

"I'm just saying. I had an important meeting that I ditched for you, and I didn't have to do that. Sulking and staring out the window and then jumping down my throat really doesn't help anything."

"Oh, excuse me, Prince Charming. Allow me to fawn all over you," I growled. "So sorry about your *date*."

"Date?" he asked with wide eyes.

I snorted. "And you didn't even notice. Wow. Same old Jordan."

"Sophia and I are not dating."

"You might be *the* most oblivious guy on the planet. Did you not see the way she fell all over herself when you showed up? Or are you just used to that from the rest of the female population?"

He gritted his teeth. "I know she's into me, but we're not dating. I don't even know why you're getting upset about this. It's not like *you* want to date me."

"You're fucking right about that."

"Annie—"

"No," I said, cutting him off. "I don't want to have this conversation."

We'd had this conversation before. Jordan and I'd had a one-night stand. One of the best nights of my life. He'd told me he was leaving, going back to Vancouver. He *hadn't* mentioned that he was moving here. Which meant, of course, that he hadn't wanted me to know. Fine by me. If that were where it'd ended, I'd have just shrugged it off, and we wouldn't have this distrust between us.

But it hadn't ended there. He'd brought his *girlfriend* to Jensen and Emery's wedding a month later, and it had all gone downhill from there. I still didn't even like to think about that wedding.

Somehow, the best night of my life had been tainted by one of the most humiliating. I'd been vulnerable with Jordan, and now, I knew better than.

"One day, we're going to have to get past this," Jordan said softly.

I tipped my head back and closed my eyes. The worst part was that he was right. One day, I would have to get past this. It wasn't like we were suddenly going to be in a different circle of friends. He was a Wright. And I'd known Sutton Wright my entire life. I was on a rec soccer team with his brother, Julian. None of this was going away or getting easier.

And my day sure as hell wasn't helping anything.

Deep down I knew that I was taking out my anger on Jordan. He was an easy target.

I deflated a little at that. Jordan was doing me a favor.

Maybe I could shelve my resentment for the next half hour and get through this day with his help.

I breathed out heavily. "Sorry," I said with a sigh. "I've had the worst day. Like, honestly, the worst day in existence."

He startled at my apology. He clearly hadn't been expecting that. "What happened?"

My body relaxed back into the seat. I hadn't even realized all the tension I was holding in my back and shoulders until he asked. "Well, my house flooded. Like, completely flooded, and I don't have a room right now." I got choked up at the thought. "I lost all my shoes!"

"Holy shit, Annie!"

"I know. I'm still recovering from the loss. The landlord is going to cover everything, and he has insurance, but it's pretty terrible. Hence the impractical snakeskin shoes."

He laughed softly. "And I just thought those were you."

"I was about to donate them. It's a mess." I shook my head. "I almost got into a car accident on the way to the party. Then all of...this." I shrugged. "Wine dilemma, car trouble..." *You.* I trailed off. Keeping *him* as the last problem to myself. Ten minutes ago, I would have slung it into his face, but there was no point now.

"I'm so sorry. That sounds terrible. No wonder you're so mad. I would be, too."

"Understatement," I agreed. "So...what was your meeting actually about? What does Wright Construction have to do with a small wine business?"

"Nothing," he said with a laugh. "You're never going to

believe this, but I'm considering going in with Julian and Hollin on buying a local winery."

My eyes widened. "*You're* going to go in on the winery?"

"I know. It's ridiculous."

"I thought that was all Julian."

Julian had always been the wide-eyed dreamer to Jordan's stoic business practicality. But their cousin Hollin Abbey had worked at a defunct winery on the outskirts of town, and at soccer matches for months, Hollin had cajoled Julian into purchasing it. I'd never have guessed that Jordan would actually want to invest in it, too.

"And how do you know about it?"

"Soccer."

"Ah," Jordan said with a nod. "Yeah, well, it was Julian's idea. Hollin's idea really. But Julian kept badgering me to run numbers and look into distribution and check something or another. I gave up fighting him on it. If I'm going to do all the legwork, then I'm going to get a piece of the pie."

I laughed. God, that was so Jordan. "So, what you mean is that you can't say no to your brother?"

He glowered at me. "Yeah, I guess."

"How do you have time for this?"

He shrugged. Which meant that he *didn't* have time for this. And like the workaholic he was, he was just going to push himself to death.

"Turn left here," I told him.

The Spirit Ranch came into view. The trees were strung with fairy lights, and the tent glowed. I could see that they were nearly finished with setup. Inside somewhere, a very anxious Cézanne was pacing, waiting for all the wine to show the fuck up. She'd probably messaged me, but I didn't have the energy to even check my phone and deal with her stress.

"Whoa," Jordan whispered. "It's actually...beautiful."

"I know, right? I love it out here. You should see it in the spring when everything's in bloom and all the peacocks are out."

His eyebrows shot up. "Peacocks?"

I laughed at his expression. It mirrored mine the first time I'd been here and seen the strutting peacocks all over the property. "Yeah. For some reason, there are peacocks. They're gorgeous."

"Lubbock is weird," he concluded.

"You are not wrong."

Jordan backed into a spot in the rear of the building, nearest to the kitchen. I hopped down onto the gravel in my too-high heels, already cursing the stupid flood again for putting me in this predicament.

A bunch of eager med students flooded out of the back of the building when they saw all the wine in his truck. Jordan went into a managerial role and directed everyone as they unloaded.

"I'm going to look for jumper cables," I told him and then headed inside without waiting for a response.

I found Cézanne pacing, just like I'd thought she'd be. Her clipboard was clutched tight in her hand, and she looked ready to bang it against someone if everything didn't settle itself out. She'd have a real career in event planning if this doctor thing didn't work out.

"Annie! Oh, thank God!" she said, pushing her one stray box braid behind her ear. "I'm assuming this means we have wine for the party."

"We do. No thanks to Bryan."

"He's been handled," Cézanne assured me.

I was sure that he had been. Until the next time he fucked up.

"It's being unloaded now. I had to recruit Jordan Wright to deliver, but yeah, it's here."

Cézanne arched her eyebrows. "Jordan Wright, huh?"

Cézanne had been there that first night I met Jordan. When I'd looked at him across a crowded bar and said if I had a type, it'd be him. I'd been right—and so damn wrong.

"Yeah. Serendipity," I muttered. "He was there for a meeting, and we got the wine in his truck. Anyway, my car died, and I don't have jumper cables. I assume you do."

She crossed her arms and smirked. "And you...drove over here in Jordan's truck?"

"Did you want your wine or what?"

"Uh-huh," she said, grinning at me in a *you can't fool me* way.

"Stop," I groaned.

"I'm over here, dealing with your friend Bryan, and you get Jordan Wright."

I rolled my eyes. "Again, Bryan is not my friend."

"If you say so." She tucked the clipboard under her arm. "Come on. *Of course* I have jumper cables. Who do you think I am?"

"Cézanne, the goddess of organization."

"Precisely."

Once we acquired the cables from Cézanne's car, she insisted on carrying them over to Jordan. He'd just finished unloading the truck. He hopped down out of the bed, landing at our feet. He slammed the tailgate closed and smiled that charismatic smile that got him anything he ever wanted. Even me.

"Hey, Cézanne," he said amicably. "You're our savior tonight."

She shot me a look. She certainly hadn't missed the use of the word *our*. I hadn't missed it either. Not just my savior...but his, too?

"Sure am." She passed him the cables. "I like saving Wrights. Always good to have a favor owed."

He shook his head. "I help Annie out and somehow end up owing everyone else favors."

"Well, you owe Annie enough to never be out of her debt."

My cheeks colored at the comment. Even in the dim light, the blush against my freckled cheeks was obvious. "Thanks, Cézanne. You're a lifesaver. Now, go kick ass at this party."

She squeezed my hand, recognizing the dismissal. I loved her to death. But anything that didn't come out of her mouth was surely written all over her face. If she liked you, you knew it. If she didn't, you sure as hell knew that too. If she thought you were an idiot, like poor Bryan, good luck ever feeling like anything else in her presence. And for Jordan Wright, well, if he hadn't known that he owed me before, he did now.

He held up the cables, his eyes lighting as they caught mine and held. "Shall we?"

I swallowed. It was probably safer to wait until after the party and take the cables with Cézanne. To keep Jordan Wright owing me favors forever. To never let him have the chance to clear what was between us. But that car ride had released a valve. What could it hurt, driving back with him?

Three years ago, I'd said that he was my type, if I'd ever had one. And that hadn't changed a bit. Because that damn smile still did me in.

"Let's do it."

5
___

JORDAN

"*O*kay, try it now," I called to Annie.

She sat in her car and turned the key, kicking the ignition into place. The car revved to life. A slow rumble and then a roar. I sighed with relief. With the day she'd been having, she needed this small victory. The last thing I'd wanted was for the battery to be dead. I didn't think my luck would have lasted against her rage.

Annie's whoop of delight was loud enough to be heard a few blocks over. She jumped out of the car, leaving the cables and conflict forgotten.

"It works!" she cried, doing a little dance. "Thank fuck!"

I laughed at her enthusiasm. At the chance to see this Annie up close and personal. It'd been so long.

"Come dance with me, Jordan," she said, still twirling in place.

I shook my head at her.

"I know you know how to move."

With a laugh, I ducked under the cables and stepped

closer to her. I grabbed her hand mid-spin and twirled her in a circle and back to me. She giggled and took my other hand, pushing and pulling us closer together and then apart. She tipped her head back as I twirled her around again in a circle.

It didn't matter that we were in the pitch-black in an empty parking lot with no music. Annie was just too happy that something had finally gone right to even consider stopping. And I didn't want this to end either.

I spun her out to arm's length and then rolled her back in, cocooning her in my embrace before dipping her. She looked up at me. All bright green eyes and teasing smile. For a moment, I thought about bridging that distance between us. All I wanted to do was capture those perfect pink lips. And for a split second, something in her eyes flashed a challenge, daring me to do it.

A beat passed, and neither of us moved. Then she let her head drop down, her hair trailing against the pavement. The moment broken. My chance gone.

I lifted her back to her feet and released her. Her smile was only slightly reduced.

"Thanks," she muttered, brushing back her red hair. "I needed that after the fucking day I've had."

"No problem. It was fun."

"It was, wasn't it?"

"Well, you probably have to get back to your party."

Annie sighed heavily and leaned her body back against her car. She tilted her head up to the sky, lifting her arms, as if she could reach out and touch it. Head off into the heavens and find real adventure.

"I never really wanted to go to the party."

"Then don't go," I said with a shrug.

She snorted. "It's not that easy. The professor who is retiring is a big deal. All the other professors will be there. It's my last semester, and those relationships mean something."

"It's one party. It can't mean the end of your career as a doctor."

"No. Just whether or not this semester is abysmal."

"One party shouldn't decide that."

Her eyes finally found mine again. "No, it shouldn't, but that doesn't mean anything is as fair as it should be."

The words hung between us. She wasn't talking entirely about medical school or even business. She was talking about us. Nothing had ever been fair when it came to Annie. Not when she'd captured me wholly that one night or the three years of fuckery afterward.

"No, I suppose it isn't."

"Cézanne is probably waiting for me."

"Yeah," I said, barely holding back my sigh.

She pushed off from the car and went to turn it off. I removed the cables and passed them to her. She tucked them into her trunk, slamming it shut behind her with such force that I knew she was irritated again.

"Well...thanks," she said.

And she actually stuck her hand out in front of her as if I were some stranger who would shake hands with her.

"Anytime," I told her, taking her hand anyway. Because maybe I wasn't a stranger, but we were strained enough for it not to matter.

Her fingers were freezing as we shook, and she barely met my gaze.

I should let her go. Watch her drive off into the night and never look back. But I didn't let her go, and I didn't release her hand.

"I guess I owe you." She didn't pull back either.

"Nah, didn't you hear Cézanne? I might never be out of your debt."

She grinned, a flush coming to her cheeks. "You don't have to listen to her. She's ridiculous."

"But right."

Annie finally must have seen sense because she withdrew her hand and rubbed it down her jacket. Then crossed her arms. I didn't know what she was thinking. How could I? If I had a way to tap into that beautiful brain, maybe I wouldn't have wrecked us already. But I did know that she was shutting herself off from me because I was getting too close. Maybe that should have made me want to walk away, to give her all the space she wanted. I just didn't want that. I didn't want space. Not when this was as close as we'd been in years.

"What if I have a better offer?" I blurted out.

She arched an eyebrow. "A better offer than what?"

"Than the party."

She shot me a skeptical look. "What's the offer?"

I tipped my head toward my truck and pulled down the tailgate.

She peered inside and then immediately started laughing. "Did you *steal* a case of wine?"

"Steal? No, of course not," I said, affronted. "Sophia gave it to me when I was loading them up. She told me to try a few bottles before our next meeting."

"Ah," she said, her voice frosting over.

"So, do you want to?"

She narrowed her eyes. "Do I want to...what?"

"Try out a few bottles?"

"What?"

"Forget the party, Annie. Forget your obligations for one night. You've had a shitty day. You don't need to spend another night schmoozing at a medical school party when everything else has gone wrong. Do you really think any *good* is going to come from you going there? After the day you've had?"

She bit her lip. "No. Not really. Bad luck is kind of clinging to me. I'll probably trip and take the whole tent down. Or hit an outdoor heater and catch the woods on fire."

I snorted. "Trip on the way to the drinks and crash down all of the wine we carted over there."

She covered her face. "Oh God! Pour wine down a professor's white dress."

"Pour wine down *your* dress," I added.

She broke into a fit of giggles at our worst-case scenario-ing. "I could see it all happening. Today has been a real shitshow."

"So, any interest in popping open a lot of expensive wine I got for free and taste-testing the bottles?"

"I don't know."

I could see her resistance slipping. That she wanted to go with me, but I wouldn't push her. Not when I'd just started to get back into her good graces.

Then she glanced up at me. "We couldn't go to my place. It's still flooded. I'm planning to crash on the couch until the water damage is fixed."

"Or we could go to my place," I offered, bracing myself for her disdain.

But it never came.

"Where do you live again?"

"Out near Landon."

When I'd first moved here, I'd been shocked by how cheap housing was. Coming from Vancouver, where every shack was a million dollars, it felt inconceivable that I could build a mansion for under a half-mil. I'd gone a little crazy at the prospect.

"We're just drinking wine," she said almost to herself.

"Yeah. My guest room is probably better than the couch."

She met my gaze. I could see her walls breaking down at the prospect of a bed. No matter how much she talked up the couch, it wasn't the same.

She finally nodded. "All right. That sounds fun."

My smile widened at her acceptance. She blushed furiously and brushed past me to her car. As if she couldn't even look at me or she'd change her mind. I was sure she was already regretting her choice.

She might have been having a terrible day, but mine had only gotten better the minute I saw her. And I wasn't ready for her to leave anytime soon.

6

ANNIE

*T*his was a really bad idea.

I hit the steering wheel savagely. I should have gone to the stupid party, even if it was the last thing I wanted to do. But Jordan's invitation sounded really tempting. Who wouldn't want to try a bunch of expensive wine on someone else's dime?

It shouldn't matter that Jordan was the only bright spot in my otherwise terrible day. But somehow, it did. Once I'd stopped taking out my anger on him, it had actually been...great. The drive there and back, getting the car started, the dance, even the carefully awkward invitation. I wanted to go. That was what it had come down to. He'd been a good guy, helping me out when he certainly didn't have to. No matter what Cézanne had said about owing me.

I rolled my eyes at myself. If he ended up being a jerk after I drank all his wine, then fine. Whatever. At least I'd get some expensive wine out of the bargain.

Anyway, I was already committed. We were driving

toward the mansions on the south side of town, toward the country club and golf course that Jordan's cousin, Landon Wright, had created. It was a swank area, mostly owned by construction executives, oil tycoons, and decorated PGA golfers, like Landon. Regular people need not apply.

And as the mansions came into view, my trepidation wore off. I hadn't been out here in a while, but *damn*! They made the rest of Lubbock look like they were living in squalor.

Sometimes, I forgot that the Wrights were heads of a Fortune 500 company and billionaires. That thought was front and center as we rolled up to Jordan's enormous two-story.

I parked next to him, killed the engine, and stepped out into the cold. My eyes going up, up, up at the beautiful home, all red brick and stone and stained wood columns for the porch and shutters. The grass was trimmed and nearly as spotless as the golf course he lived on with two towering trees that must have taken a lot of care to keep alive way out here in the dusty, arid climate.

"Wow," I whispered to Jordan as I came up to stand next to his truck. "Your house is beautiful."

"Thanks," he said with a furrow in his brow. "The garage door opener isn't working. Battery must be dead."

"Of course it isn't working. I must have killed the battery."

He chuckled as he headed toward the bed to collect the wine. "I'm sure it's just a coincidence."

I wasn't sure.

I'd been hoping to look into the garage though, if for

no other reason than to get a good look at the car I actually associated with him—a silver Tesla Model S. It was a gorgeous electric car that I'd coveted for years. I still couldn't fathom that someone who had an electric car... had purchased a diesel truck.

I patted the truck as he slammed shut the tailgate. "And apparently, you've gone full Texan."

He sighed. "I needed something for when I went to sites. I'd been putting it off."

"Do I need to get you some boots? A belt buckle?" He narrowed his eyes at me, but I couldn't stop myself. "A cowboy hat?"

"Now you've gone too far."

"You need something to go with that truck. It's heavy duty. You'll definitely need a hat and boots for the construction sites."

He shook his head and headed toward the front door. "I don't think I'll ever be that Texas."

"Oh, come on."

"No chance in hell." Then he tossed me the keys. "It's the silver one."

I found the key to the front door and turned the lock, pushing my way inside. He carried the case of wine, and I let the door close behind us. My hand went for the light switch as he hauled the case of wine to the kitchen island. But nothing happened. I narrowed my eyes and tried again but still nothing.

I fished out my phone and turned the flashlight on. "Uh, I think we have a problem."

"What's that?" he asked, going to flick on the kitchen light. Nothing turned on. "Well, fuck."

And somehow, *that* was the moment that I broke.

Not when I'd stood alone in my flooding house as I watched everything fall apart. Or the moment of sheer terror as I'd nearly been driven off the road. Or the frustration with dealing with an issue that I hadn't caused. Or finding Jordan Wright's face there when I'd just wanted to deal alone.

No, it was this moment. When, against all odds, his power was out.

The laughter bubbled up from the deep recesses of my chest before bursting out of my mouth. It was a hysterical madness that couldn't be contained. Tears came to my eyes as the compounded effect of this terrible day hit me full force.

"Annie?" Jordan asked.

But I was already leaning forward on my knees, trying to suck in air as I hiccupped around my laughter.

"What's so funny?"

"Everything," I gasped out. "This day. Just think, we came here to escape a flood, and your power is cut. It just feels too good."

"I think you've lost it."

Slowly, my laughter subsided, and I swiped at my eyes. "Maybe I have."

The anger was gone. That *end of my rope* feeling subsided, and in its place was relief. Because the day was almost over, and if it wasn't tempting fate, I'd wonder, *What else could possibly go wrong?*

Jordan used his phone as a flashlight to find a stash of candles. He lit a few of them, positioning them around the living room. The space glowed soft, ambient light. I dropped my purse on the island next to the case of wine and took in the vaulted ceiling with the enormous royal fireplace, nearly big enough to walk into. The couch and chairs matched without being too matchy, making the room feel open and inviting. The back of the house was all glass, looking out over a pool and the golf course beyond. It was a marvel, and he'd clearly spared no expense. Not surprising considering the family business.

"Here you go," Jordan said, appearing again a minute later. He held out a set of clothes.

I raised my brows. "What's this?"

"You look cold." He pushed the clothes into my hands and walked away without looking back. "Bathroom is the first door on the left."

I stared after him in confusion. This wasn't the Jordan of three years ago, who couldn't get me out of my clothes fast enough. Now he was offering me sweats and not even paying attention as he started a fire in the fireplace.

Huh. Maybe this wasn't as bad a decision as I'd thought.

I ducked into the bathroom and stripped out of my ridiculous heels and dress. He'd left me gray sweatpants, a plain blue T-shirt, a black pullover with the Wright Construction logo on it, and a pair of wool socks. I hadn't realized how cold I was until I pulled it all on. Even though it was way oversized and I had to roll the pants four times before they fit me, I was finally *warm*, which was all that mattered.

When I came back out of the bathroom, the fire was slow going, just a gentle flame in the enormous fireplace. Jordan had set up what was essentially a pillow fort on the floor in front of the fire. A dozen blankets and pillows littered the space with a few bottles of wine and glasses next to the fort, like a picnic.

"You've been busy."

"It's cold," he admitted, glancing back at me. His eyes scanned me in my oversized sweats, and something possessive flickered through that gaze. As if the sight of me in his clothes did it for him just as much as my skimpy clothing. He quickly looked away. "I contacted the power company. I guess a line was cut in our area, and they're working on it. They didn't give me an ETA on when everything would be working again."

"Idiots," I grumbled.

"Do you think you could watch this while I change?" he asked.

"Sure. I was a Girl Scout. I can manage a fire."

"Thanks," he said gratefully and then disappeared around the corner.

I craned my neck, wondering which room was his, but the place was too big. I lost him around the bend, and really, it didn't matter. It wasn't like I had any plans to see his room.

I expertly tended to the fire while he was gone until it was burning nice and hot by his return.

His eyes rounded. "You really were a Girl Scout."

"I was," I said, admiring him in casual clothes.

He wasn't exactly the *sweats and T-shirt* type. I'd mostly only seen him in suits. Otherwise I'd seen him in swim trunks and his birthday suit. This was a different Jordan. Careful. Cautious. He was trying not to scare me away.

I realized then that I didn't really want that careful, cautious fear between us. I'd been hurt by what had happened, but I was to blame for that, too. What had I been expecting out of a one-night stand? I'd been stupid enough to fall too hard and too fast. He'd been smart enough not to...and I'd seen what I'd wanted to see. Everything that had happened afterward was miscommunication and hurt feelings that we let linger.

If Jordan was making an effort, then maybe it was time for me to put the past behind us. We didn't have to be anything more than this. Someone who could be here for the other when they were in a bad place.

"Thanks for helping me today," I said finally.

He sank into the cushions next to me. "You don't have to thank me."

"Yeah, I do. You didn't have to help, and you did. So, thanks."

"You're welcome."

He nodded as if seeing the olive branch for what it was. Something passing between us that settled the past. After three long years, we were finally back on even footing.

7

ANNIE

*W*e lapsed into silence. Jordan looked through the bottles of red in front of us. He'd put the white in a wine cooler, which I shouldn't have been surprised that he had. He selected a bottle and expertly uncorked it.

"You're good at that," I told him as he tossed me the cork. I lined it up on the fireplace.

"Lots of practice. I've drunk my way through Napa a few times."

"Fancy."

"And France."

"Of course you have."

I'd never been anywhere. Not really. I was fourteen before I ever even left the state, and it was for a cheerleading competition in Oklahoma City that I thought was the coolest thing ever. Sutton and I went to New York City after high school graduation, and that was my first time on an airplane. I should have been terrified, and I'd promised myself that I'd travel more...but of course, you had to have money to travel. And I'd never really had money. My family wasn't impoverished, but my parents had other priorities—volunteering, charity, church. Our money went to those less fortunate than us, which I appreciated and understood. But I still wanted to see Europe one day...to get out of Lubbock one day. As much as I loved it—and I did *really* love it here—there was a whole wide world out there.

Jordan poured us each a tasting glass. He held it aloft between us. "To free wine and good company."

I laughed and clinked my glass against his. "Cheers."

We each took a sip of the wine. My eyes rounded to saucers.

"Whoa," I gasped. The wine was delicious. Fragrant and light with notes of cherry and something else I couldn't quite put my finger on. "What is that last taste?"

Jordan picked up the bottle and read the back label. "Cherries and plums."

"Plums!" I said with a nod. "So good. I could drink this whole bottle."

He laughed and poured me another drink as he uncorked a second bottle. I inappropriately guzzled the wine like it was water. It was too good to waste a single drop. We moved on to the next bottle and the next and the next after that. Tasting alone likely would have gotten me tipsy, but any of the ones that I loved, Jordan would pour us both extra. Which meant that even though we hadn't finished a single bottle, it was possible that we'd gone through three or four. The "tasting" was pretty deceptive.

"This one," I gasped. "This is the one!"

"I don't think we can even judge anymore," he said, taking another sip of the wine I was insisting was the best. "I don't even know what this tastes like."

"Delicious. Here, let me line them up in order."

Jordan had put stoppers in most of them, which was good because my hands were clumsy and I nearly knocked over two of them.

"Whoops," I muttered before arranging the bottles in some order. "Wait, is this the chocolate one?"

"No, that's this one."

"Okay. Put that down there."

"Annie, this is incoherent," he said with a laugh.

"Shut it, Wright. This is *the* order. It is."

His laugh continued, and he scooted in closer to examine the labels. "You didn't even like this one!"

I tried to keep the label in focus as it doubled in front of me. "I did, too!"

"No way. You said it was sour."

"You don't know anything." I pushed him lightly. But all it did was put myself off-balance. "Oh God!"

He chuckled harder, reaching out and grabbing me to keep me steady. "Maybe you're done."

"We still have a few bottles to open. What about the white?"

He shook his head. "No way. We can do the white another day."

"Jordan," I groaned. "We can do it. I believe in us."

The electricity had come back on at some point, but we'd left the fire and candles going instead of turning on any lights. I'd lost the sweatshirt and socks when I got too warm. The wine heating me up from the inside out.

Jordan's brown eyes were dark in the ambient light. I could see notes of amber around the irises and the heat hidden between us. The one that I'd been ignoring ever since I saw him at the Wine Boutique earlier that evening. And now, after hours of sipping wine in front of the fire, the space between us had diminished to nothing. His hands were still on my shoulders to keep me upright. His interest in me not hidden by his sweatpants. My tongue flicked out to taste the wine across my lips, my brain shutting down when it fought to wonder if this was a good idea.

"We should get you to bed," Jordan said. He swallowed hard, his Adam's apple bobbing in his throat.

"Should we?" I whispered.

My hand brushed across the hair falling over his forehead. He shivered at my touch. His grip tightened on my shoulder before sliding down to my waist.

We moved at the same time. I couldn't even say who started it. One minute, we were apart, and then suddenly, we were crushed together. His mouth fitted to mine. The taste of wine heady between us. His tongue opened my mouth to him, taking what he wanted from me. And I did nothing to stop it. Couldn't deny even in my addled brain that I wanted this from Jordan Wright.

One kiss.

That was all it took.

And I was *his* all over again.

Jordan broke away breathlessly, going for the hem of my T-shirt. I helped him pull it over my head and stripped his off next. Our sweats followed. A haphazard,

slightly drunken tugging of clothes and abandoning
them on the outside of our pillow fort.

There was no thinking. No wondering if this was the
right decision. No second-guessing at all. There was only
this moment where I couldn't get close enough to him,
couldn't feel enough of his heated skin against mine,
couldn't taste enough of his potent lips.

Our underwear disappeared just as quickly, and I
reached out for the hardened length of him. Jordan
groaned, pulling me back to his lips and kissing me
savagely. Like he was on fire and all he wanted was me to
stoke the flames. His hand moved lower, pressing against
my clit until I squirmed underneath him.

"Condom?" he gasped against my lips when he felt
the slick wetness between my legs.

"Birth control," I said instead.

I couldn't fathom him walking away from this
moment to go find a condom in his house. I suddenly
needed him inside of me with a feeling that bordered on
desperation. I couldn't wait any longer.

He pushed me back into the pillows. The light of the
fire casting shadows across my body, trailing a map of the
freckled constellations across my skin. His eyes roamed
the heavens before settling back on my face. He leaned
forward on his elbows and brought our lips back
together.

"I've wanted you for so long," he admitted so softly
that I almost didn't hear him.

I didn't know what to say in return. If I would admit to
wanting him, too. But then his cock settled in the apex of
my thighs, grazing against the wetness of my pussy. I

moaned, my eyes fluttered closed, and the world teetered on its axis.

"Are you sure?" he asked just once. Always a gentleman.

The head of his cock was nearly inside of me already.

"Jordan," I moaned his name, thrusting my hips upward to meet him.

He didn't need to be told twice.

Nor did I need to say anything else when my body told him precisely what I wanted.

He thrust deep inside of me. My body opening up for him and pleasure blooming through my core. Holy fuck!

I'd forgotten. Three years without him was a long time. And even though my brain had made him more gorgeous in our absence...it had not exaggerated how good he felt. In fact, he felt even *better*. A point that I hadn't thought was possible. But it was Jordan Wright; I never should have underestimated him.

Our hips moved together seamlessly. A rhythm as synchronized as the waves beating against the beach.

Our lips met again. I was drowning in him. Succumbing to the undertow. Letting him drag me under. I didn't fight it. Didn't want to. I was in a perfect state of bliss as my climax hit me full force.

I cried out, tightening around him. He grunted. His fingers brushing my hair out of my face. I looked up to find him staring down at me with adoration in his expression. I was terrified of what would come out of his mouth, so I kissed him. And he came hard and fast inside of me.

"Fuck," he moaned against me, pumping into me twice more before stilling.

"Fuck," I repeated.

He put his forehead against mine. "You're magnificent."

I smiled sleepily, sure that I looked thoroughly fucked, and then kissed him again. He pulled out of me, and I went to the bathroom to clean up. Then I collapsed down onto our pillow fort, snuggling close to the dying fire. I didn't want reality to crash back into my life just yet. So, I let Jordan pull me tight against him. My back to his chest. He drew circles on my skin until sleep was tugging me under. He kissed my shoulder once, soft and gentle.

I heard him whisper something behind me. Something that sounded a lot like, "I wish you were staying." Those traitorous, vulnerable words that I'd uttered to him the last time we did this.

But then I was asleep, and I was sure that I'd misheard.

PART II

FRIENDS WITH BENEFITS

8

JORDAN

*A*nnie was gone when I woke up.

I rubbed my eyes and stared at the empty pillow fort, half-full bottles of wine, and ash-covered fireplace. Dawn had risen bright and blinding through the living room windows. The precise reason that I'd designed my bedroom facing the other direction. I grumbled under my breath and then pulled sweats and a shirt back on.

I left the pillows strewn across the living room floor along with the bottles of wine and glasses.

Her purse was gone from the island. I trudged to the front door and saw that her car was missing as well. She'd disappeared sometime in the middle of the night without even waking me up or saying good-bye. Damn, that was cold.

I reached for my phone with a yawn and saw a dozen text messages from Julian, Hollin, and my mother but none from Annie. She'd really just ghosted.

I wasn't sure what I'd expected from her. We hadn't

even been on speaking terms until last night and then all of that had happened so fast. We probably wouldn't have even had sex if we'd both been sober. I hadn't *planned* for it, but I sure as fuck wouldn't regret it. Despite all the animosity that lingered between us, it was incredibly easy to be with Annie. It was how we'd tumbled into bed the first night. And last night too.

But if this was just another one-night stand, then fine. We'd done that once before and I was the one who left. It was only fair for her to get her chance.

I cleaned up the house, replacing the pillows, wine, and glasses before taking a scalding shower and getting dressed for my meeting with Julian and Hollin. I was supposed to have met with Sophia last night and gotten her take on the winery purchase. She worked with all the wineries in the area and had insider information that I'd told them both I needed before making a decision.

Obviously...there hadn't been a meeting.

Nothing I could do about it now.

I grabbed a coffee from a local shop on the way to the winery and guzzled it before I arrived. I should have gotten a second. My mind was still fuzzy from the night before, and I hadn't felt up to eating anything. Skipping my run had been bad enough.

When I drove into what had once been West Texas Winery, nostalgia washed over me. The barn still looked ramshackle, as if at any point, the entire thing might collapse in on itself. The surrounding vineyards, in contrast, were well maintained and beautiful, even in the barren January morning. Farther down the property was the main processing building and cellars. I'd seen detailed pictures of the facilities, but this was the first time that I'd been on the property for an assessment. First time since Annie and I had been here three years ago.

Julian and Hollin were standing in front of the barn with their arms crossed, looking up at it with broad smiles. I wasn't sure that we saw the same thing when we looked at it.

"You made it," Julian said.

He stepped away from Hollin and shook my hand. My brother was the main reason that I was here. Annie had hit it on the head when she said that I couldn't say no to Julian. I'd been his protector my entire life.

In the beginning, it had been in elementary school when other kids picked on him for siding with the less popular kids. He always had this charismatic way about him and love for those others saw as weaker. He could have handled it himself, but I scared the kids who'd picked on him, and it stopped. In high school, he was a star athlete, running circles around everyone else on the soccer pitch. Even away at college, I kept recruiters from taking advantage of his generous nature. All of that was easy. But it was our father who was the hardest thing to protect him from. Our parents had briefly split when we were younger, and our dad had started a parade of girl-friends. I took the brunt of it and kept Julian from as much of it as I could. And I tried to shield him from our father for the years of manipulative, narcissistic behavior that followed our parents getting back together. It had been a relief when we finally saw the worst of him and could cut ties after the divorce.

"I made it," I told him. "I thought this was a business meeting."

Julian looked down at his own fitted khakis, teal polo, and sharp dove-gray jacket. I was pure business, but Julian had *style*. And he prided himself on it.

"This *is* business attire for me."

Hollin just laughed and stuck his hand out. "I don't want to even know what you think about what I'm wearing."

I just shook my head.

Hollin Abbey had been born and bred a Lubbock cowboy, complete with boots and belt buckle. I'd bet real money on his hat being in his truck. He wore Wranglers, a plaid button-up, and a jean jacket layered under a leather jacket. Cowboy who rode Harleys on the weekends. A conundrum of clichés. I'd thought that the first time my mother introduced us to her brother Greg and our three cousins: Hollin, Campbell, and Nora.

It was still strange to have all this family around now. For so long, it had just been me and Julian against the world. Now we had three cousins on our mom's side and five Wright cousins on our dad's side. I worked with Jensen, Austin, and Morgan through Wright Construction and Jensen Wright Architecture. Landon was my neighbor when he was in town and not out, golfing professionally. Sutton was the youngest and Annie's best friend. So I didn't see much of her...more of her husband, David, the CFO of Wright Construction. Either way, it was a lot of family, and I was still getting used to it.

"Have you heard from the agent?" I asked them.

Hollin nodded. "Yeah, Larissa should be here in five.

She got caught with her five kids after her husband's meeting ran over."

"Perfect."

"How'd it go with Sophia?" Julian asked.

"Well," I said with a pause. It wasn't like I could tell them about Annie. Not after she'd disappeared this morning. "It didn't really happen."

"What? You've been trying to get this meeting for weeks," Julian said. "How can one woman give you this much runaround?"

"Yeah. Aren't you some heartthrob?" Hollin joked.

"That's Julian."

Julian rolled his eyes. "Not anymore. Ashleigh and I have been together for almost two years." He gestured back to me. "It'd be *you* if you didn't fuck up all your relationships."

"Solid point," I said with a shrug. "Anyway, I saw her, and she gave me a case of wine to try before our next meeting. I know in one of our messages, she had a sommelier recommendation who lives in Houston but studied in France. So, we have options for hiring if we go through with this."

"Oh, wine to try," Hollin said eagerly. "We'll all have to taste-test what she sent over."

I frowned. "I might have already tasted all the red bottles."

"Alone?" Julian asked in confusion. "You never drink alone."

He was right. I avoided that habit after seeing how it had turned my father into more of a monster than he already was. Apparently, alcoholism ran thick like a river through our family.

"No, I wasn't alone," I said, turning back to stare up at the barn.

I didn't miss the look that passed between Julian and Hollin. They'd gotten close over the last three years. They played on the same rec soccer team, and their friendship had only strengthened.

"Was it that blonde?" Julian asked with a cringe. "What was her name?"

"Leslie?" Hollin offered.

"No. It doesn't matter who it was."

"Why doesn't it matter?"

"Because it doesn't matter," I insisted, wanting to be done with this conversation. "Anyway, she'd kill me if I told you."

"So, we know her then?" Hollin asked.

I frowned. Well, shit.

"Forget I said anything."

Julian laughed. "No chance in hell." He glanced at Hollin. "Who do we know who would hate him for telling us?"

Then at the same time, they said, "Annie."

I closed my eyes in resignation. Jesus Christ, was I that transparent?

"Fine. Yes, it was Annie. Just don't tell her I told you."

"How did that even happen?" Hollin asked. He tilted his head and ran a hand through his blond beard, his light-blue eyes revealing his shock. "I thought she, like... hated you?"

"She doesn't *hate* me."

"Well, obviously not anymore," Julian said with another barely concealed laughter. His dark eyes, the mirror of mine, were full of mirth. "But you brought Missy to Jensen's wedding. No one was oblivious to the argument that ensued."

I cringed. "Yeah, that was a mistake."

"Oh, Jordan Wright makes mistakes?" Hollin said with a laugh.

Julian grinned. "Only in relationships."

"I didn't mean for all of that to happen. It was a misunderstanding."

"Meaning...you weren't really as broken up as you thought you were."

"Yeah."

"I *told* you that space didn't mean a break up."

I shrugged. "It felt concrete to me. So when I came back to Vancouver, Missy thought we were still together. I didn't know how to back out of bringing her to the wedding."

"Hi, I fucked someone else in Lubbock, it's over?" Hollin suggested with a laugh.

"Well, when she found out about Annie at the wedding, that solidified the break up," Julian said.

It sure did. And ruined any chance I had with Annie too.

"I was an idiot, all right?" I ran a hand back through my hair. "It was complicated with Missy. She was there for me when we got Mom's cancer diagnosis. It felt like the right thing at the time."

Julian nodded absentmindedly, as if he understood. Things had been different when we found out that Mom had breast cancer for a third time. Everything screeched to a halt. We'd moved here to be with her during her treatment, afraid that this was going to be the time where cancer took her from us. Everything after the diagnosis was still a bit of a blur, and I felt like maybe we should both be given a little slack for anything that happened. Not that Missy or Annie appreciated how stupid I'd been then.

Luckily, Mom was in remission and happier than ever, being back in her hometown with her siblings. She spent every weekend with her siblings, Greg and Lori, and Lori's wife, Vail.

"Yeah, but I'm still shocked Annie would talked to you. How did that happen?" Julian pushed. "She's in med school. Every time she comes for a Tacos game, she seems half-frazzled and part-manic. She constantly says she doesn't have time for anything but this one game a week."

I shrugged and was saved from answering by Larissa showing up for our meeting.

"Sorry! Sorry! I'm here," she said, brushing her dark blonde hair out of her face and striding over to meet us. "I always swear I'm going to be on time, and then five kids." She shrugged helplessly. "Happens."

"It's not a problem," I insisted and shook her hand.

"So good to see you all again. Where would you like to begin? The barn, cellars, vineyard?"

"Let's start with the barn," Hollin said cheerily.

Hollin had worked at the now-defunct West Texas Winery for years before it finally collapsed due to a loss of capital. The wine itself was delicious. I still couldn't figure out where their money problems had originated. It was a problem I'd wanted to solve before agreeing to this endeavor. Though having Hollin on board, who knew every inch of the process of the winery, made me feel a lot better.

"Barn it is!" Larissa said, taking a fortifying sip of her coffee.

I braced myself and followed them inside. I hadn't been here in three long years. Even when Julian and Hollin tried to drag me in for weekend drinks. I'd spent one night here with Annie, and the memory lingered strong enough that I didn't particularly want a repeat. Country music, line dancing, dirt floor, and cheap booze would never be my scene again.

But as soon as I stepped inside, the potential for what this place *could be* swept over me. It had character. I could almost see all the possibilities that Julian and Hollin had been trying to bang into my head since the get-go. Saw the truth in this dusty, old barn—the Wright Vineyard.

9
_____

ANNIE

"Think this is the last bag," I said, hauling the trash bag full of stuff out of my bedroom and dumping it into the mostly intact living room.

Jennifer looked on with a frown. "I cannot believe this happened. I was only gone for a couple days!"

"It wouldn't have stopped the flood if you'd been here."

"No, but I might have been home and caught it sooner. Before it decimated your room."

I nodded thoughtfully. "That would have been nice, except that it wasn't flooding when I went to sleep and something clearly *burst* in the middle of the night."

"But I would have woken up before you," Jennifer offered.

Which was true. I was as much a vampire as I could manage, and Jennifer believed that the early bird caught the worm. She probably would have noticed the flood at, like, five a.m. instead of almost noon. By that time, there had pretty much been nothing I could do, except panic. Which I'd done perfectly.

"What did the landlord say?" Jennifer asked. She stood from her seat on the undamaged living room chair and chewed on her nails. A bad habit she'd never been able to give up.

I rolled my eyes dramatically. "Bastard called me at the ass crack of dawn to come over and inspect the damage. He made some notes and then left. Said he'd be in contact."

I'd had to get over here so early that I had to ditch Jordan's place. He looked so peaceful that I didn't dare wake him. I'd left a note on his fridge, but I hadn't heard from him since. Guess that was that.

Probably for the better anyway. I had no time for... whatever that had been. The sex had been great, but if he wanted something more than sex, well, *that* wasn't happening. I'd have to chalk it up to a drunken mistake.

"Well, the wedding was at least good, wasn't it?"

Jennifer had just wandered into the kitchen and reappeared with a dreamy look in her eye and a bag of cat food. "Oh! It was amazing," she said. "Come with me to feed Avocado and Bacon and then I can show you the pics on my camera."

I couldn't keep from laughing. "You know if you *name* the stray cats then they become *your* cats, Jen."

She wrinkled her nose at me. "I don't like cats."

"You literally have cat food in your hand."

"Well, I'm not going to let them starve," she said as if that made sense.

We wandered outside and she filled two small bowls at the front of the house. I thought it was ridiculous that she was feeding two cats that didn't even belong to her. But despite her insistence that she didn't like cats, she clearly *loved* these cats. She'd named them, for God's sake.

"Cado! Bakey!" she called.

And out of the bushes came a black cat, Bacon, and an orange and white cat, Avocado.

"Here you go, guys," Jennifer said. The cats avoided her and went straight for the food. She stood as if all of this was totally normal. "Okay, my camera?"

I shook my head and followed her back inside. She disappeared into her room as I observed the wreckage with a sigh. I was going to need to go shopping or else I'd start and end my last semester of medical school with what I had in my room right this minute. Because there would be no time to go otherwise.

Jennifer reappeared with her fancy Canon Rebel and scrolled through the hundreds of images she'd taken at the wedding in Sedona this weekend. Over the last three years, she'd really embraced her photography. And as I'd always known she would be, she was now a coveted travel photographer. During the busy season, we never saw each other. Passing like boats in the breeze as I lived at the medical school all week and she darted off to unknown destinations every weekend. I'd be jealous of how much she traveled if I wasn't so damn proud of her.

A knock on the door pulled us away from the pictures, and before I could even jump up, the handle twisted, and my best friend, Sutton Wright, entered. We'd known each other since we were babies and grown up together from diapers to cheerleading uniforms to Texas Tech to now with her walking into my house without an invitation.

"Hey, girlie," Sutton said.

Her smile was bright, and her hair was a lighter blonde than it had been in a decade. All the Wrights had dark hair and eyes. It was almost jarring to see her blonde, but she loved it.

"Sut!" I said with a smile. "Did you come over to take me shopping?"

Sutton laughed and shook her head. "Soccer game, remember?"

I groaned. "Right. I almost forgot. Where are Madison and Jason?"

Sutton had a five-year-old, Jason, with her first husband, Maverick. He'd passed away four years ago now. I'd been there when it happened. It was half of the reason that I was in medical school. I'd sworn that I'd never stand by and not be able to do anything ever again.

Sut had remarried last year, and within nine months, she'd had her second baby, Madison. She was the most gorgeous kid I'd ever seen. She could be one of those baby models. I was the godmother and always itched to hold the little ball of sunshine.

"They're with David." She put her hands to her chest. "I had to pump all afternoon to make sure we had milk. I didn't have enough stocked up. Ugh! My boobs!"

Jennifer and I laughed.

"Your boobs look amazing," I told her.

"They do, don't they?" Sutton said, sticking her chest

out. "I've always had such tiny boobs. I'll be sad when these go away."

Jennifer shook her head. "You could get a boob job."

Sutton pointed at her. "Good idea."

"Let me see if my soccer bag made it through the flood," I told them and then headed back to my room.

I checked my phone along the way to see if Jordan had texted. But of course, he hadn't. I didn't even know why I cared. It had been one night. Just like last time. I'd been stupid to expect something then, and I wasn't going to be that stupid again.

My bag wasn't in my room, which was a relief, but that meant I didn't know where it was. I stepped into the garage, popped open the trunk of my car, and dug around until I found the bag. When I opened it, the smell from my last game a month ago wafted up to me. I cringed away.

"Shit," I muttered.

Good news: it hadn't been ruined by the flood.

Bad news: I'd been so worried about finals last semester that laundry slipped my mind.

I trudged back inside and threw my uniform and socks into the dryer with a wet washcloth and dryer sheet. It wasn't a perfect solution. It only took a few minutes, and I promised the uniform I'd take care of it after the game. Then I changed into the outfit—red shorts and jersey with the number six on it and our team name, The Tacos.

"Ready to go," I said to my friends as I stepped back into the living room. "Let me see if Isaac needs a ride."

"Is he back from New York?" Sutton asked.

She put her hands under her chin and looked at me dreamily. Jennifer mirrored her look.

I bit my lip and nodded. "I still can't believe it all happened!"

My brother, Isaac, had dated Peyton Medina all through high school, but she'd left to go to the New York City Ballet. They'd reconnected while she was in town for *The Nutcracker*. We were all still unbelievably happy for them. Almost seemed too good to be true. But after his first wife, Abby, had died in childbirth, I'd say that my brother deserved all the happiness in the world.

Bro, you want a ride to the Tacos match?

A second later, my phone dinged.

Appreciate it. Mom is coming over in twenty to watch Aly.

I'll come inside to kiss my favorite niece.

She's your only niece.

All the more reason.

"He's in," I told them.

"Sweet. Now that he's off the market, maybe Jennifer can stop making goo-goo eyes at him," Sutton said as we headed for her upgraded Audi SUV.

"I do *not* make goo-goo eyes at him!" Jennifer protested, slinking to the backseat.

"You kind of do," Sutton teased.

"Ew," I muttered.

"He just really knows how to play soccer. That's all I'm saying," Jennifer said. "He and Julian and Blaire really bring the team together."

Though my brother had been recruited to a Division I school and Julian had played in college, Blaire was the star of the Tacos. She was a power forward and goals from girls counted double in this league. She was the reason we'd killed it last season. Plus, she was just a really fun down to earth girl.

I couldn't resist ribbing Jennifer though. "Hey! I'm on the team, too."

Jennifer's cheeks heated. "That's not what I meant!"

"No, you meant that Isaac knows how to dribble, but *Julian*—"

"Stop!" Jennifer said.

Sutton laughed. "Don't pick on her."

"I just wish that it had worked out with you and Julian," I admitted. "No one wants to deal with Ashleigh Sinclair."

"It was one date," Jennifer said, looking down at the camera still strung around her neck.

"And the wedding!" Sutton said.

"Fine. One perfect kiss with Julian Wright." She shrugged. "And then he found someone more in his league." She didn't even sound upset about it. Just thought it was how things were. Sure didn't stop her from watching him and wishing. I knew that even if she wouldn't admit it.

"Bah!" I cried.

"Ew, don't say that," Sutton said. "Ashleigh Sinclair is not more in anyone's league. Plus, I'm a Wright and I say with certainty that if anything you're out of his league."

Jennifer grumbled under her breath. "Yeah, right."

"Chin up," I said. "We don't have to worry about any of it today."

I was glad for the change of subject, because usually, when the conversation went to Julian, it swung right around to Jordan. As much as Sutton had been against us dating her cousins when they first showed up, she was all for it now. Wanted us to be part of the family. As if *that* was ever going to happen.

Luckily, we made it to Isaac's without incident. I hopped out of the SUV and jogged inside. My mom and dad stood in the entranceway.

"I didn't know both of you were coming over!" I said, throwing my arms around them.

"Hi, sweetie," my mom said.

"Ann," my dad said, kissing my cheek. He was the only one who called me that anymore.

"Where's my favorite niece?"

"I'm here!" Aly cried, running out of her bedroom in a tutu and tights, a tiara planted in her mass of red curls.

I picked her up and swung her around in a circle. "I missed you!"

"I missed you, too, Aunt Annie."

"You were gone to New York for so long."

Aly's eyes widened. "It was magic. The buildings were so tall." She held her hand up as if to show me how tall they were. "And Peyton's house doesn't even have a yard! But you can still have dogs."

"Wow," I said with enthusiasm.

"Apartment," Isaac corrected Aly as he walked out in a matching Tacos uniform. His red hair was cut short and gelled off of his face. He was a head taller than me but still muscular and lean from years of soccer. He could have gone pro when he was younger. "Peyton lives in an apartment, remember?"

"Right. Apartment. It's small, and I got to sleep on the couch!"

"That sounds like the best adventure."

Aly nodded. "It was. I missed my house though. And dance. Dad said we could get a dog."

Aly was a budding ballerina, and even at five, she insisted on being in the studio as much as humanly possible.

"I did not say that," Isaac said with an eye roll. "Give your aunt a kiss good-bye."

Aly puckered up and plopped a wet kiss on my lips. "Have fun. Love you!"

"Love you, too, Aly Cat."

Isaac kissed his daughter next and thanked Mom and Dad before following me out to Sutton's SUV. He ruffled my hair. "Thanks for the ride."

I swatted at him, fixing the now-mussed ponytail. "You can ride in the back with Jennifer."

He snorted. "Fine. Good to see you, too."

"I missed Aly more than you."

"I feel so loved," he said sarcastically.

"Love you."

We jumped into the car, and Isaac regaled us with tales from the last couple weeks in New York City. We all listened with rapt attention. Sutton had been a bunch before, but I'd only been once, and Jennifer still hadn't had a wedding there. It was on her bucket list. We both swore we'd go for the next bachelorette party that we had to throw. Since Sutton had refused any festivities when she married David.

Sutton parked next to Cézanne's CR-V. She stepped

out of her car in The Tacos uniform at the same time as us. She hip-checked her car door as she plaited her box braids up into a ponytail and then wrapped it all up into a high bun.

"How was *your* night?" Cézanne asked with an arched eyebrow.

"Fine. How was the party?"

"Boring. You really missed out."

I chuckled. "Well, I'm so sad that I didn't go."

"No, you're not, and eventually, you're going to tell me what actually happened."

"Am I?" I asked as the group of us stepped into the indoor soccer facility.

"What's Jordan doing here?" Sutton said in surprise.

I froze in place. My eyes lifting from Cézanne's to stare up into the row of bleachers. And...yep. There was Jordan Wright seated at the end of the row, talking to Julian and Hollin. He'd never *once* come to a game before. As if he recognized it as my space. And yet, here he was.

10

ANNIE

"**W**hat is he doing here?" I hissed under my breath.

"I don't think he's ever been to a match," Sutton said.

"No, he hasn't."

So, what the hell was he doing here now? Sure, we'd kind of reconciled last night, but then I hadn't heard a peep from him today. It didn't seem like him to make a scene here. I didn't see another reason why he'd show. If he was here for Julian or Hollin, then he would have come to games sooner.

Cézanne cackled. "Oh, this is going to be good."

Jennifer and Sutton looked at each other and then to me.

"Oh boy," Jennifer muttered.

"What did you do?" Sutton asked.

"Nothing," I ground out.

Then I pushed past my friends, straight for Jordan Wright. Julian and Hollin saw me coming and beelined for the field to warm up. Which likely meant they knew.

72

Was Jordan going around and telling everyone about his latest conquest?

"What are you doing here?" I asked before he could say anything else.

"Hello, Annie. Good to see you," he said. His face was carefully blank. He'd been preparing for this moment. The inevitable fight.

"You don't come to the soccer games."

"My brother and cousin play on the team."

"So?"

"I don't see why *you're* mad about me being here. You're the one who ran out this morning."

My eyes widened. "I didn't *run* out. I had to deal with the flood in my house. I left you a note. You're the one who didn't text me."

His mask faltered. "You didn't leave me a note."

"Uh, yes, I did. I left it on the fridge."

"What? No, you didn't."

I looked to the ceiling and prayed for strength. "Fine. Believe whatever you want about me."

I turned to go, but with whip-sharp reflexes, he snagged my elbow and pulled me back to him.

"Hey, I didn't know. I thought you'd just ghosted the next morning." His voice was soft, sincere.

I wanted to believe him, but it was hard to think that he didn't have ulterior motives.

"Well, I didn't."

"Okay," he said quickly. "I believe you."

"Thank God," I said with an eye roll, pulling out of his grip. "Just...I don't have time for this."

Jordan opened his mouth, but I pushed away from

him and headed out onto the field. I was thrown by his presence. I'd thought he wasn't interested, and he'd thought I'd ghosted him. We were both wrong, and still... I hadn't lied. I really, *really* didn't have time for whatever this meant.

I needed to focus on this game and not Jordan Wright anyway. I wasn't the best soccer player by any stretch of the imagination. I mostly did it because Isaac needed extra girls to play on the coed team and stayed because I liked the team.

Blaire did most of the work. She was already running through drills, her typical baseball cap down low over her eyes, her dark hair swinging nearly to the middle of her back in a pony. She was short, quick, and fierce, running circles around everyone.

Isaac and Julian were midfielders. Both having played soccer in college, they dominated the run game. While Cézanne, Hollin, and I played defense. Which usually meant Hollin was a ball hog and Cézanne had to politely tell him to stop being a fuckface. It was entertaining as all hell when Cézanne let loose. Gerome was our mostly silent goalie, six and a half feet tall with long locs and a serious disposition. We didn't win every match, but the commentary made it worth it either way.

"Hey, Annie," Blaire said, jogging over.

We slapped hands back and forth and then a fist bump. A handshake we'd had for the last couple seasons. Blaire was one of those disarmingly beautiful people with full black hair and close-cropped bangs. Her eyes so bright blue and rimmed with black that they seemed almost too large for her face and a short, hourglass figure. She hid behind hats and baggy clothes ninety percent of the time while running the most successful Instagram account I'd ever known. I even followed her. Though I didn't have much time for social media, I loved that she focused on body positivity and mental and physical health, not just cultural stereotypes about those things.

"Hey. How's it going?"

"Good. Good. Piper and I are going for pizza after, if you're interested."

Piper Medina was Blaire's roommate, and coincidentally, Isaac's fiancée Peyton's younger sister. She was a spit fire and ran a successful vineyard in town with her father.

"Yeah, for sure, I agreed. "I might have to catch a ride with you. I came with Sutton and Jennifer."

"Invite them to come with," Blaire insisted.

"Nah, Sut will have to get back to the kiddos," I told her as we stepped together through a quick warm-up.

"Yeah, makes sense. Well, maybe next time," she said with a blindingly white smile.

"All right, Tacos," Isaac called.

We all jogged over to him, forming a loose circle as he ran through his weekly pep talk. He was good at it, too. I almost felt motivated even though I was easily the worst person on the team. Oh well. I had fun, and that was all that mattered.

Julian and Hollin fell into step with me as we broke from the circle. I sighed. This was going to be good.

"So...are you into Jordan?" Hollin asked with his shit-eating grin.

"Subtle," Julian grumbled.

"I think you should both mind your own fucking business."

"I'm just asking because—" Hollin said.

"Don't care," I interrupted. "Jordan obviously already told you."

"Well, we guessed," Julian said. He glared at Hollin. "He insisted that we don't bother you."

"Then, you failed," I told him with a shrug and a smile. "It wasn't much of anything. Just...let it go."

Hollin opened up his big mouth, but Julian hit him in the solar plexus, and he doubled over to catch his breath. I laughed and winked at Julian before taking my place in the back of the pitch.

I glanced up at the stands just once before we started and found Jordan staring right at me. He was seated next to Julian's girlfriend, Ashleigh, but he seemed to be ignoring the constant drivel she was spewing. I tilted my head in question, and he just smirked. As if he'd caught *me* looking at *him* and not the other way around.

The whistle blew, and I cursed. I needed to get Jordan Wright out of my head and get my head in the game.

* * *

I ran straight to Blaire, throwing my arms around her after she scored the winning goal and the ref blew the final whistle. The entire team congratulated her. I beamed with excitement. It had been a tough match. Our opponent was almost our equal. I'd blown a few plays, and I was glad that we had Blaire to clinch the win.

"Pizza," she insisted. "Everyone needs pizza after that."

Isaac shook his head, as always. "I need to get home to Aly, but the rest of you should go have a good time."

"We're in," Hollin said, pointing to himself and Julian.

"Gerome?" Julian asked.

Gerome shook his head and smiled. He was so quiet that I'd only heard him speak when we were playing. It was strange, considering that everyone else was such a loudmouth.

"Cézanne?" I asked.

"Nah, I need to study."

I groaned. "We're not even in rotations again until Monday, and I know that you're already prepared for clinical exams."

"What can I say? I like to succeed." She hip-checked me on her way back to the bleachers. "You have fun."

"You coming with me?" Blaire asked as she hoisted her soccer backpack onto her shoulders. One of her Instagram sponsors had provided it from a specialty company in LA. She'd taken a few pictures with it, and now, it was as beaten up as the rest of our gear.

"Yeah, just...give me a minute."

My eyes flicked up to Jordan, who looked like he would do anything to extract himself from Ashleigh Sinclair. Julian bounded up there, and they kissed in front of everyone. My heart panged as I saw Jennifer carefully look away. She still couldn't feign disinterest when it came to Julian.

"No problem," Blaire said. "Maybe Jennifer can take a

few pics for me! I'll text Pipes and tell her to get us a table."

"Sounds good."

I shouldered my own bag, a recycled Lululemon shop bag that I'd gotten when I got a sports bra on sale. Then with a deep breath, I headed over to where Jordan stood with Julian, Ashleigh, and Hollin.

Ashleigh beamed when she saw me. "Hey, Annie!"

"Ashleigh," I said, trying to make my face seem excited to see her.

I personally thought Julian was getting scammed, but I couldn't say that. Ashleigh Sinclair didn't have a sincere bone in her body. I'd known her my entire life. Her brother, Chase, and I had grown up together. He'd been my high school heartthrob until the day that he left for Yale.

"Are you going to pizza, too?"

"Yeah, I'll meet y'all there," I said as a dismissal. Then I turned to Jordan. "Can we talk?"

He arched an eyebrow and hit Hollin before he could say anything. "Sure."

We walked away from the rest of the team and out into the dark night beyond. Bright constellations beamed down at us. It was one of my favorite parts about the indoor soccer complex. It was far enough out of town that the stars were visible.

"Sorry about Julian and Hollin. I told them not to talk to you," Jordan said abruptly when we stopped in front of his Tesla. This felt more like him than that truck ever would.

"Julian said that. It's Hollin. You know his big mouth."

"That I do."

"I don't care that they know," I said, finding that it was truer than I'd thought.

"Yes, you do."

"Look, it doesn't matter." I dropped my soccer bag and leaned against his car. "We can't do this."

"Okay," he said, short and curt.

"I'm serious."

"Okay," he repeated.

I pushed off the car and crossed my arms. "I'm in medical school, and I'm too busy. I decided not to date while I was training to become a doctor. I'm in rotations all day, and when I'm not in person with patients, I'm studying for board exams and clinicals. Not to mention, we're coming up on all of my final residency interviews, and I still have to finish my research for my spring conference..." I trailed off. "It's a lot, okay?"

"I get it. I'm an executive at Wright, and I just decided to buy a vineyard. I'm not exactly full of empty time."

I paused. "You bought the vineyard?"

"We put in an offer at least, yeah. We went to look at it this morning and agreed that we were all in. I know it'll take time for the wine business to take off, but we want to use the available space for events. You know, Hollin's sister, Nora, interns with an event planner. She graduates this semester, and we were thinking of bringing her on full-time."

"Wow! That's amazing," I gushed. "I'm excited for y'all."

"Thanks," he said as if he'd been expecting another response from me. "But as you can tell, I'm also busy."

I watched the way the shadows played along his features and imagined us trying this out. The way we'd fall head over heels and, within months, completely disintegrate, hurting each other beyond repair and ruining this sort of truce we were living in where we could now occupy the same space. I didn't want that.

"I'm leaving," I blurted.

His eyebrows shot up. "What do you mean?"

"I mean that I'm leaving. I'm getting out of Lubbock. I've been interviewing for residencies all over the country the last few months. I have one in Dallas in a few weeks and my last one in Seattle in February. Then I have to rank choice my top residency programs, and Texas Tech is at the bottom of my list."

"Oh," he said softly.

"Residency is three years," I pushed on, showing him all the dire consequences of being interested in someone who wanted to become a doctor. If he was actually interested. "I want to live somewhere else. Experience somewhere else. Relationships don't survive medical school. It would never survive a three-year residency out of state. And honestly, I just don't know…"

He set his hand on my shoulder, and I trailed off.

"It's fine, Annie. I'm not expecting anything from you."

"Good," I said quickly. "Because it's not happening anyway."

"Okay, but we can be friends."

I eyed him skeptically. "Can we?"

"We were friends last night."

I laughed derisively. "Friends who fuck?"

He paused before saying, "Friends...with benefits?"

My first thought was to disagree with him. There was no way we could be that. But...what was stopping that from happening? He understood that neither of us was in a position to date right now. Would it be the worst thing to have someone like Jordan Wright around when I needed some relief, too?

No, no, it would not. It would be fucking amazing. Because the sex was beyond amazing. And I wanted more sex with him...even when I couldn't ask for more.

"Does that actually work?" I asked.

"We could make it work."

I chewed on my lip and twirled the claddagh ring on my finger that my parents had given me for my high school graduation. I never took it off even though it was a beat-up, old thing, so worn through that the band was almost cracked. But I loved it, and it was a constant source of comfort.

"Well, do friends like to eat pizza?"

"Is that a euphemism?" he asked with that indelible smirk.

"Maybe it is."

"Then I would love to eat pizza." He stepped close enough that I could smell his aftershave and had to stop myself from breathing him in. "If you'd like me to go with you to eat pizza."

We were actually doing this.

I nodded. "Yes," I breathed, sealing our fate in the winter breeze.

Jordan Wright was my friend...with benefits.

11

ANNIE

*C*apital Pizza was The Tacos' after-game celebration locale. Mostly because it was the only place still open this late at night. Consequently, the place was packed, and it took a solid thirty-minute wait to get a table big enough to seat nine.

I took a seat next to Jordan and Blaire and across from Julian, Hollin, and Ashleigh. Blaire's roommate, Piper, sat on her other side with her twin brother, Peter, and Peter's boyfriend, Jeremy, taking the end of the table. I'd never been as close to Piper as Blaire because of the soccer team, but I admired that she was a strong woman, running Sinclair Cellars. While it used to run in the Sinclair family, their grandfather had left it to the Medinas, but they'd kept the reputable name. And that was as much as I knew about the wine business in this town.

Once we were seated, we agreed to order a half-dozen pizzas to sate the giant dudes at our table. While everyone else was arguing over what toppings to put on, my gaze drifted to Jordan. He was dressed down in jeans and a button-up with the sleeves rolled up to his elbows.

"What do you prefer?" I asked him.

"Honestly shouldn't eat any," he said with a shrug. "I have five miles to run in the morning."

"Oh, come on. I feel like I just ran five miles, and I'm having some."

"Pepperoni," he said with a shrug. "Do you still run? Outside of soccer?"

I frowned. Maverick running next to me at our Fourth of July marathon. Him collapsing. The screams that had ripped out of my mouth when I realized he wasn't moving. The fastest final three miles I'd run in my life as I rushed to get Sutton once the paramedics took him away.

I shivered.

"Sometimes," I said softly. "It's hard to find time."

"I know. I'm usually up at five or six a.m., and if I have to be in the office early, then I'm running in the middle of the night."

"I used to have a schedule like that," I said. I missed it, if I was honest. But then the memory of Maverick falling down hit me hard again, and I remembered why I'd never taken it back up with such vigor.

"You're opening a winery?" a voice asked at the other end of the table.

Both Jordan and I turned to see Piper's look of disbelief and Hollin's shit-eating grin.

"Yeah, baby, *I'm* opening a winery," Hollin said.

Piper narrowed her dark eyes. "What do you know about running a winery?"

"Everything," he spat back. "I worked at West Texas Winery for years."

Piper snorted. "You managed a bar. That's not the same thing."

"If you're so afraid of the competition, just say so, Pipes," Hollin said, leaning forward.

"Don't call me Pipes," she growled.

Blaire sighed heavily and rolled her eyes. "I did ask you both to *try* to be nice to each other."

This was normal behavior for Piper and Hollin. I had no idea what had transpired to make them hate each other so much, besides Hollin's smug face, but it was constantly like a bomb had gone off in each other's presence. Right this minute, they looked ready to reach across the table and rip out each other's throats.

"You know my fondness for Sinclair Cellars," Ashleigh said conversationally, her voice nasally and grating. "But Julian is going to be investing and working at Wright Vineyard, too." She patted her boyfriend on the arm. "It's going to be great."

Piper looked over at Julian. "You let him con you into this?"

Julian laughed with that soft charism that he had to defuse a situation. "There was no conning. Wright Vineyard is going to be a new winery on the market."

I was so deeply invested in their conversation, listening to their quips back and forth, that I barely registered that Jordan had leaned in closer to me. Not until his hand landed on my thigh under the table. My eyes widened for a second as his fingers slipped lazily under the hem of my soccer shorts, brushing against my sensitive skin.

My eyes tipped back to his, and he arched an eyebrow as if to say, *What?*

No one else was paying attention. No one else could see his hand drifting ever further up my leg, a leisurely pace northward.

I swallowed hard and then reached for my water as my body heated under his rather public touches. I should have stopped him. We'd agreed that we weren't going to have a relationship. But did friends with benefits do this? I didn't know where the line was. And letting him touch me in public felt like crossing it.

Yet...I didn't mind.

Fuck.

His finger reached the apex of my thighs, dragging down my center. I forced down a shiver. I didn't want anyone to notice what the hell was happening. I didn't even know what to think about it. Besides not wanting it to stop and not knowing if that was the right reaction.

Double fuck.

He hit my clit, and I couldn't stop myself from jumping. Blaire glanced back over to me, and Jordan retreated.

"Cold?" she asked, offering me her Italian rose-embroidered jean jacket. It had to have cost a fortune. I knew she'd gotten it for free, like most of her stuff.

"Thanks," I murmured, draping it over my shoulders.

I shot Jordan a warning look, but he was a mask of innocence.

"What?" he asked.

"Don't *what* me."

He leaned forward so that only I could hear him. "Then tell me to stop."

But I wasn't going to do that. So, I settled on glaring at him. He smiled wider and started his ascent back up my legs. His fingers crested my clit faster this time. Our eyes still locked. It took everything in me not to close my eyes and give in to this. My body superheating under the table, in front of everyone. And no one else knew what was happening.

He tipped his head, as if to tell me to look away. I swallowed, scooted forward in my seat, and tried to engage in the conversation. But I couldn't hear any of the argument that was taking place between Piper and Hollin. Blaire and Julian trying to play mediators.

I just felt Jordan slowly working me to climax while he casually drank from his beer, as if nothing at all was happening.

My breath hitched as I came so close to hitting that point that I nearly tipped over my drink. Jordan pulled back then when all eyes came back to me. I shot them a weak smile and was glad that pizza appeared then to distract everyone again.

After two pieces of pepperoni pizza and an entire glass of water, I was coming down from my high. I could still feel the tingling between my legs and the wetness coating my panties.

"Hey, I can drive you home," Jordan offered offhand as soon as he finished his pizza. "I know you said that you had to do some studying tonight."

"I...do," I agreed. "That'd be great. Thanks." I handed

Blaire her jacket back. "Jordan's going to give me a ride home."

Blaire smiled wide, unassuming, unlike Julian and Hollin on the other side of the table. "No problem."

Jordan and I both handed over cash for the pizza. I was glad that I had some on me because I didn't want to be there another minute.

We walked at a normal pace to his car, but as soon as we were inside, the door closed behind us, he grabbed me from across the car, crushing our lips together. I moaned, the heat that had built between my legs not completely extinguished.

"Fuck, I want you," he ground out.

"I noticed that," I gasped.

His dark eyes gleamed. "Oh, you liked that?"

"Almost spilled my drink everywhere as I fought not to come."

"Mmm," he groaned. "I like that. Can I make you come now?"

He didn't wait for my response before his hand slipped under my shorts and slicking through my wetness.

"Fuck, Annie. You're so wet."

My body pulsed at his words. Our lips still pressed together. His hand working my clit in ways that I wasn't entirely sure were possible in his car while I was wearing all of my clothes. But the tension in the pizza parlor coupled with the very public groping had me exploding in mere minutes.

I barely came down before he had the car out of the parking lot and was driving south. Away from my house. I would have fucked him in the backseat of his car at this point, but his house was good enough for me. I didn't even complain that I didn't have time. Because I wanted this—this effortless, sexy, easy thing between us.

No commitments. No strings. No questions. Just friends...and great fucking sex.

12

ANNIE

School blew in like the first snowstorm of the year. First, a joyous run through the blinding white flakes, catching them on your tongue, and crafting snow angels and snowmen out of the winter wonderland. And then, inevitably, a hard freezing blizzard that crushed your soul and made you forget that brief moment of happiness.

I was past the blizzard and onto the dirty slush as my feet tromped through what had once been an idyllic beauty.

This rotation was with radiology. Next was anesthesia. I was really not looking forward to either, but I knew that I needed both to become the kind of emergency medicine doctor that I'd always dreamed of. I'd done two month-long rotations in emergency medicine, and I was working on getting a broader base of knowledge with my electives. Especially after spending months on the other core fields on medicine. I hadn't minded family medicine, which Cézanne was specializing in despite everyone wanting to push her into surgery, but pediatrics had been my least favorite. As an ER doctor, I knew that I'd have to deal with sick kids, but I *hated* seeing them. It was too hard not to imagine Aly or Madison or Jason all day. That had been the hardest rotation by far last semester.

I shuddered, thinking about it, as I pushed out of the hospital and toward my car. I blinked up at the dark sky overhead. Was it really that late?

I checked my phone to see that it was already six o'clock, but the damn winter made it seem so much later. Thanks, daylight saving time.

The other benefit of checking my phone was that I had a message from Jordan.

Any interest in trying the whites tonight?

A smile touched my features before exhaustion won out. As much as I'd love to do that, I couldn't. I needed sustenance and then to study for boards. No wine for me tonight.

I didn't have the energy to respond. So, I dialed his number as I got into my car.

"Hey there," he said.

I could hear typing on the other end of the line. As if he was still working. Maybe he was still at Wright Construction. He really did work as much as I did.

"Hey. I can't do wine tonight. I have to study."

"All right. You could study at my house."

I put him on speaker as I headed out of the hospital deck. "All my stuff is at my house, and I need to eat something. I only had time for a protein bar for lunch, and now, my stomach is eating itself."

"I could pick up Chinese on my way home and meet

you there. There's that new place out by my house that has the best lo mein. You like lo mein?"

"Everyone likes lo mein," I said with a laugh.

"Okay. Let me know what you like, and I'll put in an order."

"Jordan, I can't," I muttered.

Wasn't this the point of friends with benefits? That both of us were too busy for a relationship. Didn't it seem like a relationship to have him pick up dinner for me on his way home?

"It's just studying, Annie. Your house is still a disaster. Not exactly conducive to getting anything done. And I have plenty of work to keep me occupied all night. I won't be in your way."

"It sounds like a date," I told him.

He paused as if he, too, knew that it sounded like a date. But he only hesitated a moment. The businessman in him had prepared for my dissent. "I used to pick up Chinese for my friend Cush while he was going through medical school in Vancouver. I know how grueling it is, Annie. This is what friends do."

I chewed on my bottom lip as I pulled into my driveway. My house *was* a wreck. I'd had trouble already, trying to get work done when contractors kept coming by to get measurements and the landlord was about to rip out all of the hardwood due to the water damage. Plus, Chinese did sound pretty amazing.

A lingering part of me said that I should be mad at Jordan. The last three years had been rocky between us at best, openly hostile at worst. It was strange to want to ditch my own house for his mansion and peace and quiet.

I wasn't even thinking about the sex. Okay, maybe just a little.

But giving in felt like an admission. Maybe just staying home was the right idea.

"Nah, I'll pass. Thanks for the offer though."

"All right," he said, carefully masking what sounded like disappointment. "I'm about to leave the office. Text me if you change your mind."

I hung up and stepped into my own house. I'd made the right decision. I was sure of it. We weren't dating. I wasn't going to go over to his house for no reason. After I'd slept over twice this weekend.

A yawn broke free as I pushed into the living room. Sleep always got harder once the semester started.

Last semester, I'd taken much of November and December off from rotations for all of my interviews. It was a whirlwind of residency programs. I didn't get to see much of any one city, except the cab ride from the airport and the inside of the hospitals, which all looked the same. I'd lost more sleep from interviewing than from rotations, and I still hadn't caught up. Even with a few weeks ostensibly off.

Jennifer was editing images on the small breakfast nook table, which was cluttered with her equipment. I frowned. Definitely no space for me to get to work. Fuck.

"Hey, Jen," I said. "How's editing?"

"The grueling part of the job," she said as she clicked incessantly in Photoshop.

"Are you even halfway through last weekend's wedding?"

She shook her head. "Nope," she said and then

glanced up at me with a smile. The top half of her blonde bob was in a bun, and her hazel eyes glittered with excitement. This was the Jennifer that I adored. Completely unassuming, full of joy, and confident in her abilities. But when she stepped out of her circle of confidence in photography was when she fell apart. She'd had anxiety her entire life, and while it was managed, she still slipped when she got into uncomfortable situations. Like...Julian Wright.

"But it's okay. I had the most beautiful bride, and Evan was second shooter. So, we had a great time."

I smiled inwardly. She didn't realize that her second shooter, Evan, was totally into her. Not that I intended to point it out.

"I'm glad you did," I said as I retreated to my room.

My body sagged when I looked at my once-beautiful room and the mess it was now. The warped boards, the damage to the baseboards, the empty closet, a few Amazon boxes scattered around the room. I'd had to order new shoes for my upcoming interviews, and I might have gone overboard. As with everything. Suddenly, it all felt like too much. There was no way that I was going to get any work done.

I slung my backpack down on the bed and thought about screaming.

One bad day, and I'd had to suffer the consequences for months. I opted for a quick shower, towel-drying my messy red hair and pulling it up into a neat ponytail. Then I started packing a bag.

* * *

I wasn't sure when I'd decided to go to Jordan's, but suddenly, I was on his doorstep with a change of clothes and my backpack. I rang the doorbell.

Jordan appeared a minute later, opening the door cautiously. He was still in his suit. He must have just gotten home. Considering it was an hour later than when we'd talked, he must have stayed even later at work after I declined.

His eyebrows shot up. "Annie." He slipped the door open wider. "Come in."

"I should have texted," I said automatically, twirling the claddagh ring around my finger.

"You're in luck. I ordered enough Chinese for a family of four. There was a special."

I laughed softly, staring around at his mansion and marveling that someone with that much money still appreciated specials. "Sesame chicken?" I asked hopefully.

"That's my favorite," he said, shutting the door. "So definitely."

I exhaled softly. "Well, great. I like Mongolian beef, too."

"Also included in my family pack," he said, following me into the kitchen.

"Jesus," I whispered.

A dozen little white Chinese boxes were spread out like a feast. He hadn't been kidding about enough for a family of four.

"Pick your poison," he offered.

After loading up a plate with sesame chicken, Mongolian beef, lo mein, fried rice, and two egg rolls, I retreated to the enormous dining room table. My eyes widened with relief. Nothing like the tiny space I'd been using the last three years. I could probably fit all of my notes here.

I set my plate down and dug out my computer, books, and notes. Jordan ate silently across from me, scrolling leisurely on his iPad.

"What are you working on?" I asked him after downing half of my plate in a feverish haze of hunger.

"Soccer complex," he muttered, not taking his eyes from the screen.

My heart skipped. Isaac had told me about this, but it had slipped my mind. Wright Construction had gotten the contract to build an outdoor stadium for a new soccer team coming to Lubbock. It was our first professional sports team, and everyone was pretty excited. My brother was especially excited to be the on-ground project manager.

"What do you have to do for that?"

Jordan glanced up once with an amused look on his face. "I thought you had to study."

I glowered at him. "I do."

"Why'd you decide to show up?"

"Free food."

He snorted. "Doubtful."

"Jennifer is using the table for edits, and my room is still a mess from the flood," I admitted. "I was worried that I wouldn't get anything done."

"So, here and not the library?"

I gestured to the Chinese food again with a smirk. "Like I said, free food."

"I'm doing everything for the soccer complex," he admitted. "I was the one who reached out to the team to suggest a site to build."

"Whoa," I whispered. I hadn't known that. "How did you know they were looking?"

He smirked. "That's half my job. I can do all the things that Morgan and Austin and David do, but my strength really lies in making connections, pinpointing new contracts, and negotiations."

"Huh. Like how you convinced me to study here."

He managed to look smug instead of sheepish. "If you get the studying done, then does it matter?"

I laughed. "Mildly manipulative."

"It's not...manipulating. It's negotiations, love," he said with a wink and then returned to his scrolling.

I just shook my head at him and went back to my own work. I didn't mind the "negotiations." Not really. This was actually peaceful, and I felt locked into my work. Soon, the Chinese was cold and forgotten, and I was deep, deep into my studies. My eyes could barely stay open by the time I looked up from my stupor.

"Oh God, is it already midnight?" I muttered, rubbing my hands over my eyes.

Jordan had retreated to the couch at some point and was typing furiously into his laptop. "It is."

I yawned. "I should head home."

"Take the guest bedroom."

I closed my laptop and walked around to where he was sitting. His dark eyes drifted up to mine, and he quirked an eyebrow in question.

"Are you going to bed?"

He shrugged. "Soon."

A part of me knew that I should go to the guest bedroom. I'd seen it before. It was lush and probably nicer than my own bed anyway. But he'd done exactly what he'd said he'd do. He'd gotten Chinese and left me to study. I felt better prepared for tomorrow than I had in weeks...maybe months. We'd been...friends. Just like he'd said. I'd been skeptical, and he'd proven me wrong.

I reached out for his laptop, moving it to the coffee table. Then I straddled him, settling my weight down onto him. His hands moved to my waist and slid to my hips.

"This is not studying," he teased.

"It's late," I reminded him before my lips dipped to his.

He kissed me back hungrily, as if he'd barely restrained himself from kissing me all evening. The control behind that kiss revealed everything I needed to know. He wanted the benefits from this arrangement as much as the friends. And he was willing to forgo this to make me comfortable.

"Come to bed," I murmured against his lips.

He didn't need to be told twice. He stood, lifting me into the air. I wrapped my arms and legs tight around him, and then he walked me to his bedroom. No guest bedroom necessary after all.

13

JORDAN

*A*nnie started studying at my house almost every evening.

She didn't stay the night every night. Sometimes, she actually finished her work at a decent hour and went home to spend time with Jennifer. On rare occasions, she had study sessions with other fourth years, and I didn't see or hear from her at all.

Which was fine.

We weren't dating. No matter how Julian or Hollin joked when it was brought up. And if I was honest, this was much easier than any relationship I'd been in. Those relationships had always been as brittle as glass. Glossy and seemingly perfect on the outside, but one good hit to the surface, and the entire thing shattered.

"Okay," Morgan said, clicking her pen against the notebook in front of her. "I think that's a wrap. We all need lunch. We can come back in, say, an hour and a half to get back at this."

Morgan was the CEO of Wright Construction. She'd

been promoted before she was thirty, and a lot of people had been skeptical she could handle the job. Especially my asshole father, who had all but staged a coup to take the position from her. But Morgan had proven them all wrong. She was more than capable, if our stock numbers were any indication.

She was seated next to David, Sutton's husband and CFO, and her brother, Austin Wright, a senior vice president. The other vice presidents and the executive directors were present, discussing the new soccer complex.

When I'd moved here from Vancouver, there hadn't been a position for me available, but they'd added an executive director position, and I'd stepped right in. There had been a few grumbles about it until I'd proven myself with The Buddy Holly Hall, a new performing arts center that was going to bring Broadway to Lubbock.

"Excellent," Austin said. He scraped his chair back and stretched. "I could use some Hank's. Anyone else?"

"I'm in for Hank's," David agreed. It was everyone's favorite local fried chicken place.

"Jordan?" Austin asked.

I shook my head. "Count me out."

"You're not just going to sit at your desk and forget to eat again, are you?" Austin joked.

"I'm heading to Thai Pepper." I'd promised Annie that I'd bring her lunch since her rotation this week was intense and *she* had kept forgetting to break for lunch.

Morgan eyed me astutely. "Haven't y'all noticed Jordan leaving all the time for lunch now? He used to only get up from his desk once a month, and now, it's two or three times a *week*."

"Huh," Austin said. "Who's the girl?"

"No one," I said with a laugh as I stood and buttoned my suit jacket.

"No one," Austin mimicked with an eye roll. "David, do you believe him?"

He grimaced. "I mean, I might have heard who the girl is from Sutton already. It's not entirely fair."

Austin's eyes glimmered. "Spill."

"It's Annie," I said as I pushed my chair in. "We're just friends."

"Just friends," Morgan said with air quotes to punctuate the words.

"Is this like just friends, but you're really dating?" Austin asked, slinging an arm around my shoulders. "Or like just friends, but you're fucking?"

I shook my head, pushing him off of me.

"Leave him be," David said, jostling Austin. "Imagine if everyone had treated you like this about Julia."

"They did!" he insisted.

Morgan scoffed behind them. "They did not. *I* was the one who got shit about Patrick, you ass."

"Well, yeah, you were dating my best friend. What did you expect?"

Morgan swatted him on the back of the head. "Why are you the worst?"

I laughed. It had been three years since I moved, and still, I wasn't used to having this much family around. I had friends back in Vancouver who I'd always been close with but nothing like this. Nothing unconditional. It still baffled me.

We took the elevator to the bottom floor and spread out as we headed to our cars.

"Have fun," Austin said with a wink.

Morgan laughed and squeezed my arm. "Don't let him bother you. If you want to keep you and Annie a secret for longer, I don't blame you one bit. Our family is pretty intense."

She didn't let me respond before hiking across the parking lot in her four-inch heels to her new black Tesla Model S. After driving mine, she'd immediately gone and purchased one. We were still in negotiations with Tesla to get a Supercharger in Lubbock now that it was becoming a hot commodity.

I tried to let everyone's comments fall off of me. Maybe Morgan understood what was happening with Annie. But still, not quite. She and Patrick had been a secret. Annie and I weren't a secret. We just weren't... together either.

Thai Pepper was packed by the time I arrived. I was glad that I'd put in an order earlier this morning, so I just walked up to the counter and picked up our two pad thais. I drove them to the hospital and found her in the cafeteria, seated next to Cézanne, with her head buried in a book. She looked half-asleep.

"Superman!" Cézanne cheered. "Please tell me one of those is for me."

"You can have mine," I offered.

Annie's head tipped up. She had dark circles under her eyes. Even though she'd claimed to be sleeping more since staying at my house, I wasn't sure how she'd been functioning before. Still, she was beautiful. I couldn't deny that I liked her just as much in scrubs, a messy bun, and no makeup as I did when she was all done up, snake-skin heels and all.

"Hey," she said with a smile that lit up her face and dropped all of the exhaustion. "I hope you got it extra hot."

"They thought I was crazy for asking for it, but I managed." I pulled the food out of the plastic bag and passed one to her.

She opened it and shuddered just at the smell of the heat. "This is going to burn."

"I don't even know you," Cézanne said, wrinkling her nose. "That looks like a powder keg."

"Exactly. Just how I like it."

I offered mine to Cézanne. "I still have time to find something else."

She waved her hand at me. "Boy, sit down. You should eat lunch with your girl."

Annie looked up at her with fire in her eyes. "Stop it."

Cézanne grinned like she had no idea what Annie was talking about. I was about to make an excuse. I some-times brought her lunch, but we didn't eat together. She was too busy and usually only had a few minutes for lunch. I didn't mind getting her something to eat, but I didn't think that she wanted me to interrupt her day.

Then Annie looked up at me and smiled again. She patted the seat next to her. "Don't let your lunch get cold."

I decided not to second-guess her and sank onto the bench. Cézanne and Annie kept up a steady stream of conversation about their current rotations. I knew next to nothing about what they were going through. So I let the easy conversation drift over me. Even as out of place as I was in a business suit next to these doctors in white coats, they never let me feel left out.

"How's the winery going?" Cézanne asked.

"Well, it's not going anywhere yet," I said with a shrug, pushing away my empty pad thai. "We put in an offer to purchase one. At first, the owners seemed excited, and then they asked for an extension while someone else looked at it. It's frustrating since it didn't seem like anyone else had even known about the property."

"When is the extension up?" Annie asked.

"Tonight."

"Oh good. Then it'll all be over."

For some reason, I didn't think so.

Cézanne stood from her seat. "Duty calls. Are you still coming over for the study session tonight?"

"I'll be there," Annie agreed.

Cézanne left, and Annie stood, too, with a yawn.

"So, I won't see you tonight?" I ventured, collecting her empty lunch.

She shot me a mischievous grin. "Maybe when I need to sleep."

Fuck, I wanted to kiss her.

"Why do I think we're not talking about sleep?"

"Because tomorrow is Saturday. So, no work tomorrow," she said. "We can actually sleep in."

"My little vampire wants me to keep her up all night."

She twirled her claddagh ring around her finger. She did it all the time. Especially when she was trying to make a decision. Then she bit her lip and nodded.

"It'll be late," she warned me.

"I'll be up."

It took everything in me not to wrap my arm around her waist and pull her into me. But we weren't dating. We were friends. And friends didn't kiss in front of coworkers. The benefits were reserved for less public places.

"Then, deal."

"Don't forget to bring your workout clothes."

She pouted. "I hate that I told you I wanted to work out more. Don't you know I'd rather sleep?"

I laughed, and despite myself, I stepped forward and hooked my pinkie around hers. Her eyes shot up to mine. For a second, we just stood there. Questions in her emerald-green eyes. A heartbeat too long for friends. A breath too long for benefits.

She swallowed and then pulled back, breaking contact and running a shaky hand back through her hair. "Change of clothes. Got it. Let me know how it goes with the winery extension."

I nodded. "I will. Good luck at the study session."

Annie smiled again. It was only half as bright as when she'd first seen me, and then she disappeared back to work. Still, I couldn't bring myself to regret that one bit of contact. Even though I knew she'd found it more forward than the hours lost in my sheets, where I fucked her brains out.

* * *

Did you hear from Larissa?

Julian texted me for the tenth time today. But no, in fact, I hadn't heard from Larissa. And I was starting to get pissed off. It was nearly five o'clock, and I could hardly concentrate on my own work while waiting for her call about the winery.

I hadn't even wanted this stupid winery, and now that I was invested, it seemed to be taking over my life. I was about to text Larissa for an update when her number flashed on my screen.

"Hey, Larissa," I said.

"Jordan."

"Cutting it a little close."

She exhaled in frustration. "I've been trying to sort this mess out so that you don't have to."

I sat up straighter. "What mess?"

"The winery has had a second offer come in. It's higher than yours. Though not significantly so. We could go over it easily."

"Who is it?"

She sighed again. "That's the tricky part. They won't tell me. They said it was an anonymous offer. No matter how much I tried to find out, they stuck to their guns."

"Frustrating. What do you suggest?"

"I think we need to go big or go home. If this is the property you want, we should show that we're serious. Scare off the competition."

"How much?"

She threw out a number, and I gritted my teeth. Of course. Some asshole had had to come in and mess up the plan that I'd set up. I'd have to rerun the numbers to make sure it was feasible. We had the money. That wasn't really the problem. But I wanted it to still be a sound business decision.

"If you don't want to go that high, we can always go lower," Larissa said instantly. "The property has a history of problems, as you know. So, it could be that we skirt the issue and see if the anonymous person comes back with something else."

"No," I said at once. "Your idea makes sense. I run it by Julian and Hollin. How long do we have?"

She paused a little too long. "They want an answer today."

"What?" I ground out. "They made us wait an extra week, and now, they're riding us hard?"

"I did say the property has issues."

Haunted. That was the word she wasn't using. I'd heard that from multiple people since I'd looked into purchasing it. The property had had too many issues over the years for it not to get a reputation for being haunted despite the fact that no one had ever died at the place. Well, as far as I knew.

"Give me an hour," I told her. "I'll get back to you."

"Sounds good. Thanks, Jordan."

I hung up the phone and stood with such force that my chair smacked hard into the bookshelves behind me. This was all Julian's and Hollin's fault. They'd dragged me into it, and now, I had to deal with all the fallout. Story of my fucking life.

It wasn't even really a decision. I knew what they'd say. That as long as I okayed the finances, they were in. Of course they would be. It was their pet project. It was my *investment*. Two different things.

I ran the numbers first before calling Julian and Hollin. We put the higher offer in an hour later. I still wasn't happy about it even though they were. It was a risk. As a businessman, I accepted a certain level of risk in my life, but a haunted winery? That might be taking it too far.

I didn't stay my irritation until Annie crawled into my bed just after midnight. Her hands tugging off my boxers, her mouth falling hot and needy on my cock. My hands threaded through her hair as she made me forget all about my abysmal afternoon.

14

ANNIE

*T*he smell of coffee woke me.

I groaned and peeled my eyes open. Jordan stood with two steaming mugs in his hands. He was shirtless in nothing but a pair of black boxers. His hair was wet and floppy, as if he'd just gotten out of the shower.

"Is that for me?" I whispered, rubbing my bleary eyes.

"It's almost noon."

I yawned again as I took the coffee from his hand. "I was so tired."

"I noticed that."

"Did you already shower?" I pouted. "Without me?"

He laughed, sinking into the bed next to me. "I worked out this morning. Needed the shower."

"How long have you been up?" I asked between sips of coffee.

The first time I'd stayed the night, Jordan had made the mistake of trying to talk to me before I had my coffee. And I wasn't coherent enough for that. I wasn't picky about coffee, but he was. He liked a French press or a

Chemex or a cold brew. Anything but a pot or a Keurig. I'd rolled my eyes at him, but if he wanted to make me fancy coffee, then I wouldn't complain.

"A couple hours. You looked like you needed the sleep. I wore you out last night."

I snorted. "You mean, *I* wore *you* out."

He grinned devilishly. "I could fix that." He set his mug down and crawled onto the bed toward me.

I squeaked as I put down my precious life force. His lips landed on mine. He tasted like espresso and hazelnuts, and I could have drowned in his caffeinated kisses.

He rolled me over so that I was on top of him. I could feel him hardening underneath me, and I twirled my hips in a figure eight. He groaned, skimming his hands up to my face and pulling me in for another hot kiss.

"What are your plans for today?" I whispered against his lips.

"You."

I laughed as he flipped me back over with him on top, pressing his cock against the front of my green lace panties. His hands roaming freely under the oversized white T-shirt he'd given me to sleep in last night.

"All day?" I teased as he pinched my nipple, forcing me to arch up against his hand.

"Have somewhere else to be, love?" He pushed up the shirt and replaced his mouth where his hand had just been.

I should have told him to stop calling me love. It wasn't the first time though. I'd thought it was just a joke. He always said it in such a teasing manner that it had to be. He knew the arrangement. He was also too busy for anything but whatever we were doing right now.

Not that it explained him reaching for my hand in the hospital cafeteria.

"Work," I finally got out as he slid down my front.

His mouth landed hot on my core as he blew against my panties. I squirmed uncontrollably. Then he hooked his fingers underneath the material, slipping two fingers inside of me before I could say anything else.

"Work can wait," he told me.

And he wasn't wrong. It could wait.

He worked me until I nearly climaxed before removing his fingers from inside of me. I clenched down, trying to hold him there, trying to reach that point where I fell over and off into oblivion. But he just smirked at me as he pulled the panties off and tossed them to the floor along with his boxers.

His hands gripped my hips, and he flipped me over, pulling my ass high into the air before settling between my legs.

"Mmm," he purred.

He slid his still-wet fingers over my opening. Swirling them around and around until I thought I'd come. I was teetering on the edge. Then his cock pressed against the opening of my pussy, and he slid in easily. I was so worked up that it took no effort, even from that angle. In one deep, long thrust, he was inside of me. Then he built a rhythm that bordered on painful. If I hadn't been so turned on, it would have hurt more. But right now, all I could feel was how fucking amazing this all was until I was screaming into the pillow as I came apart.

Jordan kept going. Holding on as I finished, and then just as I came all the way down, he let go, digging his fingers into my hips and emptying himself inside of me.

We both collapsed, breathing heavy, before I padded to the bathroom to clean up. I returned to the bedroom with him naked and satisfied on the bed. He was lying in repose, his eyes closed, face tranquil, and arms over his head.

"Good morning," I murmured, taking a sip of my coffee, which had since gone cool.

He cracked open an eye. "Morning."

I grinned, downed the rest of the coffee, and snuggled into bed next to him. "What do you have to do today?"

"I already told you."

I giggled as he nuzzled my neck. "Yeah, but besides me."

He groaned. "Are you making me think about work after fucking you so thoroughly?"

"How'd the winery thing go yesterday? You never told me."

He buried his head between my breasts and murmured incoherently.

"That bad?"

He looked up at me with his big brown eyes. "Someone made a higher offer. We countered. We'll find out today if the other people make another offer."

"And what happens if they do?"

"I curse Julian and Hollin for ever involving me in this."

I chuckled and brushed my fingers across his brow.

"You want it, too. I know you do. Who put in the other offer?"

He propped himself up on his elbow. "That's the thing. It was anonymous. They don't have to tell us even if it's not, but Larissa is good at her job. We got her because she has an eye for these things."

"Frustrating."

He shrugged. "What do you have for work?"

"I need to study later, but I promised Jen I'd meet her at Sutton's work. She's taking some pictures for the bakery."

He nodded thoughtfully. "Sounds nice."

"And Sutton said she'd go with me to find something to wear to my Dallas interview."

"That's next weekend?"

"Yeah, I leave Thursday. I've had a ton of interviews, and it still makes me nervous to think about."

"I can understand that. You never know what to expect." He ran his fingers through my hair. "What are your plans until you meet your friends?"

I snuggled in closer as an answer.

"Why don't we go for a run?"

I groaned and rolled over. "Must we?"

"You said you wanted to start working out again."

That wasn't what I'd meant. Just the thought sent shivers down my skin and made my throat close up.

"Yeah, but running..."

"You used to run all the time."

"I know," I said.

But Jordan didn't know the specifics of why I'd stopped running. He didn't know about Maverick. He didn't know about any of it. And I didn't have any desire to tell him.

I scrambled out of bed. "You've already worked out. You don't need a run, too."

"Annie...is everything all right?"

"Fine," I ground out. "It's fine. I just don't want to run, okay?"

"All right," he said, holding his hands out. "We don't have to run. Would you like breakfast?"

"You know, I think I'm going to go." I found my bag, pulling on sweats, a T-shirt, and a hoodie.

Jordan threw his feet over the side, and I could feel his stare on me. "Did I say something wrong?"

"Wrong?" I asked as if I were confused. "No."

He huffed as if I was being purposefully dense. I was. I didn't want to talk about Maverick. I didn't want to go running. It had been four years since he collapsed next to me, but after three years in med school, I was prepared to fix the situation now. Not discuss it.

"You don't have to go," he insisted.

"I know." I ran a hand down my face as I shouldered my bag. "It's fine. I have so much studying to do anyway this weekend. I shouldn't just lie in bed."

He shot me a disbelieving look. "Are you sure? I could make breakfast. I'm pretty handy with French toast."

I smiled, tight and guarded. I couldn't manage my more carefree smile. "That's all right. I'm not hungry."

He followed me as I headed for the front door. "Are you going to tell me what happened here?"

"Nothing. I just need to study."

Jordan reached out and took my shoulder. "Hey. You know you can talk to me, right?"

"We're not dating, Jordan," I said, sharper than I'd intended.

"I know that," he said tersely. I narrowed my eyes at him, but he held his ground. "We're just friends. And friends tell each other why they just freaked out."

"I didn't freak out," I said with an eye roll. "I just don't want to run."

"Then we don't have to run, but you don't have to run out of here either."

I closed my eyes and sighed. "This is why I can't do relationships right now."

"Why?" he demanded.

"Because I don't have time for this."

He kept his deep, dark eyes on mine. "Fine, Annie. Run out of here and don't explain yourself. Use our arrangement as your scapegoat." He shrugged and crossed his arms. "Are you coming over tonight?"

"No," I bit out. "I'm going to study."

"All right," he said, just as irritated as I was.

I could see the frustration roiling through him. That I wouldn't tell him what this was all about.

But it wasn't that I wouldn't.

I just...couldn't.

No part of me was ready for that conversation, and I certainly wasn't going to have it here.

So, I turned on my heel and left. Left behind all the unanswered questions and expectations. We weren't dating, and I didn't owe him anything.

15

JORDAN

*W*ell, what the fuck was that about?

I slammed the door shut behind Annie. So much for friends with benefits not being complicated. Things had been going so well. And now... whatever that was.

My anger simmered in my gut, threatening to boil over if I didn't give it an outlet. I'd always had a short temper. Courtesy of my asshole father. But I'd learned to rein it in when I had to in business. In my personal life, it was my weakest link, and I didn't want to let it loose here. Even though I *was* frustrated and wanted to.

I threw on running clothes and forced myself to go for that run anyway. Annie didn't want to go, but now, I needed to go. The first few steps were too fast. I knew it wasn't a sustainable mile, but I didn't care. I just ran and let the anger out on the pavement.

My breath frosted in front of me, but I wasn't cold. And for the first time in a long while, I missed Vancouver. Missed the run along the Stanley Park Seawall, the way the sun shimmered along the waterfront in the winter, the eclectic food options, the vibrancy of my home. I even missed the rain. Fuck, who knew I'd ever miss the rain? But I was used to it raining what felt like half of the year, and now, it never rained in Lubbock's arid climate.

A few miles in, I slowed my pace. The nostalgia of Vancouver had brought my temper back to normal. Whatever had upset Annie wasn't my concern. If she didn't want to tell me and she didn't want to run, then fine. I'd run without her.

Six miles later, I returned to my house and took another shower. I found my phone where I'd left it charging. I had a missed call from Larissa.

My heart skipped. I'd been so occupied with Annie that I forgot we'd hear from the winery seller today. She'd kept me so thoroughly fixated that I forgot business. Who the hell was I?

I called Larissa back. "Hey, Larissa. Sorry about that. I was out for a run."

"Jordan, good to hear from you."

"Do you have news?"

"I do. I wanted to call to deliver this: you got the winery!"

I released a relieved breath. "That's *great* news, Larissa. Really great news."

"I'll let you deliver it to Julian and Hollin."

"Of course."

"I'm sending the contract your way right now. Everything looks good to me, but look it over and tell me if there's anything you want to change."

"Will do. Did you hear anything else from the other

people who offered?"

She sighed. "I didn't. I know that they went back to them to ask if they'd go over our asking price, and they said no. So, it's yours!"

I nodded in relief. It was still strange to me. Usually, I knew who I was going up against in business. I didn't particularly like thinking that my opponent was a ghost.

Larissa congratulated me again and then got off the phone. I read the entire contract before calling Julian and Hollin and asking them to meet me at Walkers.

I staked out an oversized booth at the coffee shop and bar and ordered a latte from the barista. Walkers was actually the first place I'd ever met Annie. She'd been standing against the bar at a medical school orientation happy hour. She'd been shockingly aggressive, and I'd been into it. I still thought about her when I walked into the darkened interior with all of its hardwood booths and glossy bar. During the day, it was a coffee bar, and as the sun set, it turned into a real bar, serving all sorts of libations. I came here frequently enough that I had other memories layered over my first one with Annie.

Julian and Hollin showed up together, finding my table immediately and heading toward me. Hollin in jeans and a button-up, belt buckle, and boots and all. Julian in crisp maroon pants, a white polo, and gray cardigan. They were a mismatched pair and still had turned into the closest of friends. It was one of Julian's specialties.

"What's all this about?" Julian asked, shaking my hand when I slid out of the booth to meet them.

I grinned. "We got the winery."

"What?" Julian gasped.

Hollin's eyes widened. "We did?"

"I wanted to tell you in person."

"Holy shit!" Hollin crowed.

Julian looked amazed and jubilant. He threw his arms around me in a careless way I hadn't seen since we were kids. "You did it!"

I laughed and released him, shaking Hollin's hand. "I didn't do much."

"Whatever, man," Hollin said. "We never would have gotten here without you."

They were probably right, but I just laughed them off. I was far too buoyant from our victory. They pulled me over to the bar. I couldn't even find it in me to argue when they convinced the barista to pour us shots of something clear. I had a way with business, and they had their own charismatic specialties. Apparently, getting drinks out of a barista was one of Hollin's.

One drink turned into five, which turned into ten. I stopped counting as we celebrated well into the evening, forgetting all about the work I should have been doing and the earlier argument with Annie.

When David showed up with Jensen, Austin, Landon, and Patrick in tow, it was only then that I remembered why I'd chosen Walkers to begin with. It was David's birthday. All of the guys had taken the night off and planned to start festivities at Walkers.

I clapped David on the back. "Happy fucking birthday."

David cracked up. "Looks like someone started celebrating without me."

I laughed. "We got the winery."

"That's incredible," David said, shaking my hand. "I'm happy for you all. I know you've been busy with it."

"What winery?" Jensen asked. He appeared at my other side with a bourbon in his hand. Top-shelf likely. Jensen was the oldest Wright. He'd been CEO and given it up to pursue his love of architecture. It was his wedding to Emery where I'd managed to fuck everything up with both Annie and Missy. A talent, I know.

"We bought West Texas Winery," I told him.

Austin wrinkled his nose. "That shithole?"

His best friend, Patrick, elbowed him in the side. "Dude."

"It is," I agreed anyway. "But we have big plans for it."

"Isn't it haunted?" Landon asked with a laugh.

"If you believe in that sort of thing," I said with a shrug.

"It's had one too many problems not to blame it on something," Austin added.

Jensen rolled his eyes. "It's not haunted. That's ridiculous."

"I'll blame it on mismanagement."

"Seems more reasonable," Jensen said. "Haunted."

"It's what everyone says," Landon added.

Julian appeared then with another shot.

I took it from him and lifted it into the air. "To David's birthday and owning a haunted winery."

All the other guys raised their glasses at the toast. We all drank deep. The tequila hardly even burned. I didn't even need a chaser. That was probably a problem. I hadn't let loose like this in Lubbock in years. Not since the night our mom's cancer had gone into remission. We'd celebrated for three straight days. We hadn't thought she'd make it this time, but a year of chemotherapy, and they'd declared her cancer-free. This didn't feel quite like that, but it was definitely worth celebrating.

The conversation turned to work, as it so often did with so many from Wright in one place. I wasn't even sure when Morgan had turned up to make fun of us all for talking work at a birthday party.

"You all are the absolute worst," she said with an eye roll. "I'm going to get another drink to avoid this conversation."

I laughed, finishing off number thirteen...or was it fifteen? Uncertain. I was drunk. That was for sure.

David pushed past me and straight toward the entrance. I turned and found Sutton standing in the entranceway. He picked her up and swung her in a circle like they were in some fucking Hallmark movie. But it wasn't Sutton that stopped me in my tracks. It was the woman standing next to her—Annie.

She was in a black dress that I'd never seen before. It hugged her features to her hips and then flared out in a flowy skirt to her knees. Her wild red hair had been tamed into some intricate updo, and she had on more makeup than I'd seen from her in weeks.

She was deep in conversation with Jennifer, who tugged her toward the bar. Neither of them noticed that I was even here. After our fight this morning, I probably should give her space.

But I didn't.

I stepped right up to her, leaning into the bar and

sliding my hand up her waist. She jumped almost out of her skin before she saw it was me.

"Jordan," she gasped. "What are you doing here?"

I arched an eyebrow. "It's David's birthday."

"Right," she whispered.

I moved in even closer so that we were nearly touching. My fingers found hers in the empty space between our bodies. She flushed and tugged back.

"Stop it," she hissed.

"Why?"

"We're in public."

"So?"

She took a deep breath and shook her head. "Don't. Not tonight."

Jennifer passed her a drink and shot me a pained look. "I'm going to go find Sutton."

Then she scampered off, leaving us alone.

"I thought you were studying," I said as my brain remembered her words to me this morning.

"Not that it's any of your business," she got out, "but Sutton insisted I come with her since she got a sitter for Jason and Madison. I agreed to one drink."

"How exactly is that none of my business?"

"I don't have to tell you where I am." She took a sip of her drink, averting her gaze.

"You didn't have to *lie* to me."

My temper was a caged animal, threatening to rip free and devastate everything in its path. I wished that I'd had a longer leash. That I had found a way to channel my anger into something productive. And while sometimes I could, when I was drunk...all bets were off.

"I didn't lie," Annie shot back. "I had planned to study all evening. I told Sutton that I wasn't going out this semester at all because I was too busy. But she's my best friend, so...here I am."

"You had to know that I was going to be here."

"And how would I know that?" she snapped. "You didn't tell me that you were coming to David's party."

"Not after you had a meltdown at my house this morning."

She took a step back. "Fuck you, Jordan."

She turned away from me, but I grasped her arm.

"We are *not* dating," she spat at me. She shook with the control to not raise her voice. "We're *not*."

"I heard you, Annie," I growled. "We're not dating. We're fucking. Friends with benefits. Whatever you want to call it."

"Fucking is fine with me." Her eyes were twin flames. "Because right now, I'm not sure we're even friends."

"Fine," I said.

"Fine," she repeated through gritted teeth.

She jerked out of my grip and stalked across the room. She stood like a sentinel next to Jennifer and Sutton. They all laughed and joked while Annie sipped her drink and pointedly avoided my gaze. She finished her one drink, hugged her friends, and then headed for the door.

She really *had* come for only one drink.

I'd been in conversation with Julian and Hollin about the winery when I saw her slip out. I didn't even make an excuse; I just darted for the exit.

I caught up to her on the sidewalk next to her car.

"Annie."

She sighed heavily and then turned to face me. Her eyes glittered in the moonlight. I wanted to kiss her, to brush aside all the harsh words we'd said to each other. Just to take her home and forget it'd all happened.

"What do you want, Jordan?"

"I don't want this to be the end."

It wasn't what I'd meant to say. Instead, it was the truth.

"Whatever it is, Jordan, it has to end eventually," she said, defeated. "I'm leaving. I told you that from the start. I'm leaving in a few months, and you're staying. We can't date."

"Okay," I said calmly, stepping closer to her. "I know you don't want to date."

"No," she said with a shake of her head. "We *can't* date." She drew an imaginary line between our bodies. "This is the line in the sand."

"And if I want more?" I asked stupidly, drunkenly. A question I never would have asked sober. Not in a million years when she was right there in my grasp.

She crossed her arms, blocking me from her body. "If you can't stay on your side of the line, then that's that."

I didn't know what to say to that. Because Annie and I worked. We worked just how we fucking were. I'd be an idiot to fuck with that. But I was drunk and honest, and I couldn't deny that crossing that fucking line sounded like the right move.

So, when Annie opened the door and got inside her car, I let her drive away. I wouldn't push her for something she didn't want. Even if she was what I wanted.

PART III

LINE IN THE SAND

16

ANNIE

"*W*elcome to UT Southwestern," Kimi said cheerfully from the front of our small group of medical students. "We're the only emergency medicine residency in Dallas and proud of it. As a third-year resident myself, I'm here to answer any questions about what goes into the residency program, the interviews, and tours."

I covered my yawn with my notepad.

I'd arrived in Dallas the previous day, and unlike a lot of the other interviews I'd been to, I was paired with a current resident, Prisha. The hospital had put me up in Prisha's house, and she'd taken me out to a local barbeque place. We came home early. I'd only had one drink. I should have slept great, but I'd tossed and turned all night. Actually, I hadn't had a restful night of sleep since the argument with Jordan on Saturday.

I'd wanted to go over and spend the night in his comfy bed and study at his enormous dining room table and eat takeout like normal humans. But I'd drawn the line in the sand. I wasn't going to be the one to cross it.

With another yawn, I followed Kimi through the hospital. Apparently, she was always this chipper. I'd never been a morning person. So, I trudged through the tour, happy that we stopped for coffee long enough that I could become a human again.

"This is so boring, right?" whispered another resident-hopeful. He was a tall white guy with loose blond curls and wide eyes the color of the Caribbean Sea.

I grinned. "So boring. As if we haven't all seen a dozen of these hospitals."

"All hospitals look the same."

"Tell me about it."

He held his hand out. "Cord."

"Annie."

We shook, and he winked at me before turning back to Kimi.

"When's your interview?" Cord asked as we continued through the hospital.

I checked my phone. "In, like, three hours."

"Mine too. Where else have you interviewed?"

"Oh God, so many places. Atlanta, Houston, Austin, D.C., Chicago..." I trailed off.

"I'm from Atlanta. So, I interviewed there, too. Emory?"

"Yep. I liked their program."

And suddenly, the tour was less boring. Cord and I compared all the programs that we'd been to.

By the time we had to head to our respective interviews, I'd had more fun than any of my other interviews.

Not that other medical students were bland, but Cord was so much more outgoing, like me. He was definitely the kind of resident I'd want on my team to keep me up when we had to do morning shifts or overnights.

"I heard a few residents talking about going out to a bar nearby after dinner tonight. You interested?" Cord asked.

"Definitely. I only have a seven a.m. flight to catch. What could go wrong?"

He grinned. "Great. Let me get your number, and I can text you when we head out."

We exchanged phone numbers, and he texted me a smiley face.

I held the phone up. "Got it."

"Good luck. Not that you need it," Cord said.

"You too."

We parted as I headed down the hallway toward my impending interview. I already liked Dallas more than everywhere, except maybe Atlanta. That had been my top program before I got here. The benefit of Dallas was that it was only five hours from home and had a killer airport.

I stopped in front of my designated interview spot.

"Annie Donoghue," a voice called.

I smoothed down my skirt and took a deep breath. *Here goes nothing.*

* * *

Dinner was a local taco shack that had to-die-for coconut-shrimp tacos. I hadn't been sure that anywhere had this sort of food off the coast, but Dallas was proving me wrong.

When the rest of the residents showed up together, I flagged Cord down, and he took the seat next to me. Prisha and Cord's resident, Taureen, slipped into the seats across from us. We spent the entire meal discussing our interviews and work and what came after this.

After this, we were going a bar where Taureen promised the best night. "You all coming to JRs?"

Prisha wrinkled her nose and ran a hand back through her short, dark cut. "Count me out. Annie?"

"I'm in."

"Come on, Prish. It's right down the street."

"You know I don't dance," Prisha said. "And my girl-friend is in town."

"Tell Virginia to get her ass out here."

Prisha sighed heavily but started texting her girl-friend to meet us at JRs. Most of the residents headed over to the bar, which was a hole in the wall not too far from the hospital. It was apparently everyone's favorite spot and owned by a husband of one of the doctors. Jared Ross, i.e. JRs. The place was every bar I'd ever been to in —dark, loud music, and full of booze. I liked it.

I fell into the easy rhythm. Besides the one harried drink with Sutton last weekend, I hadn't gone out just for fun since Christmas. I'd already had a pretty good toler-ance, which I was thankful for. It meant I could have a few drinks and still be coherent. It was walking past a few drinks that was usually a problem for me.

And shots.

So many shots.

Cord pulled me onto the dance floor, and we danced

to the rap music that blared through the speakers. He had great rhythm. Our bodies moved in time together. It was fun and mindless. And I wasn't at all thinking about Jordan Wright back home.

Prisha waved us back over now that her girlfriend, Virginia, had arrived. I hadn't known what to expect, but she was drop-dead gorgeous. The same light-brown skin as Prisha with long black curls and a body people would kill for.

More drinks.

More shots.

The evening blurred together. So much dancing and drinking and laughing. Everything was so much funnier.

"Picture," I cried. "Everyone, get together."

I held my phone aloft in front of all of us. Cord slipped an arm around my waist and leaned in close. Prisha and Virginia drew in. Taureen grabbed another group of residents. We all beamed at the photo.

Switching to my text message, I pressed J and sent the photo to Jennifer with a text.

Having the best time!

I slid my phone back into my purse and went back to dancing. I was perfectly content to let the alcohol whisk me away. After all, this was what my life would be like in a few short months. Far away in a place I'd never lived before, where no one knew who I was. That was what I wanted...right?

17

JORDAN

*M*y phone buzzed noisily in my pocket.

"Excuse me for a minute," I said.

I stepped away from Sophia as she lingered over the cellar barrels. She waved me off, unperturbed by the interruption.

A text waited for me from Annie. I gritted my teeth. I couldn't decide if this was going to be good or bad. With Annie, I could never tell anymore. Especially after how she'd left it at the bar.

I'd been drunk enough not to remember the rest of the night, but I had crystal-clear images of Annie telling me it was this or nothing. When we'd started, I'd thought, *What's the harm?* Annie and I fit, and it was better than being at each other's throats. I hadn't thought that it would be anything more than that. Hadn't thought I'd want anything more.

And now...I was uncertain.

And she didn't care.

So, why the hell was she texting me?

I opened the message and immediately went cold.

It was a picture of Annie with what I was guessing were other residents or resident-hopefuls in Dallas. I zeroed in on the guy next to her. Tall and blond and, I could even admit, attractive. He looked like summer to my winter. Light to my dark. A cutting baby face and probably a pretentious prick.

I glowered at the shot. He had his hands all over her. His arm around her waist. Low. Touching her hip, dragging her in closer to him. His chest pressed nearly into her back.

Other people occupied the frame—a Black guy in a pink shirt with short hair, a short Indian woman with eyes only for the woman next to her, who looked like an actress I was certain I should have recognized, and a few others in the background. None of them seemed to be a threat. Except the blond guy...touching Annie.

Why the hell had she sent me this?

My anger flared hot in a second, and I thought about sending her a picture of Sophia and me together just for spite. But it cooled instantly.

Sophia and I weren't here for pleasure...only business. I didn't know what Annie was doing out at a bar with this guy, but I was jumping to conclusions, assuming that she was there with him for anything but business. Would I fault her for cozying up to the residents so that they'd recommend her? No.

I clenched my jaw, indecision warring through me. An unfamiliar feeling to be sure. Not responding would send a message. Responding would send a message. I needed to choose my words carefully.

"Everything all right?" Sophia asked.

She wore a low-cut blouse and a fitted black pencil skirt. She was still bent over, looking at a barrel, but her eyes were on mine. Had she chosen that pose so that I'd see nothing but ass and tits?

I averted my gaze. She was attractive, but...

But what?

Why *shouldn't* I be interested in her? She wasn't stringing me along. She wanted more than friends with benefits. She was clearly *here* right now.

"Fine," I said. "Just a friend."

I looked down at the picture again and sighed, sending off a message back.

Glad you're having a good time, Annie.

Then I turned the ringer off and stuffed it back in my pocket. No more distractions.

"All set."

"Well, I think you have an excellent starting point here. These barrels are in great condition. It's lucky that they left you so much equipment," Sophia said, finally standing and brushing her hands off on her skirt.

"Hollin said the same thing."

"You're lucky to have him on board, too."

"We wouldn't even be doing this if it wasn't for him."

Sophia smiled. "Well, I'm sorry we had to reschedule so many times, but I'm glad that I was able to see the property. It's a smaller operation than the vineyards I worked at in Napa. With some care, I think it'll be a great contender in the state. Get a good sommelier in here, get the right blend going, and you could be on your way to winning awards in a year or two."

"Not that soon," I insisted.

"You'd be surprised at how fast it can happen if the grapes are already set. If you're starting with fresh grapes..." She waved her hand as if that would be the worst thing imaginable. "I was in Napa one year when a wildfire caught the edge of a grapevine. The whole field went up in a matter of hours. Six years of careful tending, gone."

I blanched. "That's horrifying."

"It was," she said with a sigh. "Truly. Now, what else can I do for you?"

"Honestly, I think that's all for now. We're having Wright Construction work on the barn. Hollin is managing the wine production. Julian is hiring. I told him that's where I drew the line."

Sophia laughed softly. "Well, if you get my sommelier to come interview, then be there with Julian. You'll want to meet her. She's whip-smart, really knows her stuff."

"Deal."

We headed back toward the entrance together. The night was beautiful in Lubbock this time of year. We were far enough out in the country that the stars were bright overhead, and the soft swish of the wind carried a tune with it. A chill, too. Sophia tucked her coat tight around her.

"Do you have plans tonight?" Sophia asked once we finally made it back to the cars.

"I...don't," I admitted.

"Care to get a drink? La Sirena has the best wine selection or the Funky Door?"

I wanted to say yes. No, actually, I didn't want to say

yes. I wanted to *want* to say yes, which felt even more ridiculous than the other options.

Truly, I just wished this were Annie and she wasn't hundreds of miles away, doing who knew what with some blond dude. Unfortunately, I was my father's son. And that temper led to possessive, jealous tendencies. All I wanted to do was convince Jensen to lend me the jet, so I could fly out there and figure out what the fuck was going on. But I knew that would be psychotic. Or at least, she'd take it that way. If she'd drawn a line in the sand at much simple things, then that would surely be literally flying over it.

"I think that we should keep our relationship related to business," I said as gently as possible.

Sophia still colored. "Oh. Well, yes, of course. I understand."

"I'd hate to lose your friendship."

Which I was sure was the wrong thing to say as her blush darkened.

Then she stuck out her hand, ever the professional. "It was a pleasure doing business with you, Jordan. Let me know if you need anything or if you hear from my sommelier."

"I will."

We shook, and then she got into her car and sped off. I leaned back against my truck. What the fuck was I doing? If Annie was really leaving in a matter of months, was any of this worth it? Should we be doing this at all?

It wasn't like friends with benefits kept either of us from getting hurt in all of this. And I'd broken enough hearts to know that I didn't want to be the one hurting at the end of it all.

Still, I could have fucked Sophia tonight, and the inclination wasn't even there. Not even a little. Maybe it was already too late.

18

ANNIE

*H*ours passed.

I'd stopped drinking so that I could sober up enough to get home and sleep instead of puke my guts up. Prisha and Virginia had left at some point. I'd waved them off, promising that I'd grab an Uber.

The rest of us stayed out until bar close. Taureen had an arm over Cord's shoulders. Cord had an arm over my shoulders. We stumbled to the sidewalk to wait for our Uber as we all sang whatever the last song had been in the club. We were ridiculous but happy. The night had been incredible, and even better, Taureen lived in the same neighborhood as Prisha. So, we could all ride together.

We tumbled into the backseat and drove the short distance back to their place. I was sober enough by now to tell our Uber driver was irritated with us, but still drunk enough not to care.

"You can keep driving to Prisha's," Taureen said, pointing down the street. He was already stumbling back

138

into his house, leaving Cord and me alone out on the street.

"I could walk you instead," Cord offered.

"Sounds like a good idea," I agreed.

The Uber zoomed away without another word.

"Ass," Cord said, kicking his foot out as if he could kick the car.

I giggled, tugging my jacket tighter around me. "We're all drunk. I'm sure he hates drunk people in his car."

"Probably."

I pulled Prisha's address up on my phone. Taureen was right. It was only a few blocks away. Cord glanced over my shoulder at the map.

"See, not far," Cord insisted.

"Will you be okay getting back?" I asked him.

He grinned. "I think I can manage."

We were silent on the walk to the house. As if the dark night had swept in and sucked all the words out from us. Covering us in shadows and sealing us in with the black of night.

The brisk walk cleared my head. Made me look back at the night we'd had. I blinked and cringed. I saw where this walk was heading before we even reached Prisha's. Knew what was coming next. And felt my feet slowing down, trying to stretch it out so that this didn't have to happen.

"What?" Cord asked. He slowed next to me. His big blue eyes suddenly concerned.

"It's just there." I pointed at the next house. As if it wasn't already obvious. "I can walk the rest of the way."

He turned to face me, stopping us both on the sidewalk. He stepped close, running his hand down my sleeve to my hand. Then he took it in his. "You shouldn't go the rest of the way alone."

I took my hand back quickly. "It's fine. Really."

"I could...come in with you."

Of course. Of course that was what he was going to say. How could I have been so stupid? I had known where this was going, and at every turn, I hadn't said no. I hadn't walked away. I hadn't discouraged him. And now, we were one house from where I was staying, and I had no backup plan.

I was alone with a relative stranger on a dark street. Cord seemed like a nice guy, but how many nice guys did I know who had done bad things? Wasn't that what they always said on the news? *Oh, he was such a nice guy.* I gulped. If I didn't manage this correctly, I could be in a lot of trouble.

My body shook from the cold and worry.

"I..." I bit my lip and glanced down and then back up into his eyes. Let him see my decision was made. The alcohol had dissipated some. "Thanks, but no. I have an early flight."

"Annie," he whispered. He leaned forward as if he was about to kiss me, and I took another step back, putting the distance between us. His face didn't immediately turn angry but back to concerned. "What is it? Are you seeing someone?"

I hesitated on the question. Was I? Not technically. I'd drawn that line myself. But it didn't feel right to be here with Cord right now either.

"No," I finally admitted.

"Then, what?" he asked as if that were the only possible explanation.

"I don't have to be seeing someone to not want to do this."

He sighed and nodded his head. "No, you don't. I just...I thought we had something." His shoulders slumped. "I had a nice night." He brushed a lock of hair behind my ear and pressed a kiss to my temple. "I hope you did, too. And that I see you at other interviews...and maybe if we both go to the same place, we can pick this back up."

Then he turned and walked away.

I released my breath. That could have been very, very bad. I was lucky that Cord wasn't a predator...and instead just a guy who was into me. And why wouldn't he be? We'd hung out all day. We'd danced all night. It could have easily gone that direction. Fuck.

I hurried back into Prisha's house, closing and locking the door up. She and Virginia were fast asleep as I padded into the guest bedroom. I peeled off the clothes I'd worn all day and into nightclothes. Then I crawled into bed, finally feeling safe, and checked my phone.

My stomach dropped when I saw the text message from Jordan.

"Oh fuck," I whispered.

When I'd pressed J on my phone, it had defaulted to Jordan instead of Jennifer. The picture had been sent to him and not my friend.

I cringed and looked at the image again. The way Cord was leaning into me so casually. Fuck, fuck, fuck.

Panic clawed at my throat. I'd drawn the line, but I

hadn't wanted to do this to him. He definitely didn't deserve it. Even if I was mad at him for pressing for more when I'd told him from the beginning that this was all it was.

His message hung there between us.

Glad you're having a good time, Annie.

I swallowed and closed my eyes. My stomach was in knots. I was sure that he was thinking the worst of me right now. He had no way of knowing that I'd turned Cord down. That I'd had no interest in him.

I debated what the hell I was doing, but I was still a little drunk. So, I snapped a selfie of me in bed. Alone.

Then I sent it to Jordan on purpose this time.

I miss your stupid face.

Even though it was almost three in the morning, another message dinged on my phone a minute later. A picture of Jordan, shirtless and in bed.

I miss yours, too.

I hugged my phone to my chest with a sigh. And finally got a good night's sleep.

19

ANNIE

*D*espite the texts, I didn't see Jordan when I got home. I had too much work to do, especially after missing two days for the interview.

I moved back into an emergency medicine rotation, which was my specialty and also meant strange hours. We were supposed to get used to working all potential shifts, which meant all hours of the day. I'd apparently drawn the short straw and started with overnights, getting into the ER at midnight. It was a long night ahead of me, but emergencies never ceased, and the hours rushed by.

It was still two hours until eight, which was when I got off. I knew they were being generous, doing eight-hour shifts with four days on, two days off. In residency, I'd heard horror stories of working thirty-six hours straight and up to a hundred hours a week. But I'd take it for now even if my schedule was all whack with these overnight shifts.

As I finished off my last couple of charts, my mind

was still on Jordan. I needed to decide what to do about us. He'd clearly said that he wanted more, and I just... couldn't give him that. Could I? I'd been avoiding him and relationships more broadly since I started medical school. And with the prospect of leaving Lubbock looking more and more like a for-sure thing, it felt wrong to push forward.

I set my last chart aside just as a new patient was rushed into the hospital.

"Dr. Donoghue," the attending physician, Dr. Lee, called as the man was wheeled off of the ambulance.

I rushed after him. My mind immediately went blank. Nothing mattered, except what was right in front of me. About saving lives.

Dr. Lee was calmly issuing instructions, and the nurses broke into emergency mode, moving us all in time. The patient was young. He was about my age, not even thirty if I had to guess. The next two words from Dr. Lee nearly stopped me in my tracks—*heart attack*.

He was too young for that.

But apparently, that didn't matter.

The next half hour was a blur as we worked diligently to save this young man's life. We did everything we could, but there was something else wrong with his heart. Even as we physically kept his heart beating, it wouldn't do it on its own. And then the machine couldn't do it either. It had all gone catastrophically wrong.

"Call it," the doctor said, stepping backward.

"Time of death. Six thirty-seven a.m.," one of the nurses said.

I was still standing over him, prepared to step in. Prepared to get his heart pumping. Prepared to *fix it*.

But there was no fixing this.

There was nothing to be done.

And he was dead.

Thirty years old, and he was dead.

Dr. Lee put his hand on my shoulder and guided me out of the room. I yanked off my mask with trembling hands, sucking air in deep, barely hearing the doctor say that we needed to speak with his family.

That was part of my job, of course. An essential part of my job. And I was frozen in place. I couldn't do it. I'd had to tell Sutton. I couldn't do it this time. Oh God.

"Dr. Donoghue."

I didn't respond.

"Annie," he said more gently, forcing me to look at him. "Is this the first one you've lost?"

I nodded even though it felt like a lie. It was the first I'd lost in the ER.

He nodded and patted my shoulder. "I remember my first, too. I'll speak with the family. You go home."

"I have another hour and a half."

"Not anymore you don't. Go home. Get some sleep."

"Sir—"

But he was already turning away. Going to tell someone's family that they no longer had their husband, father, brother, son.

And I was here, still shaking so bad that I couldn't get my gloves off. I yelled and yanked them off, throwing them in the trash. The shaking had moved from my hands to the rest of my body. I darted for the physicians' lounge.

A few other doctors were in there, but no one looked up when I walked in. I grabbed my stuff out of my locker, shrugged my jacket on, and headed out without a word.

I had no recollection of driving. No idea how I managed it with the way I was feeling. But somehow, I pulled up in front of Jordan's house.

My bag was still in the back of my car, and I wrenched it out of the backseat before heading for the front door. I rang the doorbell and tried to twist the knob, but the door was locked.

A minute later, Jordan appeared in a pair of sweats and a T-shirt. He rubbed his eyes as he opened the door. I must have woken him.

He startled at the sight of me. "Annie?"

"Can we go for that run?"

He opened the door wider to let me inside. "What are you doing awake? It's…" He checked his watch. "It's not even seven in the morning."

"I worked an overnight."

"Shouldn't you be sleeping then?"

"Can't sleep," I said as I headed for his room, intending to change.

He followed in my wake. "So, you want to run? I thought you didn't want to run."

"Changed my mind."

"Slow down." He pulled me toward him and looked me in the eyes. "Are you okay?"

I clenched my jaw and slowly shook my head. "Can we run…please?"

"It looks like a storm out there."

"I don't care."

He nodded, seeing that I was telling the truth. "Okay. Okay, let's run."

Then he released me tenderly, the look in his eyes one of absolute concern. I hadn't seen him in over a week, and now I was here, acting like a crazy person. One who couldn't sleep and was going back on everything I'd said to him. And still, he just stepped aside and found running clothes.

I changed out of my scrubs as quickly as possible, half-considering burning them. The thought of wearing them again made me sick to my stomach. I turned away, so I didn't have to look at them again. I'd had training for this. Yet nothing could prepare a person to watch someone die especially with what I'd gone through. And every time I closed my eyes, I saw his heart stop and the doctor call it and the world close up.

"Ready?" Jordan asked.

"Sure."

We took off with Jordan guiding us toward the golf course. Dark clouds loomed in front of us, and the course was empty. No golf carts rushing about the track or tiny balls flying through the air. Just the two of us trekking past the holes and their little flags. Jordan had clearly run this way often, probably got up early enough to miss the morning golfers. That seemed like a respectable thing he'd do.

The farther we ran, the deeper the burn in my legs and lungs and heart. I hadn't run like this in years. Not unless you counted the occasional soccer game, which I didn't. Everything hurt, and yet I welcomed it. At least I was feeling that instead of the pain from the hospital.

My breathing was ragged, and soon, I was panting. Jordan shot me a worried look. He wasn't even breathing hard. In fact, it looked more like he was jogging next to me than running.

Whatever. I wasn't going to stop. I was just going to keep going.

Breathe in. Breathe out. Arms pumping. Feet pounding the pavement.

Better than anything else. Better than trying to sleep when I was sure that I'd only see the flatline monitor, his chest stop moving, the sound of death.

See Mav falling and not getting up.

Nothing I could have done. Nothing I *could* do.

Nearly four years of medical school, and Mav would still have died. He still would have died on my table or in my arms or on the pavement.

I jogged to a stop. My heart pounded in my chest. I'd pushed it too far. Just like Mav had that day. I put my hands on my knees, gasping for breath. I could hardly breathe, hardly think. Just memories on repeat, over and over and over.

I was going to be sick.

Oh God.

I turned away from Jordan and threw up everything I'd eaten in the last twenty-four hours. I coughed and spat, wiping my mouth with the back of my hand.

"Gross," I groaned.

Jordan reached out and touched my shoulder and then the other one. "You're shaking."

"Am I?"

Which was when I realized that I was in fact shaking like a leaf. My body responding involuntarily to the reminder that I'd seen someone *die* today. That I'd seen someone die...again.

And as that cruel thought split through my head, the universe listened to my mood and escalated the situation.

The skies opened, and suddenly, it was pouring.

Thick sheets of rain that had come completely out of nowhere. The skies had been dark, but it hadn't even been misting or sprinkling or anything. And now, we were caught in a deluge, still a hundred yards or more from the nearest building.

I tilted my head up to the sky.

And then the tears finally came.

Deep, racking sobs.

And I couldn't stop it.

I mourned.

20

JORDAN

*S*omething in my strong, beautiful girl was broken.

I didn't know what had happened. I didn't need to know. All that mattered was that she was crying in the pouring rain. All that mattered was that she was hurting.

I didn't say a word. I didn't try to get her to talk.

I just stepped forward and drew her into my arms. She held stiff for a moment, her body rigid, her hands covering her face as the tears flowed. But still, I held her.

Then something released, and she threw her arms around my neck, holding me tight and fast against her. She buried her head into my shoulder. The sobs shaking her entire body.

I ran my hand up and down her back, not caring that we were soaked through in seconds. That everything was probably flooding thanks to Lubbock caprock, and getting back to the house was going to. But none of that was important. What was a little rain when Annie was crying?

Then abruptly, she pushed away and stalked across the golf course.

I followed her onto the grass. "Annie!"

"Just let me go, Jordan."

"No!" I yelled back. "I'm not going to let you go. I'm not going to let you walk off into the grass when you're not okay."

She whirled on me. "That's right. I'm not okay. So, just...let me be."

"Why won't you talk to me?"

"I don't want to! I don't want to talk to you or anyone."

"I can see that, but it's not healthy."

She ground her teeth together and paced farther away from me. The rain was coming down harder, beating down on my skin and matting my hair to my face. Then just when I thought I might have to run after her again, she walked back toward me. Her eyes were fiery.

"Just talk to me! What's the harm in that?" I called over the rain.

"Because then it's real!" she shouted. And the fire dimmed. "Then, it's real. Then, someone died and there's nothing I can do and it's just *over*."

I stopped in my tracks. "Someone died?"

She flung her hands wide. "Yep. I killed him."

"Annie...you didn't kill anyone."

"I might as well have. I was there when he came in with a heart attack. I stood over him as I tried to fix his broken heart, and I couldn't *do anything*. What's the point of this damn degree if I'm going to lose people anyway?"

"You're saving people," I insisted, stepping closer. "That's what makes the difference. Maybe you lost this one person, Annie, but that doesn't mean it's all pointless. You're making a difference in people's lives."

"I couldn't save him then, and I can't save him now," she said, still frantic.

I drew a blank. "Couldn't save who?"

"Maverick!" she yelled as if it were obvious.

Then it all clicked. I'd heard the story about how Sutton's husband had died. That he'd had a rare heart condition and died on the Fourth of July a few years back. What had they said about Annie?

"You were there." The pieces fell together. "You were running the same race as him."

She nodded as the tears started again. "I watched him collapse. I ran the rest of the race to tell Sutton what had happened. I couldn't do anything to save him."

"And now, you're a doctor. You became a doctor to save lives. So you didn't have to stand on the sidelines anymore." My heart broke for her. "What happened to Maverick was a terrible accident. You can't blame yourself."

"I know," she said, barely loud enough. Then louder. "I know! But it doesn't change the fact that it still feels like my goddamn fault!"

I reached for her, and she let me draw her against me again. "It's not your fault. Not Maverick. Not the person who died today."

"I know," she repeated.

She cried into my shoulder and didn't fight my hold on her as all of her grief finally released her.

* * *

W hen she finally stopped crying, we jogged to the country club and stepped into the lobby. We were drowned rats, but the staff hurriedly brought over towels and blankets to dry us off.

Annie took a seat next to the fireplace and stared off into it like it had the answers to the universe. I left her there, only coming to her side to pass her tea. The last thing I wanted was for her to get sick. She was dealing with enough.

Twenty minutes later, the rain finally let up, and the country club staff offered to drive us to my house in a golf cart. It was a quick drive back, and after I got Annie inside, I came outside with a hefty tip for everyone involved. The college student looked like she was going to fall over as she thanked me profusely.

I waved her off and then came back inside to find Annie staring blankly around the house.

"Come on," I said gently.

After stripping us both out of our sodden clothes, I directed her into a steamy shower, washing her clean of the hospital and rain and the entire day. She tipped her head back into the spray and sighed. Some of the heartache seemed to loosen from her shoulders. When we stepped out, I bundled her in fluffy white towels and got her into bed.

"Jordan," she whispered.

"Yeah?" I asked as she finally lay back against the pillow and closed her eyes.

"Thank you for taking care of me."

"Of course."

I bent down and kissed her forehead. She was out almost instantly, and I hoped she stayed that way for a while. She needed a solid eight or nine hours of sleep to feel even partially human after this.

I changed into jeans and a sweater and then headed down the hall to my at-home office. Though I practically lived at the office, I liked having an office in my house for emergencies. Like right now. Usually, I used it for late-night working or weekends.

When I reached the office, sinking into the black leather chair I loved, I called Morgan.

"Jordan, how can I help you?"

"I'm not coming in today."

Morgan was silent for a minute. "Are you okay? What's wrong? Are you hurt? Sick? Bleeding out?"

I laughed softly. "Nothing. None of that. I just have to take care of some things here. I'll still be working from home, but I won't be as available as normal."

"I'm concerned. I don't think you've taken a day off in three years, Jordan."

I sighed, realizing I was going to have to give her something. This was unusual for me. And I wouldn't put it past Morgan to come over here and find out if I was really okay. She was that kind of boss. Really, the best kind.

"It's not me. Annie...she had a rough shift at the hospital. I don't feel comfortable leaving her."

Morgan softened immediately. "I'm so sorry. Is she going to be okay? Anything I can do?"

"She'll be okay. She just needs some time."

"Give her my best."

"I will. Thanks, Mor."

We hung up the phone, and I got to work.

* * *

"Hey," a voice said hoarsely from the doorway.

I nearly jumped out of my skin. I'd been in so deep on the soccer complex project that I didn't even hear footsteps. I glanced up at Annie, who looked a wreck but...settled. "Hey, how are you feeling?"

She shrugged. "I've been better. What are you doing here? It's three in the afternoon. Shouldn't you be at work?"

"I called out."

She blinked. "What?"

"I told Morgan that I couldn't come in. I hope you don't mind that I told her you were having a rough day. She worries."

"It's fine," she said softly. "But...you called out of work? You never do that."

"No. I don't think I've called out of work...ever. Yeah, maybe ever."

Her mouth opened slightly. "Then, why did you do it today?"

"I was worried about you. I knew that you were going to be sleeping...or at least, I hoped you would sleep. But I wanted to be here in case you needed me."

"That's very considerate." She fidgeted with her claddagh ring, turning it around and around. "I guess I should go. I haven't eaten or anything, and I have work and..."

"How about this?" I said, pushing away from my desk and coming to stand before her. "How about we go to Rosa's and get some margaritas and queso? Tacos are good recovery food."

She looked at me to see if there was a catch to it. "I don't know how to say no to that."

I laughed. "Then don't."

"Okay. Margs and queso and tacos it is."

I tried to keep a self-satisfied smile off of my face as she darted back into the bedroom to change. I absolutely wanted to make sure that she was okay. I was worried about her. But taking her out for Mexican was definitely a date. Whether she wanted to admit it or not.

She came back out in distressed jeans and a sweater. Her red hair pulled back into a messy bun. No makeup. She was stunning. "All right. I'm ready."

We took my Tesla to the restaurant, which was completely dead. Most people had already eaten lunch, and it wasn't quite time for dinner. It was more like breakfast for Annie, but she accepted the frozen margarita with extra salt on the rim and extra limes with a smile. We ate our weight in queso and chips before tacos even arrived.

"I appreciate this," she said, just a little bit tipsy from our second margarita.

"Mexican food?"

She laughed gingerly, as if it still hurt to move her face like that. "For Mexican food and the run and the shower and taking the day off—all of it. I know that I don't really deserve any of this from you."

"Oh?"

She flinched. "Well, what went down at Walkers and

then that picture I sent you." She looked up at me hesitantly. "It was supposed to go to Jennifer. And it didn't mean anything. I mean, Cord, the guy in the picture, and I...nothing happened."

"That's good to hear," I admitted. "I thought you might have sent it as a reminder of the line you had drawn."

"I didn't mean it like that. I don't..." She sighed heavily and took another sip of her margarita. "I'm not seeing anyone else."

"Right, because you're leaving in a few months."

"Right," she muttered. "That reason. And also... because of you."

I arched an eyebrow. "Annie, are you saying that we're dating?"

"No!" she said automatically.

I laughed. "We're just exclusive and friends with benefits?"

"Well," she said, her face turning red, "I'm not seeing anyone else."

"Me either," I told her and took her hand across the table. She looked down at it for a second and then twined our fingers together. "What are you doing Sunday?"

She scrunched up her face. "I don't know. Maybe working?"

"Still overnights?"

She nodded. "For the foreseeable future."

"Jensen is throwing a Super Bowl party because the Chiefs are playing, and everyone in this town loves Patrick Mahomes since he went to Texas Tech. Do you have any interest in going?"

"Sutton mentioned it. I was planning to go if I didn't have to work. I think I can make it."

"I could pick you up before the game," I offered.

I waited for her to see it as the date it was. Like she should have seen that this was. But she didn't back down from it or say any of the things I'd expected.

"Okay. That'd be great."

"Sounds good," I told her with a wide smile.

I'd won this round. And she didn't even know we were playing.

But when we finished, I paid for the entire check, and she only protested a little. I'd call it a win.

21

ANNIE

"*Y*ou're spending an awfully long time on your hair and makeup for a Super Bowl party," Jennifer said.

She leaned against the bathroom door on the thankfully new hardwood floor. All remnants of the terrible flood were now gone.

"I just want to look nice."

"Because it's a date?"

"No," I grumbled.

"But Jordan is picking you up instead of you just going with me?"

"Well...yes," I admitted.

"Okay. So...it's a date."

"It's not," I cried, throwing a tube of lipstick at her.

She laughed and darted away. "I'm glad that y'all reconciled. You seem happier despite the crazier hours and stuff. When do you leave for your Seattle interview?"

"Next weekend," I said with a grin. "I'm so excited."

Seattle was my dream city. I'd always wanted to visit,

and their emergency medicine residency was top of the line. I knew that I'd get only the best if I went there. Unfortunately, it hadn't fit into my interview schedule until the very last weekend. So, I'd been bouncing off the walls all winter with excitement to go there.

The doorbell rang.

Jennifer winked. "I'll get it. It's probably your date."

"It's not a date!" I called after her.

It wasn't. Right?

I fluffed my hair and pursed my freshly painted lips. Okay, so maybe I was going overboard. That line I'd drawn in the sand was still there, but it was blurry...like someone had stepped on it.

After what had happened at the hospital earlier this week, I couldn't get over how Jordan had taken care of me. Not just going for a run and letting me sleep at his house, but also all the little things that he hadn't had to do. Like getting me into the shower and calling out of work and insisting on taking me for margaritas. For not judging me for what I'd gone through and not giving me looks of deep pity, which I had never been able to stand. Just...being there.

And now, I didn't know *where* we stood. We weren't simply friends with benefits. Not after last week. But we weren't dating either.

I was leaving. In a few short months, I was leaving. I couldn't fall for Jordan Wright in the meantime.

"Annie, Jordan's here!" Jennifer called.

I straightened my Chiefs jersey, grabbed my purse and jacket, and then headed out to the living room. "Hey!"

He turned his attention to me, and it suddenly felt like I was standing in the sun. His smile was so bright. His eyes on mine, looking me up and down. That gleam in his eyes that said he wouldn't mind taking me back into my room and undressing me.

"Hey, you ready to go?" he asked, sliding his hands into the pockets of his slacks.

Because, of course, he was wearing slacks. Blue dress pants at that with a white button-up tucked in and sleeves rolled up.

"I should have bought you a jersey."

He gave me an incredulous look. "Not really my style."

"Obviously," I said with a laugh, mock straightening his nonexistent tie. "You're just missing a tie."

He swatted me away playfully. "Hey. This is dressed down."

I rolled my eyes. "Sure it is." I looked back to Jennifer with a smile. "Are you sure you don't want to come with us?"

"Oh no!" she said, wide-eyed and emphatic. "I have some edits to finish and feed Cado and Bakey again."

"Cado and Bakey?" Jordan asked.

"Don't bother," I said with a laugh.

"I didn't think you could have pets."

"Oh, we don't have pets," Jennifer said easily.

"They're stray cats. She named them Avocado and Bacon. She also feeds them and pretends that she doesn't like them."

"I don't! I'm not even a cat person."

Jordan looked between us in confusion. "You're not supposed to feed stray cats."

"I don't want them to starve." Jennifer rolled her eyes. "You know what? Never mind. Have fun at the party. I'll see you later."

I suppressed my laugh and waved at my roomie. She was doing her best to not interfere on our "date." She really wanted us to end up together. And I just wanted her to kick Ashleigh Sinclair out of the picture and take back Julian, but this was Jennifer. So, I didn't know if that was ever going to happen.

We waved good-bye and headed outside. I was surprised to see Jordan had the truck today and not his Tesla. I raised an eyebrow.

He just shrugged. "It's growing on me."

"Texas."

He agreed, "Texas."

Jordan had a Top 40 station playing as we drove over to Jensen's mansion on the south side of town. Despite my nerves, things seemed completely normal with Jordan. Maybe this wasn't a date after all, and I was over-reacting to how we'd been together this week. We were probably going to have to discuss this eventually, but I sure hoped it could last a little longer. I was leaving for Seattle soon and then Match Day and then I'd be gone. We had so little time, which was why I hadn't wanted to do anything in the first place.

All of that swirling through my head made me jittery. My leg was bouncing in time with the music, and I kept stealing glances in his direction. So much for subtlety.

Jordan reached across the seat and put his hand on my leg. "What are you thinking about?"

Us. But I didn't say that. The last thing I wanted was to broach that topic right now. Even though it hung in the air between us.

"Sorry," I said instead, deflecting.

He shot me a look like he knew *exactly* what I was thinking and then left his hand on my leg. I bit my lip and let him draw lazy circles into my skin. Because, of course, I'd worn a jean miniskirt with my jersey and boots. It was impractical for the weather, but it was cute as hell. And now, it had the added benefit of Jordan's hand on my leg with nothing between us.

Jordan didn't push the matter, thankfully. We parked on the street near Jensen's house. Cars lined the road in both directions, and we were lucky to find a spot Jordan could expertly parallel park into. Even in his huge truck.

"That was impressive," I told him as we headed to the house together.

He shrugged. "Vancouver. There's not a lot of parking, and you get used to it."

I hadn't really thought about that fact as I followed my dreams to a bigger city. Maybe I could take public transit and not have to drive much.

I knocked on the door, and Emery's smiling face appeared first and her pregnant belly second.

"Ahhh, Em," I gushed. "Look at you."

Jensen and Emery had been married for more than three years now, and this was their first kid. She was due this spring and was glowing.

She put her hand on her stomach. "I know. I keep *growing.*"

I laughed as she let us inside. "You look incredible. Like the cutest pregnant person ever. Don't let Sutton hear me say that."

Emery shook her head with a grin. "Well, thanks. Heidi keeps reminding me that I'll bounce back fast or whatever. She did." She rolled her eyes about her cheery best friend, who was married to Landon, and had a two-year-old son, Holden. "Of course, Heidi is a freak of nature."

"I can hear you!" Heidi called from a room over.

"That was the plan!" Emery yelled back. She winked at me and Jordan. "The rest of the Wrights have the pregame bullshit on in the living room. Feel free to go forth and listen to their antagonism."

"We can hear you!" Jensen called from the living room.

She grinned from ear to ear. "Again, that was the plan, babe."

Jensen stepped out of the living room and came over to his wife. He pressed a kiss against her lips. "You know I love you."

"You'd better, or we'd be having a discussion about this." She gestured to her oversized belly.

He shot her that insufferable, impossible Wright smile that I knew *all* too well. Then he kissed her again, long and deep. I flushed. It was almost embarrassing, witnessing their love.

"I'm open to discussion," he said. "Maybe another one?"

She groaned. "Can't I pop this one out first before we talk about *more*?"

"I love you, Emery Robinson Wright."

She cracked. "I love you, too."

Jensen stuck his hand out to shake Jordan's as Sutton darted into the entranceway. She pulled me into a hug.

"So glad you made it," she said, glancing over her shoulder.

"Me too. What are you looking at?"

She laughed. "I, uh...just escaped the kids."

I shook my head. "Escaped?"

"I need a minute to breathe, all right?" she said with a smile.

Her eyes were still on her kids, who were being entertained by Holden and Emery's sister, Kimber's, kids—Lilyanne and Bethany. Jensen's son from his first marriage, Colton, was currently trying to ignore all of them. He was twelve and veering into those impossible teenage years. Though Lilyanne was only two years younger, he was apparently already in that *I'm too cool* stage. He was shaping up to look just like his dad. Lord, help the middle school girls.

I followed Sutton into the kitchen and grabbed a Coke from the fridge. I tried to smother a yawn. The overnights were not my friend. I still had to work tonight at midnight, and my brain was not firing on all cylinders.

"So," Sutton said expectantly.

"So?"

"You and Jordan?"

"Oh yeah, I don't know." I took a sip of my Coke, so I didn't have to say more.

"You showed up together," Sutton prodded.

"They sure did," Morgan said, entering the kitchen. "And they've been having lunch together for weeks."

I nearly choked on my drink. "How do you know that?"

Morgan eyed me skeptically. "I'm the CEO and his boss. Who do you think he had to call out to this week?"

"He called out of work?" Sutton asked.

"To spend the day with her," Morgan crooned.

I held my hands up. "It wasn't like that, and I don't need the Wright sisters ganging up on me."

"We're not ganging up," Sutton said. "We're just excited that you're dating our cousin."

"Who moved here three years ago and hasn't dated anyone seriously," Morgan added.

"Yeah, I'm sure it was so hard to come from Vancouver."

Morgan nodded with a wicked grin. "I've done the hide-the-relationship thing. I understand how overbearing our family is. I wouldn't recommend trying it."

"Yeah, but you and Patrick are so happy!" I sputtered.

"Now!" she gushed, reaching across me to the charcuterie board. "But can you imagine how Austin reacted when he found out I was dating his best friend?"

I cringed. "I can imagine that. I have an older brother."

"And if you and Jordan get together, maybe it'll take the pressure off of the rest of us," Morgan grumbled.

Sutton laughed. "Oh, please! You're not getting out of this. We're all wondering when Patrick is going to pop the question!"

"Why won't anyone bother Austin and Julia? They've been together longer than us, you know!"

"Because they're Austin and Julia," I said automatically.

"Exactly," Sutton said. "They do their own thing."

"I do my own thing," Morgan grumbled under her breath.

"Well, if he asked..." Sutton hypothesized.

Morgan rolled her eyes and stuffed her mouth full of cheese.

"She'd say yes," I answered for her.

Morgan shot us a look of betrayal. She finished the cheese she was eating. "I thought we were ganging up on Annie. This isn't fair."

We all laughed and headed into the living room with our drinks. Jordan was talking with the boys. Someone had handed him a beer. His eyes met mine across the room, and he smiled before being dragged back into the conversation.

Maybe this wouldn't be so bad. Even if it was a date.

Another knock came from the door. Emery had sat down in one of the plush living room chairs. She tried to shove herself out of it and failed spectacularly.

"Fuck," she grumbled loud enough for some of the kids to start repeating it. "Sorry. Sorry." She held her hands up to the disgruntled parents. "I can't get up. Someone else answer the door."

"I got it," Sutton said.

I followed her to the front door, and Jordan appeared next to us.

"I think it's Julian," he told me.

Ah, that made sense. He was the only Wright missing. Everyone else was already here.

Sutton pulled open the door to find Julian and his girlfriend, Ashleigh, standing in the entranceway.

"Sutton," Ashleigh practically shrieked. "I brought dessert!"

Ashleigh held out a platter of store-bought cookies and passed them to my best friend. Sutton, of all people, who owned and worked in a bakery downtown. Sutton looked at the gift like it was a ticking time bomb.

"That's so nice of you," I said to Ashleigh. I'd had more experience dealing with her, and it was better to pretend like nothing had happened.

Julian stepped inside and shook Jordan's hand. "Hey, bro."

"How's it going?"

Julian shrugged. "I think I need a beer."

I tried to smother a laugh. Julian had been dating Ashleigh for two years, and that was the first indication that her over-the-top attitude got to him like it did everyone else. At least he was human.

"Oh! I brought you a surprise, too, Annie," Ashleigh said.

"Uh, you did?" I asked in confusion.

And then another person stepped into view.

My heart stopped. My jaw dropped. Everything seemed to stand still. It couldn't be. There was only one person I'd ever fallen in love with. My best friend, my ex-boyfriend, my hope-for-forever guy.

"Chase?" I gasped.

22

ANNIE

*C*hase Sinclair was my first everything.

Even before I'd met Sutton, he was my first friend.. My first boyfriend. My first kiss. My first time. We hadn't dated my entire life or anything, but we'd always been inseparable. Until he left for Yale after high school graduation and I was stuck in Lubbock at Texas Tech.

That summer, we'd made a pact that if we weren't married by the time we were thirty, we'd get married. We were only twenty-seven right now, but looking up into his crystal-clear blue eyes, I was suddenly reminded of the fact.

"Oh my God!" I cried, throwing myself into his arms. "What are you doing here? You didn't come home for Christmas or all summer. What does that law firm in Houston have you doing?"

He laughed, easy and so comfortable, and pulled me tight against him. "It's good to see you, too, Annie."

I pulled back to look up at him. The same blond hair and blue eyes, that sharp jaw and high cheekbones, the pouty lips. We'd seen each other on and off over the years when he came back for holidays, but it wasn't the same.

"I can't believe you're here. It's been almost a year, Chase."

He ran a hand back through his sandy hair. "I know. I know. I've been busy."

A throat cleared noisily behind us. And that was when I realized that our entire reunion was taking place in front of everyone. I glanced back to see Sutton wide-eyed and incredulous. Ashleigh looked giddy. Julian was facing Jordan, as if ready to apologize. Jordan's eyes were narrowed, his arms crossed. Oh yeah, um...not good.

I stepped back from Chase. "Why don't you come inside?"

"Actually, can we talk?" Chase asked, the sincerest look in his eyes.

My eyes flicked back to Jordan, my not-boyfriend but not-quite friends with benefits. Yeah, I didn't know what to do about that. But Chase was my oldest friend, and I hadn't seen him in a year. I couldn't deny him a thing.

"Yeah, sure," I said quickly. I looked to Jordan. "I'll be right back."

Ashleigh waved at us and then yanked the door closed. I cringed at the finality as it snapped shut.

Welp, Jordan was probably going to be pissed. Okay... he was definitely going to be pissed. But it wasn't like I was going to walk with Chase to make out or something equally childish. I hadn't hooked up with Cord when I could have. Though Chase Sinclair was altogether different, it didn't change anything about me and Jordan.

"Shall we?" he asked, holding his arm out.

I chuckled softly and stepped up next to him. I didn't take his arm, and he didn't say anything about it. We headed down the front walk and onto the sidewalk. It was probably too cold for me to be outside in a miniskirt, but I hadn't anticipated any of this when I left the house this afternoon.

"So, what are you doing here?" I asked. "You haven't been home in forever."

"I know. I missed you."

"I missed you, too." It had been nine years since Chase and I parted ways, but I still considered him my best friend. This walk felt like stepping back in time. Everything settling into the way it had been. Like no time had passed at all. I nudged him. "You could have called."

"People use phones for that purpose now?"

I snorted. "Fine. You could have texted. Or I don't know...gotten on social media."

"LinkedIn?"

I wrinkled my nose at him. "Not the same."

"How's school?"

"Almost done," I said with a sigh of relief. "I mean, three more years of residency, but I actually get paid for that instead of, you know, crippling debt."

"Law school," he said, pointing at himself.

I tried not to roll my eyes. I doubted Chase had taken any debt for his fancy-schmancy law degree. Not when his parents were the largest real estate investors in Lubbock. They had money similar to the Wrights. It was outrageous.

We stopped when we came up to a little park near Jensen's house. It was full of families playing football before the big game, people walking their dogs, runners, and all manner of children enjoying the waning sunshine.

Chase gestured to an empty bench, and we sat. I yelped at the first contact of the cold metal against my bare skin.

"Didn't plan for this," I said, gritting my teeth as my skin adjusted.

"Want my jacket?"

I shook my head. "I'm fine. But tell me about you. I know you too well to know that you're avoiding questions."

He laughed and winked at me. "You're right. You know me too well. I'm here, closing on a house."

"Excuse me?" I asked with raised eyebrows.

"I'm moving home, Annie."

My jaw dropped for a second time that day. "What the hell?" I gasped. "When did you decide this? What's happening with your job?"

"I'm actually opening my own firm here in town. My dad is lending me the capital to get started, and I'm going in with a friend from Houston."

I shrieked. "That's so incredible! Congratulations!"

I threw myself into his arms again. I couldn't believe this. Chase was moving back home...right as I was planning to leave Lubbock behind.

He chuckled into my hair before releasing me. "Yeah. I could have stayed in Houston and worked to make partner, but I always knew I wanted to come home. When the opportunity arose, I couldn't say no."

"No, of course not."

"And I'll be back next week."

"Wow," I whispered. "That's so great."

Something flipped in my stomach. Was this the moment? Was this when he said that after all that time he'd been away, we finally had our shot? Did I even want that? I loved him. I'd always loved him, but he'd been gone. I hadn't thought of our promise to marry at thirty in so long. For a while, it had seemed inevitable. It was why I'd never gotten too involved with anyone, but that had been years ago. Now what?

And what about Jordan? That was just...starting. It was too much, too fast.

"I have one more thing to tell you," Chase said.

I held my breath.

"I'm seeing someone."

"Oh," I whispered. My head cleared. This wasn't...it wasn't at all what I'd thought. "Is it...is it serious?"

Chase reached into his pocket and produced a small blue box. *Tiffany & Co.* written on the top. He popped it open and showed off the insane ring inside. I'd pictured this moment so many times when I was younger. When we'd been together. But now, he was showing me the ring he had gotten for someone else.

"Chase," I managed to get out. My throat felt like it was full of cotton.

"I'm going to ask her once we move," he said. "I wanted you to know."

"I'm so happy for you."

"Yeah?"

I nodded vigorously. "Of course! I want you to be happy."

"I'm glad. I was kind of nervous to tell you."

"Don't be nervous with me, Chase," I said, reaching out and taking his hand. "We've known each other our *entire* lives. You can tell me anything. I know we were together before, but that shouldn't matter. Anyway, I'm kind of seeing someone, too."

"Yeah?" he asked again.

I nodded. I couldn't say this to my other friends. Could hardly say it to myself, but I was being purposefully dense by saying Jordan and I weren't together. We'd have to figure it out, but I hadn't gone to him last week for no reason. I hadn't avoided a hookup for no reason. I wanted Jordan Wright. Damn it all! Who knew seeing Chase was all I needed to realize that?

"Good. I'm glad you're happy." He looked down to where I still clutched his hand and then back up to me. "You ever think about that pact we made?"

I laughed, pulling my hand back. "Oh God, I haven't thought of that in *years!*" I lied. "What even made you think of it?"

"Oh, you know, I just always thought, one day...you and I..."

"That sort of thing only happens in fairy tales and romance novels," I said, forcing out another laugh.

"Yeah. You're right." He looked down and then up at me again. "You know that I'll always love you, right, Annie?"

I swallowed hard and nodded. "Feeling's mutual. I want the best for you. Whether that's a fairy-tale pact or this." I gestured to the wedding ring. "That's what I want for you."

"You're the best."

"Now...we should introduce you to my boyfriend," I said, tasting the word on my tongue. "He's probably not happy."

Chase chuckled, closing the box and standing. "If I were him, I'd want to kill me."

"Let's hope it doesn't come to that."

But I didn't think he was wrong.

23

JORDAN

*W*ell...fuck.

"Dude, I had no idea what I was bringing onto your doorstep," Julian said immediately.

Ashleigh had already scampered off to get a drink. While the rest of us just stood there, cringing.

"It's fine," I lied.

I'd never heard of this Chase guy before in my life. He'd waltzed in and swept Annie off of her feet, literally. I was as equally confused as I was pissed off. She'd barely given me a glance before walking out of the house with him. As if that had always been her expectation.

"Maybe you should go after her," Julian said.

I shook my head. There was no way that I was going to run after her. I was pissed off, and then if I followed, *she* would be pissed off. We weren't quite on steady footing yet. This was only a maybe date since neither of us had confirmed it either way. There was still a blurry line in the sand, and barging out of here and confronting her would draw it more firmly.

"I don't think that's a good idea," I said.

Sutton agreed, "Yeah, probably for the best."

"But who is he to Annie?" Julian asked, trying his best to look out for me. "I just thought he was Ashleigh's brother. I didn't know anything else."

"He is Ashleigh's brother," Sutton said. "Chase and Annie grew up together. They've been friends, I don't know, longer than us."

"Friends," Julian said dubiously.

Sutton looked away but not before I saw the wince on her face.

"Sutton," I said softly.

She shrugged. "Look, I don't think I should be the one talking to you about this."

"What's there to talk about?"

"Nothing."

Ashleigh sauntered back in with some clear beverage and looked between the three of us. "What are y'all standing around for?"

"We're discussing your brother," Julian said. He pulled her closer.

I still couldn't figure out what he saw in her, but Julian liked to be charmed as much as he charmed others.

"What about him?"

"His history with Annie."

Ashleigh sighed in that dreamy sort of way as she looked up and clutched her hands around her drink and brought it to her chest. She looked like a Disney character. "They're destiny."

I squeezed the beer I was holding and looked at her incredulously. "What does that mean?"

"Ashleigh," Sutton warned.

"Well, they're going to get married," she said as if it were obvious. "They have a pact that if they're not married by the time they're thirty then they'll get married. Now, he's moving home. They're fated."

I blinked. Was she serious? This was the sort of thing that people talked about in movies, but it wasn't reality. People didn't actually make those promises. Who wanted to marry someone they'd known at eighteen anyway? You'd both change beyond comprehension.

"It's not like that," Sutton said quickly. But her eyes said it *was* like that. "They're just friends."

Ashleigh rolled her eyes and took a sip of her drink. "Whatever, Sutton. You just don't believe in true love." Then she stepped around her and walked off.

Sutton staggered back a step at the comment. She looked like a wounded bird. She closed her eyes briefly around the pain of what Ashleigh had said. I actually stepped forward to catch her in case she fainted.

"Are you all right?" I asked.

Sutton clenched her jaw and opened her eyes. "Fine. And I *do* believe in true love. In fact, I believe that if you're lucky, it can happen more than once," she said defensively as her eyes flitted to David across the room. "I wouldn't listen to Ashleigh's ramblings. Annie and Chase dated. They broke up. They made this silly pact because he was moving across the country and likely never coming home. It's nothing more than that."

Then she nodded at us both and returned to David's side. He pulled her in close and kissed the top of her head. Ashleigh's comment had been callous. I disliked her even more for it.

"Seriously, I didn't mean—" Julian began.

I interrupted him and waved it away, "Let's forget it. You didn't know who he was to Annie." I glared at the door. "Nor did I, apparently. But there's nothing I can do about it until she gets back."

"You sure you don't want to go after her?"

"Positive," I told him.

I clapped a hand on his shoulder and directed him to the living room.

A Super Bowl party game had been set up. Everyone dropped in twenty dollars to pick three tickets. Every twenty dollars got you more tickets. Each ticket had a phrase on it, such as, *This ticket wins if the national anthem is longer than two minutes*. Then a raffle would be held at the end of the game for all the winning tickets, and the names drawn would win some of the pot money.

I blindly dropped down two hundred dollars for tickets. I'd been warned about the game and planned to buy enough for both Annie and me to play. But right now, I needed the distraction of sorting through the tickets, so I wouldn't think about her absence.

I won the national anthem ticket and dropped it into the collection bin that Jensen held out. He stood next to me as the game got geared up.

"Who are you rooting for?" I asked absentmindedly.

Jensen didn't answer. He just gave me a look. "You know, I always admired your work ethic and your complete hold on control at the office, even when things didn't go your way. But I don't know how you're standing here right now."

I met his gaze. My cousin and the only person who had ever felt like an older brother to me. "You're right."

I passed him my beer and left. Annie still wasn't back. It had been long enough. She wasn't going to like me stepping in, but she was going to have to deal with that. I tried to tamp down on the anger. I didn't want to blow up on her and lose all the ground that we'd gained. But it was hard to temper my rising fears and redirect them to something manageable.

I wrenched open the front door, prepared to head out into the darkened exterior and find Annie. But before I took the first step out, Annie stumbled forward, her hand on the doorknob.

"Oh," she gasped with a laugh. Her eyes lifted to mine. "Jordan, hey!"

"Sorry," I said automatically. "I didn't know you were there."

Obviously.

"No problem," she said, straightening. "It got dark really fast. We didn't realize how late it was."

I stepped back to let her inside.

Chase followed behind her. He shot me a smug smirk. "You must be the boyfriend."

The boyfriend? The *boyfriend*? Was I the boyfriend? Had she told him that? Or was he fucking with me? From the look on his face, I was a hundred percent certain that he was fucking with me.

"Be nice," Annie said with another carefree laugh. "Jordan, this is Chase. Chase, Jordan."

I closed the door behind them and turned to face Chase Sinclair. He held his hand out, and I put mine in his. We both squeezed harder than necessary. Until my hand was cramping and I could see the wince in his eyes before he abruptly let go. I tried not to look self-satisfied, but I'd clearly failed because Annie sighed in frustration.

"Chase and I grew up together," Annie explained. "He's in town to buying a house."

"You're moving here?" I asked, sizing him up.

He was such a fucking pretty boy. I couldn't believe that Annie had ever been into this guy. She didn't seem the type to want a guy who spent more time getting ready than she did. I was being petty and didn't fucking care.

"Yeah. Next week," Chase said smoothly. "We'll be seeing a lot more of each other."

I could hear the threat in his voice and wanted to punch him in the face. I clenched my hands into fists. Tried to remember all the reasons not to deck this guy as he'd all but said he was gunning for Annie.

"Jordan, let's go get a drink," Annie said. She stepped between us, putting her hand on my arm, as if she could tell that I was about to blow my top. She smiled at Chase. "Need anything? We can get it."

"I'm good," Chase said and then left for the living room.

Annie dragged me into the kitchen and away from the rest of the party. Thankfully, the kitchen had cleared out. The game was about to start, and everyone wanted to watch kickoff. I had a ticket for how far kickoff went, but I couldn't seem to care.

"All right," she said, opening the fridge and looking

through the choices. "What are you drinking? Shiner Bock? I don't know if I'm up for beer."

"Annie," I said carefully.

She pulled out a wine cooler with a shrug and then smiled up at me. "You look mad," she said, deflating.

"I'm not mad." Yes, I was. "I'm trying to figure out what happened."

"Chase is a really old friend."

"Ashleigh mentioned a pact?"

She sighed. "Ashleigh should mind her own business."

"Is she wrong?"

"No," Annie said as she popped the top on her drink. "But Chase and I aren't like that anymore. We're just friends."

"We've been telling everyone that *we're* just friends, too, Annie."

She cringed. "That's not what I meant. We dated in high school. That pact was just..." She trailed off and waved her hand. "Anyway, he only wanted to talk because he's dating someone serious. He wanted to tell me in person and show me the ring."

I released a breath, unclenching my hands. "You could have led with that."

She laughed and leaned into me. "And miss watching you sweat?"

"Cruel and unusual punishment, love."

"Even if he wasn't, you don't have anything to worry about, Jordan. Didn't you hear what he said when he came in?"

"What was that?"

"That you're my...boyfriend," she said the last word softly, looking down.

I paused. "I thought he was fucking with me."

She met my gaze. "He wasn't."

"Am I...your boyfriend?"

She bit her lip. "Do you want to be?"

"I don't want to be if you're only doing it because your ex showed up."

"That's not why," she said in exasperation.

"You drew the line in the sand."

"And I'm the one crossing it."

She pressed her lips to mine, and I pulled her tight against me. She tasted like home, and I didn't want to fucking let her go. If seeing her ex was the way that she'd realized we were finally dating, I guessed I'd take that.

My hand slipped lower to the hem of her skirt and then ran up her leg. I pressed her back into the kitchen counter. She made a breathy sound of protest but kept kissing me. I wanted to go further, heft her up onto the granite countertop, hike her skirt up, and take her right here.

Just as I considered how to do that fast enough so we wouldn't be interrupted, a throat cleared behind us. We pulled apart, and I found Emery standing in the entrance.

"The game started," she said with a gleam in her eye.

"Thanks," Annie said breathlessly. "We'll be right there."

Emery nodded, grabbing a water out of the fridge and disappearing again.

Annie tilted her head back and laughed. "Whoops."

"I have no regrets."

"Me either," she said, pressing a kiss to my lips again. "But we should probably go."

"Yeah, I need to see if I won any of these." I dug the tickets out of my pocket.

Annie laughed and grabbed a few of them, reading them to herself. "Oh, perfect! I want the jackpot!"

I grinned at her as she headed back toward the living room. But then I snagged her before she walked through the doorway.

"What?" she asked, looking up from the tickets.

"If I'm your boyfriend now," I said carefully, "can I make a request of you?"

She arched an eyebrow. "What do you have in mind?"

"I want to go to Seattle with you."

She startled. "For my interview?"

"Yeah. A lot of my friends live in Seattle, and I haven't seen most of them in a few years. Plus, I wouldn't mind getting away with my girl."

She melted. "With your girl?"

"Yeah. What do you think? We could go early and see the city."

"Well, I already have my ticket and room. I don't think that I could get it moved," she said, worry coming to her voice.

"Why don't you let me take care of all of that?"

She narrowed her eyes. "Why does that concern me?"

"Come on. You've always wanted to see Seattle. Let me show you."

She wavered for a second before nodding. "I'd love that."

PART IV

THE BOYFRIEND

24

ANNIE

*J*ordan had promised to "take care" of everything for this trip to Seattle. In fact, he'd told me to cancel my flight and the hotel I'd booked near Harborview Medical Center. The hospital was near downtown Seattle and the site of the University of Washington's emergency medicine residency program. I wasn't exactly sad about the hotel. It was the cheapest option that I could find in the area that wasn't a total dump. But still, I'd chosen it, and I didn't know what Jordan would choose.

We were in his truck at some ungodly hour. I held my coffee mug tight to my body, promising to never forsake it. We took the turnoff for the airport, and my knee jiggled nervously. I twirled my claddagh ring around and around and around in between sips of coffee.

Jordan just smiled at me. He could tell that I was nervous, but it wasn't about us. I actually felt pretty great about us at this point. I'd been avoiding it for so long, but now that we were dating, we fit together perfectly. Like we were always meant to do this.

It was more that I liked being in control. I'd been one of those weirdos who hated surprises and snuck in to find out what my Christmas presents were so that I didn't have to wait. And now, I wanted to know all the secrets he held up his sleeve.

Instead of heading into the regular airport, Jordan directed me to another entrance.

"What's this?"

"You'll see," he said.

I could do nothing but follow. We walked through a small security area that I'd never seen before and then directly onto the tarmac.

I froze in place.

"Jordan," I whispered.

He smiled brilliantly, that blinding smile. "Come on, Annie."

"What are you doing?"

"Flying you to Seattle."

"Yourself?" I squeaked.

He laughed. "No, I'm not flying the plane, but we are taking the Wright jet."

"We're flying private?"

He walked back to me and put an arm around my waist. "I told you that I'd take care of it."

"I've never flown private. This is...too much."

"It's really nothing. Jensen uses it primarily to see Colton. He wasn't flying this weekend, so he said it was free."

"Jordan," I groaned again.

It was one thing to know that your boyfriend was a billionaire with a private jet. It was another thing to see it in person.

He smiled and moved me forward to the awaiting plane. A man approached and took our luggage to be stored below. Then I was climbing the stairs and into the private jet.

It was everything I'd expected and more. Plush leather seats with plenty of open room to walk around. A full-service bar with dining seating.

"There's a bedroom in the back, too," Jordan said as I marveled at the expensive interior.

"You're joking."

He laughed. "Go check it out."

I rushed like a kid in a candy store straight to the back of the private plane. I passed the flight attendant, who chuckled as I opened a door that led into a small bedroom. It was mostly a bed, but who the fuck cared? It was a bedroom in a plane, and I was flying on it. What even?

I darted back out to the cabin and found Jordan sliding a computer out of his bag. "There's a bedroom."

He nodded. "There is."

"Are you going to work?"

"I have some things to catch up on, but I don't plan to work the whole time."

"Oh good. There's a bedroom," I repeated.

He grinned. "Yes."

I was definitely planning to join the Mile-High Club later, and was reconsidering my thoughts about surprises.

Maybe Jordan could surprise me if *this* was his idea of a surprise.

* * *

The benefit of a bed on the plane was that after we joined the Mile-High Club, I could sleep a few extra hours. So, when we finally touched down in Seattle, I was rested. It was hard, switching my schedule around for the interview. This would help me adjust back to daytime.

A black Mercedes waited to pick us up at the airport. I shouldn't have been surprised, but somehow, I was. I peered out the window of the car as we drove toward downtown.

It was a typical Seattle day—foggy, overcast, and rainy. So, I couldn't see much of anything. Just hazy buildings and people walking the streets, huddled over in rain jackets.

"There aren't that many people with umbrellas," I mentioned.

Jordan glanced out my window. "Yeah, you get used to the rain. It's like this in Vancouver."

"Huh. I guess that makes sense."

We were in his territory now. I was out of my depth, and I loved it. I just wanted to dive out into the rain and explore.

The Mercedes parked out in front of the Four Seasons. I managed to keep my jaw from dropping as we were whisked inside the hotel with soaring ceilings and marble everything. Jordan checked us in, and we took an elevator up to the very tip-top floor.

"What did you do?" I asked again as I stepped into the penthouse suite.

It was *enormous*. Way, way too big and too fancy for two people. It should have housed celebrities...not me.

"Jordan," I whispered.

"You let me take you away," he said, as if that were answer enough.

I plastered myself to the full glass windows overlooking Pike Place Market and the bay beyond. It was still cloudy, but enough light peeked through to give me an uninterrupted view of Seattle. I was already in love.

Jordan moved to stand next to me. When I glanced at him, it looked as if he were seeing something other than Seattle from the window. He almost looked sad.

"Does it rain like this in Vancouver?"

"Yeah. Just like this."

"It's not far from here, right?"

"No, it isn't."

I saw the nostalgia in his eyes. "Do you miss it?"

"Sometimes," he said, pushing away from the window. "I miss all the luxuries of living in a big city and my friends, of course. But I've learned to like the sunshine."

"And you have family in Lubbock."

"Yeah. I wouldn't say I'm used to that yet. It's growing on me that I don't only have Julian to rely on."

I reached out and threaded our fingers together. "They like having you there, too."

"I'm glad. It wasn't an easy decision to make."

"Why did you end up making it?"

He shrugged out of his jacket and tossed it onto an armchair before running his hand down his face and sinking into it. "I don't know. Part of me still thinks it was because of you."

"What?" I asked. "But...I don't understand."

"I'd been thinking about it for a long time. I couldn't reconcile how I could leave the company I was running in Vancouver, but I wanted to go with my mom and Julian. Jensen tried to convince me, but I turned him down. So, I think it was because when I was with you, you made me feel like I was finally free."

I stared at him in shock. "But...we didn't date."

"No, you hated me for so long because of Missy, which was definitely a mistake on my part. I didn't know that before I moved there. I was just chasing that feeling." He shrugged. "I wanted to be there for my family anyway. So, it worked out."

"Did you want to date me all this time?" I asked softly. A thought I had never considered.

My heart was pounding. This was revelatory. Surely, Jordan Wright hadn't been...waiting for me.

"Yes."

I sank into the chair across from him, my hand going to my mouth. "Why didn't you...do anything before this?"

He chuckled derisively and held his hand out. "I did. Multiple times. You turned me down, and then you started avoiding me."

I flashed back to when he'd first moved to town. How he tried to put the whole *bringing his girlfriend to the wedding* thing behind us. He *did* try to ask me out, and I laughed in his face. He did it again, and I was sure he was being an ass. Making fun of me or something. That he was purposefully cruel. And then I *had* started avoiding him. It had been easier.

"Wait...you were for real when you first moved here? I thought you were joking!"

"I was serious. I was interested in you."

"Wow."

I was still processing when he came to stand before me. He held his hand out, pulling me up.

"The past is the past. We can't make up for the last three years when we were both technically too busy to be dating anyway. So, why don't we go out and enjoy the rainy day while we can?"

I nodded. "I'd like that."

We set out from the Four Seasons and straight to Pike Place Market. I convinced someone to take a picture of us posed in front of the famous red sign. Then we wandered through the market stalls. We watched people throwing fish at the Fish Market and drank coffee at a local spot.

By the time we got back that night, I was exhausted, brimming with excitement and freezing from the perpetual rain. Jordan stripped my clothes off and tugged me into the shower as soon as we got back.

From there, we tumbled straight into the enormous bed, and I lost myself in this amazing guy. The one who had wanted me from the beginning. Who had put up with the *friends with benefits* scenario. And who had done all of *this* as soon as I was finally his.

On our one-night stand, I'd fallen for Jordan Wright. And now, I was pretty sure I was in love with him.

25

JORDAN

*W*hen Annie got ready to go to the hospital for her tour and interview, I was still in bed. We'd been up way too long. Probably later than we should have been, all things considered. Even though I should have gone for a run and checked in at work, I lounged lazily in bed.

"Jordan!" Annie called from the bathroom.

I leaned up on my elbows at the concern in her voice. "Yeah?"

She ran back inside. "Have you seen my claddagh ring?"

"Uh, no. Where did you last have it?"

She shook her head. "I don't know. I had it in the car on the way here because I was playing with it. I don't remember after that."

"I'm sure it's here."

I hopped out of bed and started a meticulous search of the suite. It was large enough that it could be anywhere. But it could be on the plane or at the market or the coffee shop, too. She was already panicking though, so I didn't say any of that.

"Any luck?" she asked, her voice laced with hysteria.

"No."

"I think I had it before the shower. I remember taking it off and leaving it by the sink." Tears welled in her eyes as she looked at the sink. "What if it fell down the drain? I've had that since I was eighteen."

"It's okay, Annie. We'll find it."

"I don't want to go to my interview without it."

"I know you don't, but you don't need it either," I said, taking her by the shoulders and forcing her to look at me.

She bit her lip. "I've had it forever. My parents gave it to me at high school graduation."

"Hey, listen, you're an amazing doctor, and you're going to kill this interview. A ring isn't going to change that."

She nodded slowly, swiping at the tears on her cheeks. "You're right. You're right. I don't have time for this. Can you keep looking and let me know if you find it?"

"Of course. I'll retrace our steps yesterday and see if someone found it."

She beamed. "That's a great idea. Thank you."

"Anytime."

After I got her calmed down enough to function, she threw a jacket on over her suit and headed out the door. I had a car waiting for her on the curb, and she texted me when she realized it.

You didn't have to do that!

That was the reason I'd done it.

Then, instead of spending my morning getting caught up on work, I got dressed again and walked every step we'd walked the day before, even going inside the coffee shop to see if anyone had found a ring. No one had, of course. If it wasn't lost somewhere in Pike Place Market, then it had fallen down the drain, and we'd never see it again.

I decided to let Annie know.

Hope everything is going well for you. No luck with the ring.

She responded almost instantly.

I hated that I couldn't fix this for her. I knew what that ring meant to her, but there was nothing more I could do. I should have returned to the hotel and worked the remainder of the afternoon. Instead, I trudged down the bleak Seattle streets in the fog and misty rain. It felt like *home*.

Annie had asked if I missed it, and I'd said I did, but being out here showed me how much I had missed it. I'd never lived anywhere but Vancouver and a four-year stint in Seattle for college. And Lubbock was about as opposite as it could get. Who knew the Pacific Northwest would hold on to my heart so decisively? That I'd want to wander through the mercurial weather just to feel like I lived here again.

I ended up in front of the bay when my phone rang. Hollin's number was on the screen.

"Hey," I answered.

"Jordan, sorry to bother you on vacation."

"I'm always available. You know that."

"For sure, dude. There's a guy here at the winery who says he's with the health department."

"The health department?" I asked incredulously. "What does he want?"

"I don't know. He said he got a complaint and needs to do a full inspection of the location."

"We're not even open."

"I know, dude," Hollin said in frustration.

"And he wants to do the inspection right now?"

"Yeah."

I tapped my finger on the railing. "I'll look into it. Let him do the inspection if he must. I don't know what he could possibly find, considering we're not even fully operational yet."

"All right."

"See if he has an order or knows who filed the complaint. I want to follow up with it. I'll check with his superior."

"Okay. I'll get on it."

I hung up the phone and wanted to chuck it into the bay. When we'd been told that the winery was haunted, we'd thought it was a joke. That all the bad luck was of the supernatural variety was outrageous. I never would have believed it until the last couple weeks of ownership. This health inspection was the last of a line of things that had gone wrong, starting with the higher offer. At some point, the electricity was cut for no particular reason. We had a containment permit, which we were certain had already been filed, go missing. We just had to refile it and get it approved, but still, it made no sense.

Then Hollin had had one too many workers back out of employment contracts right before signing to work with us.

It was maddening. I was starting to think less ghost and more that *someone* was doing this to us.

I just had no idea who.

* * *

Annie returned to the hotel long enough to change for dinner and go out again. They'd set up a special dinner for those interviewing this weekend. I ordered takeout from a local Ethiopian restaurant. One of the things I missed most about Vancouver: the food.

She came back two hours later, a little tipsy from wine at dinner, and immediately started digging through the bathroom again.

"No luck." She pouted. "I just...I don't know how I lost it. I've had it for almost a decade. Fuck."

"I know. I looked everywhere."

She sighed and shook her head. "Nothing I can do about it, I guess. Are we still going out?"

"If you're up for it."

"I am. Just let me change."

"Cush said he'd meet us in an hour."

She smiled and headed back into the bathroom. Thirty minutes later, she returned as a sex goddess. She wore a slinky black dress and thigh-high boots. Her red hair was down past her shoulders in large curls, and she had on sexy, smoky makeup that only highlighted her bright green eyes and the pout of her red lips.

"Fuck," I growled, stepping up and running my hands down her sides. "We might need more time."

"Oh yeah?" She giggled.

"I might need to bend you over this bed before we go."

"I might like that. Do we have time?"

"We can make time," I told her.

She laughed as I herded her toward the bed. "I want to, but I want to meet your friends. You know all of my friends."

I adjusted my erection and groaned. "Annie, love."

"Come on," she teased. "You can imagine fucking me all night and then come home and do it."

"I don't want to be hard all night."

She leaned in and kissed my lips. "It'll be sweeter when you come home and rip my dress off to get inside of me."

"You're speaking my language."

"I thought I might be," she said with a laugh, squeezing my ass. "Now, let's go."

She wiggled out from under me and headed toward the door. I let out a long, restrained sigh, adjusted myself again, and followed her. This was going to be a long night.

The trip to the club was a twenty-minute drive despite the fact that the Four Seasons was directly downtown. I sure didn't miss the traffic.

"So, who are we meeting again?" Annie asked, staring out at the misting sky.

"Should just be a small thing. Cush, Georgia, and Tye."

"And Cush is the one who's a doctor?"

"Yeah. Cush, Tye, and I went to Washington together for undergrad. Then Cush went to medical school in Vancouver. He's now a surgeon here in Seattle. Georgia is his fiancée. She's a higher up for Nordstrom. Their head-quarters are here. Tye and I were roommates. He was a music major and does equipment work with the stadi-ums, plays in a few local bands, helps at music festivals." I shrugged. Hard to pin down Tye. "He does a bit of everything."

"That's cool," she said as we rolled up to the front of the building.

She was back to bouncy Annie. I hadn't thought she'd be this excited to meet a few of my friends, but leave it to Annie for her extroversion to take over.

The valet opened the door and helped Annie out of the car. I followed her, and we walked right past the line of people waiting to get inside. A red rope was swung open wide at our appearance.

Annie's eyes were wide. "Is that normal?"

"For me," I told her.

And it used to be. This used to be my life. Nightclubs and galas and models and lots of alcohol. We'd all been young and stupid. Invincible. Now, it would be fun for a night, but they couldn't pay me to go back to this.

We entered the club, which was standard-issue Cush —over the top, girls dancing in cages, music blaring— and headed straight for the VIP section. I spotted Cush by the mop of shoulder-length blond hair, pale skin, and Neanderthal physique. He'd taken to wearing his hair in a man bun, as it had become fashion, and I still couldn't get over it.

"Jordan!" Cush yelled. "My main man has arrived!"

Georgia was as stunning as ever with light-brown skin that practically glowed in this lighting. Her natural corkscrew curls had been left loose in a small Afro. She was tall, lithe, and had been inseparable from Cush for at least a decade.

As soon as she saw Annie, she elbowed Cush out of the way to get to us first. "You must be Annie!" she gushed, throwing her arms around Annie as if they were lifelong friends.

Annie laughed and went with it. "Georgia, I'm guessing."

"The one and only. Come do a shot with me before the boys bombard you!"

Georgia pulled Annie to the bartender for our booth and gestured for shots. Annie's eyes were wide, but I couldn't keep the laugh from lighting in my eyes.

"Georgia," Tye said in exasperation. He wore a band shirt that revealed both full-tattooed sleeves. His hair had been recently buzzed, and I could see the outline of a cigarette packet in the pocket of his loose jeans. Old habits died hard. "Don't overwhelm the poor girl. It's bad enough she's dating Jordan."

"You're still an asshole, I see," I said to Tye and stepped into their booth, holding my hand out to shake.

We were an odd trio if there ever was one, but we'd known each other too long for us to not fit.

Tye shrugged. "I'm still me."

"You couldn't convince Logan to join us?" I asked about his husband.

Tye shook his head. "He said to send his regards. He's been working doubles right now on the docks."

"Sad I missed him," I told him, clapping him on the back.

Cush threw his arms around both of us. "Hell yeah. It's like college all over again! No chicks, no dicks!"

Georgia rolled her eyes, after finishing the shot she took with Annie. "I am standing right here, babe."

Cush sighed. "Fine. Maybe not *just* like college."

Annie giggled. "Who knew Jordan Wright was such a party animal?"

Cush, Georgia, and Tye all turned to look at her at once. I nearly put my face in my hands. Oh boy.

"That's a joke, right?" Georgia asked.

"She's definitely joking," Tye agreed.

Cush burst out, "Jordan Wright is *the* party animal."

Annie looked between them all incredulously before landing back on me. "*You're* the party animal."

"Let me learn you a thing or two," Cush said, wrapping an arm around her and pulling her deeper into the booth.

Tonight was going to be interesting.

26

ANNIE

*O*f all the things I'd anticipated about meeting Jordan's friends, this was the most surprising. Jordan spent more time at work than I thought was humanly possible. He was hardly a party animal. The only time I'd seen him out was the time I invited him the night of our one-night stand. Actually, maybe that was why he'd said yes without question. I just thought he wanted to get into my pants.

"No way," I said with a laugh.

"I thought you said this was your girlfriend, Jor," Cush said.

Georgia elbowed him in the side. "Shut up, Cush."

Jordan shook his head and took a seat in the booth. "That's who I used to be, Cush."

"Jordan went out every night," Cush informed me.

"Not every night," Georgia said with an eye roll. "Could you please let the experts tell this story?"

"Thursday, Friday, and Saturday nights," Tye added. "Minimum."

"Half the time, it was to see you play," Jordan countered.

"Well, yeah, but what about the other half of the time?"

Georgia cackled. "The other half was for all of you to chase ass."

"We were young," I offered.

Cush arched his eyebrows. "Young? You were still doing this shit in Vancouver up until you left. What happened?"

Jordan shrugged. "There aren't clubs in Lubbock."

I laughed. "Yes, there are. You just don't go to them."

"You've domesticated him," Georgia said with a wink. "We all do at some point."

"Not me!" Cush cheered.

Georgia shot me a look. "Even Cush. This isn't normal for us anymore. We were lucky that these were his days off in surgery."

It was hard to imagine that this had been Jordan's life. It didn't mesh with what I'd seen of him the last three years. But I liked getting a more complete picture of who he was and had been. No wonder Lubbock felt so simple to him and he had so much to get used to. He'd gained a family and lost everything else.

Cush turned away from the group to order drinks from their private bartender and returned a minute later with a shot-laden tray. He passed them out efficiently.

"Cush was a bartender in college," Jordan said, pulling me down next to him and wrapping an arm around my waist. "He hates having other people pour our drinks, but he endures."

Cush held the drink aloft. "To friends, old and new!"

We all held our drinks up and yelled, "Cheers!"

I downed the shot, letting the vodka course through my system. It was going to be quite a night indeed.

An hour later, we were all thoroughly tipsy, and Cush was regaling us with stories of their college adventures and all the ways Jordan had apparently gotten out of things by having too much money.

"And there we were," Cush said dramatically, "about to be arrested because someone had vomited in public."

"That was you," Tye drawled.

"Whatever," Cush said, pushing it aside.

"It was him," Jordan said to me. His hand was still around me. His face nuzzled into my neck.

"And Jordan started pulling out hundred-dollar bills."

Jordan shook his head as he kissed my shoulder. "It was twenties, and we were drunk."

"Hundreds sounds better," Tye conceded.

"He told the cops that they should just let us go."

Georgia rolled her eyes. "And they fucking did because you're white boys."

"Aww, baby," Cush said, pulling her against him. "You're ruining the story."

"With the truth?"

I snorted. "I think you'd like my friend Cézanne."

Jordan groaned. "We shouldn't put them together in the same place."

"Afraid we'd take over the world?" Georgia countered.

"I'd happily let you take over the world, G," Jordan said, coming to his feet and pulling me up, too. "You and Cézanne together would burn it down."

"Then I definitely want to meet her," Georgia said conclusively.

"Dance with me," Jordan said with a laugh.

I followed him out onto the dance floor. It was slammed with people now. The music had a heady beat, and we were pulled into the flux instantly.

"Your friends are nice," I told him.

He slipped his hands around my waist, sliding down to my ass and pressing me against him. "They're ridiculous."

"They love you."

He nodded. "They do. I didn't realize how much I'd missed them. It's so easy to be around them."

"Like with Jen and Sutton."

"Just like that."

Jordan took my hand, twirling me in place so that my ass was back against his hips. Then he bent me forward slightly at the waist. I flipped my hair and shook my ass. I could feel every single inch of him press against me as we danced seductively to the music.

His hands slid up my bare thighs, hiking my skirt higher and higher up until it was nearly around my hips. I shivered as his hand slipped under my dress and ran along the seam of my thong. I gasped, but it was lost to the music and the press of bodies around us.

He didn't go any further. Just danced and teased and worked me up into a frenzy. I supposed I deserved it after teasing the shit out of him earlier in the hotel room, but damn! If it wasn't rude, I'd ditch all of his friends and head straight back to the hotel.

I turned back into his arms, letting my skirt fall back into place. "Tease!" I accused.

He laughed, as carefree as I'd ever seen him. "From the queen of tease, that's a compliment."

"Was this really your life?" I asked into his ear as we swayed to the music.

"Yeah. It's strange to look back now, but I was always the one pushing everyone to go out."

"Doesn't seem like the Jordan I know."

"I think I was looking for something," he admitted. "I was chasing the high I get every day with you."

My heart constricted around the words. "Jordan."

"I kept coming out, dancing, drinking, sex. But it never filled me up, so I did it over and over again. Relationships fell through my fingers like sand in a sieve. I thought that was just me, just who I was. But here, with you, I don't feel like that at all." His hands tightened around me. "I don't feel like you're set to slip away from me."

It was a dangerous thing to say, considering that I had every intention of leaving Lubbock and going away for residency. But right now, it felt like we could make anything happen. That we could survive anything. And I didn't want to crush that thought by bringing in reality.

"I'm not slipping away," I told him.

After a few songs, we headed back to the booth, staying until close, drinking and reminiscing. If we were going to be in Seattle longer, I would have been happy to go to one of Tye's shows and meet his husband, Logan. To see the new art opening that Georgia's sister, Tosh, was having next week. To talk doctor to doctor with Cush about what it was really like in surgery. But we didn't have more time. We only had tonight.

So, we made the most of it and then pulled each of them in for a hug before leaving.

"We'll come back, I promise," I insisted as I hugged Georgia.

"You'd better," she said. "Pick Seattle, so we can see you all the time."

I grinned. "That's the dream."

Jordan hugged Georgia one more time, punched Cush on the arm, and nodded at Tye before piling us both into the car and returning to the hotel. I leaned my head on his shoulder as we drove back. I was little bit past tipsy and straight into drunk, but it was a happy, lazy drunk. A great-night drunk.

Jordan kissed the top of my head.

"I'm glad you invited yourself to my interview."

He chuckled. "I'm glad, too."

"Would you ever want to move back to Vancouver?"

He ran his fingers in circles around my knee. "It'd depend."

"On what?"

"Where you were."

I looked up at him and pressed my lips to his. He drew me in deeper, his tongue opening the seam of my lips and massaging my own. I groaned into his embrace. I wanted nothing more than to climb into his lap and fuck him right then and there. But even drunk, I restrained myself until we climbed out of the car and hurried up to our penthouse suite.

Jordan slammed me back against the door of our

room, kissing me breathless as he fiddled with the lock to let us inside. Finally, the lock released, and we all but tumbled backward into the room. I teetered on my heels, and Jordan wrapped his arms around me to keep me upright.

"Easy there, love." He toed the door closed.

He slipped his hands to my thighs and hoisted me into the air. I wrapped my legs around his waist as he carried us into the bedroom. His lips still pressed against mine.

My feet hit the floor as my hands went to the buttons on his shirt. When I reached the bottom, I flicked the button open on his pants and slid the zipper down. Meanwhile, his hands were roaming all over my body, slinking under the hem of my dress.

He growled in the back of his throat as I ran a finger down the length of him through his boxers. "Annie," he groaned.

Then he flipped me around and pushed me face-first into the bed. My heels were still on, my dress riding up to show my ass and the lacy black of my thong. He hooked a finger under the lace and dragged it down my legs and pushed my dress up higher, so it was around my waist.

"Jordan, please," I moaned into the comforter.

But he just brushed his hand across back reassuringly and then sank to his knees behind me. The first touch of his tongue against my clit sent me jerking against the bed. My hands clenched the comforter for dear life.

A finger slicked through my core. "You're so wet."

"You were practically fingering me in public."

He chuckled. "And why would I stop when you

seemed to like it so much?"

Truth was that I didn't want him to stop. Not in public. Not right now.

Any resistance I'd built up against Jordan Wright had evaporated.

I was his. *All* his.

One finger pushed forward into me and then a second until I squirmed, wanting more, more, more. Wanting his cock inside of me, filling me. He was making me wait because I'd made him wait, and I couldn't even regret it. Because it was always better between us when he took control.

He nudged my legs further apart, opening me wider as he flicked his tongue against my clit. I buried my head into the covers. Between his tongue and the slow swirl of his fingers reaching up to my G-spot, I was going to explode already. All that waiting had primed me, and now, I was beyond sensitive.

"Come for me, love," he commanded.

His thumb ran in tight circles around my clit, and suddenly, I came completely undone, coming on his fingers as he held me bent over. He kept swirling past the point, and I squirmed harder underneath him.

"Se-sensitive," I stuttered.

"Just how I like you."

Then he withdrew his fingers and stood. I collapsed forward against the bed, glad for the short reprieve to recover. My legs shook uncontrollably, and I was breathing hard.

Then, I heard the whoosh of his pants hitting the ground, and he settled himself between my legs. His hands spread my ass cheeks as he positioned his cock at my entrance.

"Oh fuck," was all I got out before he thrust forward inside of me.

My eyes rolled into the back of my head. He was so big, kept me so full. At this angle, I could barely resist feeling as if he'd impaled me, and God, did I fucking love it.

"I wanted to do this all night."

"Fuck me?"

He collected all of my messy red hair and then moved it to one hand, giving it an experimental tug.

"Oh," I gasped as my head dipped backward, the leverage he needed to drive into me again and again and again.

My back arched, my neck stretched, my hair pulled and pulled and pulled. And I loved every fucking minute of it. I was on fire. Every thrust a hard hit, bouncing my ass and jerking my head back a little further. I was thankful for all those years of flexibility training.

"Fuck," he groaned. "Annie"—*smack*—"you feel"—*smack*—"so fucking"—*smack*—"good."

"Please, Jordan," I gasped. "Please, I'm so close."

He released my hair, letting it fall like a waterfall to frame my face. Then he grasped my hips and pounded deeper into me. My orgasm held tight and ready at the surface, as if waiting for the chance to unleash.

Sis thumb slicked through the wetness at my pussy before slipping up to my asshole. I saw black as he pushed down, breaching my hole. Everything inside of me tightened and then exploded.

I came hard and fast, rocking back against him and crying out into the night. He removed his finger as I tightened around him. Then he jerked into me one more time as he unloaded with a primal growl.

We both collapsed at the same time. All the fight leaving our bodies and pure satisfaction taking over. After a few seconds, Jordan withdrew, and I stumbled to the bathroom on shaky legs to clean up. Then I crawled into the huge bed and felt him come in after me, pulling me close.

He kissed my cheek. "You're amazing."

"I don't think I did much, honestly," I said around a laugh.

"No, I just mean...you, as you are, you're amazing."

I snuggled in tighter. "You're pretty amazing yourself."

He held me close, and I could feel myself drifting off. The past two days catching up with me.

Then Jordan spoke softly, "I could be happy here."

I blinked awake again, unsure what he meant. "Yeah?"

He waited another second, as if he didn't know whether or not to respond. "If you picked Seattle, I could be happy here, too."

My eyes widened in the bed, and I looked up into his perfectly sincere face. "What are you saying?"

"I think you know."

"You'd move here with me?" I asked.

He nodded once. "If this was what you wanted."

And I didn't have words for that gift, so I kissed him and let my body say everything I couldn't bring myself to say.

27

ANNIE

*R*eturning to normal life was a struggle. I wanted the life that we'd had together in Seattle. The wave of fresh and new, Jordan's friends nearby, the incredible team at the University of Washington residency. I wanted it all.

And Jordan had just offered it to me on a platter.

He'd said that he'd actually move with me.

It felt...too good to be true. I'd avoided dating for so long, thinking that I couldn't get with anyone that I was going to have to leave behind...like Chase had left me behind. But now, Jordan was saying that I could have it all. That he'd go with me.

I just had to get together my list of residency programs for selection. It was the single most important decision of my career, and I didn't want to fuck it up. I'd been moving programs up and down the list since I started interviewing.

In a week, I had to make my final choice.

And I'd just moved Seattle to the top.

1. *Seattle—University of Washington*
2. *Baltimore—Johns Hopkins (unlikely but necessary)*
3. *Atlanta—Emory*
4. *Los Angeles—University of Southern California*
5. *Dallas—University of Texas, Southwestern*

The entire list was sixteen total schools with Texas Tech at the bottom. I'd probably partner with a school before Tech, but it was good to have a safety school on the list, just in case.

I stared down at the list on my phone as Jennifer pulled up to the soccer complex. I'd missed a few indoor meets because of interviewing and overnights at the hospital. Isaac had said that it was fine and that they'd gotten someone else to sub in. But I'd gotten texts from Cézanne and Julian, asking if I was coming today. Apparently, Blaire had gotten Piper to sub, and she and Hollin had been at each other's throats the entire time. Everyone was glad to have me back.

I hopped out of Bertha—Jennifer's wreck of a car—grabbing my bag out of the back, and walked with her into the complex. Jordan and Julian were standing near the entrance, huddled together with the woman I recognized as their mother. I'd seen her around at Wright events, though I wasn't sure we'd ever been formally introduced.

"Annie," Jordan said, waving me over.

Go ahead," Jennifer said.

"See you after," I told her.

Then, I headed toward Jordan as she walked toward Blaire and Piper since Sutton wasn't at this game.

"Hey, babe," Jordan said.

He reached for my hand, lacing our fingers together. I flushed at the easy contact. Things had changed in Seattle when we got to be ourselves without any other eyes on us. But here, I still wasn't entirely used to it...even if I didn't mind.

"Hey," I said with a smile.

"I wanted to introduce you to my mom," Jordan said.

"You must be the Annie I've heard so much about. I'm Helene." She pulled me into a hug in lieu of shaking hands. "It's so nice to meet you. Jordan and Julian speak so highly of you, and I'm glad to see Jordan finally happy again."

"I've been happy, Mom," Jordan said with a laugh.

Julian eyed him skeptically. "Yeah, right."

"You've been pouting since we left Vancouver," Helene said.

I covered my laugh. "I didn't really know the differ- ence until we went to Seattle and I saw him with his friends."

"Cush?" Julian guessed.

Helene sighed in exasperation. "That boy! He can eat you out of house and home. Did you see Tye, too? He's such a sweetheart."

"Yes, Mom, We saw Cush and Tye. Georgia was with them, too."

"You should invite them down," Helene said. "I'll make that peach pie they all devoured."

"I'll let them know," he said with a laugh.

"And you're welcome to come to dinner, dear," she added to me.

"Thank you so much, but I actually have a hospital shift after I leave here."

"Next time you're free then,"

"I'd love to."

"See now, Jordan, you can't hide her from us anymore," his mother said. She winked at me and then headed into the stands to watch the game.

Jordan shook his head. "It's so fun when you guys gang up on me."

Julian shrugged. "Only way we know how to show our love."

Jordan rolled his eyes. Julian punched his arm and then headed out to the field to warm up.

"I should go, too," I told him. "I feel sloppy, having not been here in a few weeks."

"I'm sure you'll be great. When are you going back to the hospital?"

"This is my last week of overnights, and then I'm back to mids. Thank God."

"Shower, dinner, and then work?"

I nodded. "That's the plan."

"I like the plan."

A figure appeared next to me, and I found Isaac standing with crossed arms.

"Hey, Isaac," Jordan said, holding his hand out.

Isaac glanced between us with a total big-brother look. Welp. I hadn't mentioned to him that I was seeing Jordan. And technically, Jordan was Isaac's boss. So, maybe that should have come up.

"What's going on here?" Isaac asked.

I laughed. "Stop that." I smacked his arm, and he released a smile. "Jordan and I are dating."

Jordan looked a little put out. "I probably should have mentioned…"

Isaac waved him away, taking his hand and shaking once vigorously. "Forget it. Apparently, I'm the last to know. I was trying to be an overbearing big brother. How'd I do?"

"Terrible," I said, bumping against him.

"Why wouldn't I be happy that you're dating my little sister?" Isaac asked with a smile. "We've worked together for three years. I know the kind of person you are by now."

Jordan relaxed at the comment. "Well, still, I've heard that older brothers have the tendency to punch the new guy their sister is dating."

"Should I punch you?" Isaac asked with mock seriousness.

"If it'll make you feel better," Jordan said with a barely contained smile.

"I think I'm good. I'm going to steal Annie so that we can play soccer. We can discuss ways in which I need to assert my masculinity later."

Jordan snorted. "Sounds good. Good luck out there."

I shook my head and followed Isaac out to the field.

"You're happy?" he asked me.

"I am."

"Good. That's all I care about."

Then he started to run drills before the game. He was still in tip-top shape from years of playing soccer, and I was envious of how easy he moved. I felt sluggish even stretching. Tonight was going to be rough.

"Tell them, Hollin," Julian said, smacking Hollin in the chest.

They were stretching with Blaire, Cézanne, and Gerome.

I sidled up to the group, leaving Isaac to his warm-up drills. "Tell them what?"

Julian glanced over at me, and his face split. "We're throwing a party at the winery."

"Already? Is it ready?"

"Well, not officially. It's not, like, the grand opening. But we've had enough of the construction finished and all the permits in order that we can have a friends-and-family thing. But that's not the best part."

Hollin finally chimed in, "Campbell said that Cosmere was going to be traveling nearby on tour, and he'd stop by to perform."

"Oh my God!"

My jaw dropped. That *was* news.

Campbell was Hollin's younger brother and probably the most famous musician to come out of Lubbock after Buddy Holly and Natalie Maines of The Chicks. He sang lead for the band Cosmere, a group he'd joined out in LA after high school graduation. They were constantly hailed as the next Maroon 5. Understandably, Campbell hadn't been back in Lubbock much since breaking out a few years ago.

"Holy shit," Cézanne said. "I don't even like their music, and holy shit! We never get bands that big in town."

Blaire had gone pale. "They're coming here?"

"Yes!" Hollin said. "Well, Campbell will be here for the friends-and-family thing. Not the whole band. He said he could do a few acoustic songs." He waved his hands, as if there were no difference. "But he said he'd try to convince the entire band to show up for the grand opening!"

"That would be incredible for the winery," I said. "You'd sell out."

Hollin laughed. "I know. I figured it's the best I can do for it, considering the Wrights fronted the money."

Julian kicked him in the shin. "Shut up. You're doing all the heavy lifting."

"So, just to confirm," Blaire said, clearing her throat as she got to her feet, "Campbell is coming here for your party? And that's when again?"

"Two weeks!" Julian said.

"Oh, hey," Hollin said as if it'd just hit him. "Didn't you two graduate together?"

Blaire clenched her jaw and shrugged. "Yeah. But he was, like, cool."

"Says the Instagram Influencer," I said with a laugh.

But I could see her discomfort from a mile off. Of course, the boys were oblivious.

"Yeah, you're the coolest person I know," Cézanne said.

Blaire forced a laugh. "I managed to be cool after high school, but back then, I was a huge nerd. My mom was a psychiatrist, and it was just..." She trailed off and made a face. "Campbell Abbey didn't even know my name."

I highly doubted that.

"Okay, let's play!" Isaac said.

We all stood from where we'd been stretching, huddled together for one of Isaac's pep talks, and then broke and ran into position.

Cézanne glanced at me. "So, Seattle?"

I nodded. "I think it's going to be number one. You?"

"Tech."

"Really? Top of the class and all those interviews, and you still want to stay here?" I asked as the whistle blew.

"If I can do some good in my community here in Lubbock, then I don't need to go anywhere else," she said as if it were obvious.

And maybe it was. I'd never thought of it that way.

* * *

We won the game thirteen to nothing.

Isaac had actually pulled Blaire back from forward after her fifth goal. Girls got two points for every goal. Julian scored the next three, and the ref called a mercy rule. I hadn't even known there was a mercy rule. But I was glad for it. Not that I'd done much to help win. I wasn't a soccer player, and I felt like I'd been run over by the end of it. We slapped hands with the other team, and then I ran to the sidelines to guzzle my water bottle.

Blaire invited everyone out for our typical pizza. I bowed out since I had to work and found Jennifer and Jordan waiting for me.

"You did great!" Jen said.

I laughed. "I was terrible."

"Same thing," she said. "You played the sports balls, and the team won. So, you won."

"I love you."

She made a cute face like she was going to rub her nose against mine. It was so adorable. "Love you, too. I'm going to get pizza." She glanced at Jordan. "Can you get her home?"

"Already the plan," he said easily.

"Thanks!"

"I'll see you later."

"Bye!" Jennifer said, waving at us and then running to catch up with Blaire.

"Shall we?" Jordan asked.

I nodded, stretching my arms overhead and yawning. "Why am I tired already?"

"Because just ran for an hour and you've been working overnights."

"Right," I said with a soft laugh. "Of course."

We reached his truck, and Jordan came around to my side to let me in. But before he opened the door, he turned to face me. "Before we go, I wanted to give you something."

"Oh?"

Then he produced a small box...a jewelry box. My mind stopped, and everything in the entire universe screeched to a halt. I mean, he'd said that he was willing to move with me, but that couldn't be what *that* was, right? *Right?*

He laughed when he saw my face. "Breathe, Annie. I'm not proposing." Then he considered it. "Not yet."

I flushed all over at that comment. "Jordan..."

"Shh," he said playfully and then handed me the box. "Just open it."

My mouth opened and closed as the box settled in my hand. I swallowed, wondering what the hell he could be surprising me with. And why I hadn't recoiled at the thought of him one day proposing?

I opened the box and gasped, my hand going to my mouth. Nestled in red velvet was a small claddagh ring.

"Jordan," I breathed. "You didn't!"

"I know it's not the same as the one your parents gave you." He plucked the ring from the box as I stood there, frozen, trying not to cry at the thoughtful gift. "But I wanted you to have something at least."

"Thank you so much," I whispered. "It's perfect."

He went to slide it onto my finger, but I stopped him.

"The claddagh is a traditional Irish ring with three parts. The hands represent friendship, the crown represents loyalty, and the heart is for love. If you're single, you wear the ring with the heart facing out," I told him, showing him that was the way he was about to put the ring on my finger. I turned the ring around. "If the heart is facing inward, it means that you're taken and your heart is guarded." I slipped the ring on and looked up at him tenderly. "Now, you're guarding my heart."

"Yes, I am," he said and then kissed me.

28

JORDAN

*A*nnie had agreed to have dinner with my mom tonight. It was her first day off after her overnights, and she had said that she wouldn't be fully adjusted but didn't know when she'd have another day with end of term rapidly approaching. My mom was thrilled.

That left one thing I needed to do. I'd been putting it off for days, and I needed to get it over with. It wasn't going to be pleasant, but it was necessary to at least lay the groundwork.

I shoved away from my desk and headed out of my office.

"Anything I can help you with today, Mr. Wright?" my assistant, Michael, asked.

He was a twenty-something who had been passed to me late last year. He handled my calendar and phone calls. I probably didn't utilize him as well as I could have because I was a control freak.

"No, thank you, Michael. I'm going to go discuss something with Morgan."

He checked my calendar. "You don't have an appointment scheduled with Ms. Wright."

"No, I don't. Is there anything on her schedule?"

His eyes scanned the computer. "She has a video conference in twenty. You should be clear. Is that all, Mr. Wright?"

I tapped Michael's desk. "That's all."

"I could get you coffee."

"I'm fine." And I arched an eyebrow. "Why don't you go get yourself coffee?"

Michael still thought I was strange to work for. His last boss must have been a hard-ass, and he kept expecting me to make him pay his dues. It was frankly an outdated model.

I strolled down to Morgan's office and rapped on her door. Her assistant glanced up as if to stop me but then thought better of it.

"Come in," Morgan called.

I pushed the door open and found Morgan busy at work, typing away. She gave me a half-look before returning to her typing.

"What's up, Jordan?"

"Can I talk to you?" I asked.

"You are talking to me."

"Without a monitor between us."

She huffed, finished her next sentence, and then leaned back. "Take a seat. What's this about?"

After I sat, I cleared my throat. She wasn't going to like this. "So, just hypothetically, if I moved to Seattle—"

Morgan straightened abruptly, her seat snapping as it righted its position. "Come again?"

"Well, if I moved to Seattle, I wanted to see what my options were with the company."

She blinked. "Excuse me?"

I ran a hand back through my hair but didn't drop her gaze. "It's theoretical, but if I moved, could we open a new office in Seattle?"

"You're moving to Seattle?"

"Theoretically," I reiterated.

This was why I hadn't wanted to do it. There was a chance that Annie wouldn't be chosen for Seattle and that she'd end up somewhere else. But I thought her chances were good that she'd get her top pick. And I needed to figure this out before we got to that day and I blindsided Morgan with a transfer request.

"Seattle is handled by the Vancouver office," she said evenly. "As you know."

"Right. As I know." I leaned forward. "But wouldn't it be better to have someone on the ground in Seattle to help with the projects there?" I'd done my research. "We have that new wing at the University of Washington, and we're building that new Hyatt downtown."

"Someone...like you?"

"Right."

Morgan sighed dramatically. "But I *like* you, Jordan," she groaned. "We made this position for you, and I was uncertain at first that we really needed it. And now, I have you here, and I *do* need that position. I like having you here. You work harder than Austin."

I laughed at the compliment. "Low bar?" I joked.

She waved her hand. "Probably. Are you really moving?"

"I don't know. I won't know what's going to happen until the end of March, but I wanted to run it by you first. Before it became a real problem."

"I appreciate that," she said with a sigh. "Of course we'd figure something out for you. Maybe a part-time office in Seattle, and you could commute to Vancouver or something every other week."

I breathed a sigh of relief. "Thank you, Morgan."

"Anything for family, Jordan. You should know that."

I should, but I hadn't been sure. Three years, and I still didn't know that they'd do anything for family. I was starting to get it...and worried I was going to miss it.

* * *

"Flowers!" Annie gushed when I showed up to her house a few hours later. She put the blooms to her nose and breathed deeply. "I love them."

"I'm glad."

"You didn't have to do this." She headed into the kitchen and pulled a vase out. After filling it with water, she put the flowers in it and rearranged them to her specifications. "Gah, they're so pretty."

"Like you." I tugged her toward me. "And it's worth all the flowers to see that smile."

She giggled and pressed a kiss to my lips. "Stop. You're too romantic. It's gross."

I laughed at her assessment. "Then I'll just have to be gross," I told her with another kiss.

"Okay. Fine," she admitted. "I don't mind."

"I thought not." I took her hand. "Come on. Let's go."

She ran a nervous hand down the front of her sweater. I could tell she was second-guessing her outfit—pink sweater, black leggings, knee-length black boots. But she had no reason for nerves. My mom liked basically everyone she'd ever met.

"You look great," I assured her.

She smiled again, returning to normal, over-confident Annie. "Thanks."

My mom's house was closer to Annie's than my house. Really only around the corner as far as Lubbock was concerned. I parked in the driveway next to Julian's tricked-out Audi SUV. He cared way too much about that car.

I didn't bother knocking, just walked inside and announced us. "We're here!"

"In here, dear," my mom called from the kitchen.

Even though we'd all wanted to build her a huge, new property here in Lubbock, she'd insisted on something small and homey with character, built in the '70s with a step down into a sunken living room, and the intercom system still worked. She'd agreed that we could renovate the bathrooms eventually, but she liked its personality—the textured wallpaper, painted brick, and quirky, tiled bonus room. And I just wanted her to be happy, so I'd shut up about it real quick.

Annie and I headed to the dining room. Ashleigh was seated already, deep into her phone. Julian was in the kitchen, sautéing vegetables, as my mom pulled out a fresh pie from the oven. Julian had been graced with all of the culinary skills. I knew how to order takeout, and that was about as far as I went other than some breakfast.

"Glad you made it," my mom said, coming over and kissing me on the cheek. She pulled Annie into a hug.

Annie retrieved the wine she'd taken with her. "I brought this with me. It's a Burklee Hill red."

"Oh, wonderful. I've been meaning to try all the local wineries, so I have a way to determine whether my sons' new venture is worth anything."

Annie laughed. Julian just glanced over at me with an eye roll. Typical.

"Do you need help with anything?" Annie asked. "I'm not super great in the kitchen, but I can serve or plate."

"No, no. None of that. I want you to relax," she said. She passed me a corkscrew. "Pop that open and pour your girlfriend a drink. I don't want you touching any of the food."

I shook my head. "I'm not going to burn anything, Mom."

She shot Annie a look of despair. "I apologize that Jordan doesn't know his way around a kitchen. He has that huge kitchen back at his house and only eats Chinese."

"Luckily, I like Chinese," Annie volunteered.

I popped the cork, which I was actually excellent at, and found glasses in my mother's dining hutch. I poured glasses for everyone, passing them out.

"Ashleigh?" I said, offering her a drink.

She wrinkled her nose. "I actually only drink hard liquor."

I nearly choked. "All right." I turned back to Annie and found her trying not to laugh as she sipped her wine.

"We don't keep hard liquor in the house," my mom grumbled under her breath.

Because my dad was an alcoholic.

Okay, when I'd said that my mom liked everyone, I meant, almost everyone. Because I had never seen her dislike *anyone* like she disliked Ashleigh Sinclair. To be fair, none of us really liked her, but Julian did, and we'd learn to deal.

My mom tapped me to carry food out to the table, and then we were all seated, loading our plates with the roasted chicken and vegetables, fruit salad, and creamed corn. My mom was an excellent cook, and we all dug in. The pie still needed to cool, but I had every intention of devouring it after eating.

"So, Annie, tell us about medical school," my mom said. "How does that all work?"

"Well, I'm in an emergency medicine rotation, where I work at the hospital with a doctor on staff. I want to be an ER doctor. So, I've been interviewing for residency programs. ER residency is three years, and then I go full-time."

"And where are you going for residency?" she asked.

"I'm not sure yet. We have to submit our top choices soon. We find out where we're going on Match Day at the end of next month."

"Exciting!" my mom said.

"Why would you want to be an ER doctor?" Ashleigh asked. "There's, like, dermatology and plastic surgery and shit."

"We need ER doctors, Ash," Julian jumped in.

"Yeah, but...still."

"Well, I watched someone I care about die, and if there's another emergency, I want to be able to help. So, I chose to work in the ER."

"I think it's admirable," my mom said.

I squeezed Annie's hand under the table. "She's great at it, too."

"Sounds terrible," Ashleigh blurted, looking down at her phone again.

My mom clenched her jaw. "Why don't we do pie?"

She stumbled as she entered the kitchen again, nearly falling. Julian jumped to his feet and was at her side almost instantly. She laughed, waving him away.

"I'm fine. Just tripped."

I frowned. My mom had never been clumsy. What was that all about?

Julian followed her into the kitchen anyway and served up a blackberry pie that was maybe the best thing I'd ever eaten.

"You are going to have to give me this recipe," Annie said. "It's incredible. I'll probably butcher it, but I could try."

"I'll make you a card," my mom said with a wide smile. She loved to hand out recipes. She had an enormous book of them.

"I might have to make Sutton help me, so I don't screw it up."

"Oh, I love her little bakery downtown, Death by Chocolate. The chocolate-mousse cups are my favorite," my mom said with relish.

"It's okay," Ashleigh said. "I mean, I like that other place better. What's it called? In Cactus Alley."

Julian shrugged, trying and failing to rein in his girlfriend. "I don't know. I like Death by Chocolate."

"I guess." Ashleigh still looked at her phone.

What the hell was wrong with her?

Annie tried to engage her in conversation, but Ashleigh was on a full rampage today. She clearly didn't want to be here. I didn't even know why she'd bothered to come if she was going to act like this.

The rest of the evening was awkward, and Julian eventually said that he was going to get Ashleigh home. She jumped up like her ass was lit on fire.

"We should probably go, too," I said. "Annie is still adjusting to the time difference."

She looked up sheepishly . "But we'll have to do this again. I loved it so much."

"Anytime, dear. Anytime. Jordan, do you think you could stay behind for a minute with Julian?"

"Sure," I said with furrowed brows. I passed Annie the keys. "Want to get it started?"

"Of course," she said before heading out.

"What's going on?"

My mom didn't beat around the bush. She looked at me and my brother and sighed. "It's back."

Julian stiffened.

I stared in horror. "What is?"

But I knew.

I knew before the words left her mouth.

"The cancer."

My vision went blurry. Everything turned to static.

Julian hugged her, promised to be there for her. She told us the diagnosis. The chances of success for *another* time were low. But she was a fighter. She was going to fight.

"I love you, Mom," I told her, hugging her.

She choked up. "I love you, too."

Then I left. Because I couldn't stay there for another minute. I couldn't even breathe.

I dropped into the passenger seat and sat facing forward like a ghost. Completely drained of all thought.

"Jordan?" Annie whispered softly. "Is everything all right?"

"Her cancer is back."

She gasped, "Oh, Jordan. I'm...I'm so sorry."

Her hands wrapped around me. I should have felt something. Should have broken down like Julian had as he cried on my mom's shoulder. But I felt nothing. Just numbness.

I didn't know if she'd make it this time. And I'd moved to Lubbock last time to be here when she went through her care. What if I was *gone* this time for it? Fuck.

29

ANNIE

*J*ordan dropped me back off at home. He wanted to be alone despite all of my protests. So, I slunk back to my house, nudging a meowing Avocado out my way, as I worried about him. I knew exactly what I needed to do.

I pulled my laptop out and opened my ranks.

1. *Seattle—University of Washington*
2. *Baltimore—Johns Hopkins*
3. *Atlanta—Emory*
4. *Los Angeles—University of Southern California*
5. *Dallas—University of Texas, Southwestern*

Seattle right there at the top, like I'd always wanted. I still had a few days before I needed to commit and submit the official form. I probably should have talked to someone about it, but I'd already made up my mind. As soon as Jordan had sunk down into the driver's seat, I'd known what it meant.

His mom had cancer. He'd moved here, primarily, to be with her for the worst of it. He and Julian had literally given up their entire life to take care of her. They were only now getting back on their feet, and now...it was happening all over again.

Right after Jordan had agreed to move with me to Seattle.

As much as I tried to avoid worst-case scenarios and look on the bright side and all that, I was a medical student. I knew the likelihood of her recovering after her fourth—or was it fifth?—time with breast cancer. It didn't look good. Would he hate me forever for taking him away if something went wrong?

I closed my eyes and tried not to cry.

I couldn't take him away. That much was obvious.

The Submit button hovered invitingly. But despite how much wanted Seattle...it had always been a pipe dream. I'd rather be here and happy with Jordan than away and have him resent me. I reordered my choices.

1. *Lubbock—Texas Tech University*
2. *Seattle—University of Washington*
3. *Baltimore—Johns Hopkins*
4. *Atlanta—Emory*
5. *Los Angeles—University of Southern California*

...

. . .

I pressed Submit on my dreams.
    And I went to bed.

* * *

Everything changed after that day.
    Not in any meaningful, measurable way.
But it all still floundered.

Today was my day off, and I really should have been at work. I needed the stress of the emergency room to clear my head. To make me not obsess about this. Jordan had claimed he had to be at work late the next couple days. But I guessed he was doing what I wished I could have done at the hospital. Jennifer was away for the week at an elopement in Denver, which left the house too quiet. I could have run, but I was too down. I should have been studying, but the words all blurred together on the pages.

So, when the text came through, I jumped to answer it. Anything to keep me from wallowing.

Hey you! If you're free today, you should swing by and check out my new place. Could use someone's advice on filling the space. Can probably provide pizza in exchange.

Chase Sinclair. Needing interior decorating advice. Hilarious.

I knew from Ashleigh that his girlfriend—fiancée?—wasn't moving in for another couple weeks because of her job back in Houston. Which probably meant that it still looked like a bachelor pad.

Pizza is a fair exchange, Sinclair. You better get the pepper-
oni, sausage, Canadian bacon.

Done.

He shot me the address, and I thanked whoever was listening for giving me an out. I changed into jeans and a sweatshirt and then headed out. The house was in Rush, on the north side of town, farther away from everyone else. The southside was where everything was growing, but Rush was all this gorgeous and enormous post-war housing. Most of the interiors had been completely gutted and redone into stunning, modern looks.

Chase's new house seemed to fit the mold. Fifties era with all the new, ritzy upkeeps on the outside—fresh paint, new shutters, dark-stained wood accents. I knew instantly why he'd decided on it.

I knocked, holding up a cold six-pack of his favorite beer when he answered.

"Donoghue, you're a dream," he said with a laugh as he took the beer. "Pizza is on its way."

The house was bare bones and still so pretty on the inside. Someone had spent *a lot* of money on it. All new hardwood floor, crystal chandelier, a new coat of paint, crown moldings, new kitchen. I was almost a little bit jealous. I was used to Jordan's brand-new construction, but this had its own character.

"I'm ordering new furniture," he explained when I stepped into the empty living room. All that was inside was the TV on the floor, a poof, and some folding chairs.

I laughed. "I think this needs more than interior design help. The folding chairs, Chase?"

He shrugged, popping my beer into his bare fridge. "I

have a bed and an office. That's about all I need right now."

"You're a wreck. When does Kennedy get here?" I asked, remembering the name he'd casually dropped into conversation at the Super Bowl party.

"Not until May. She's been delayed further," he said into the fridge. "Her company doesn't want her to go remote."

"What does she do?"

"Sales," he said vaguely. He and passed me a beer.

"Surely, she's coming up to see you though, right?"

He gestured for me to follow him around the house for a tour. "Sure. Probably."

I narrowed my eyes at his back. Why wouldn't she be dying to move up here with him? Lubbock wasn't a dream come true or anything. It had three hundred thousand people instead of a couple million and much smaller airports. But still, they were serious, right? Chase was being weird about the whole thing. But whatever. I was only here as a friend and for interior design advice. I didn't need to barge into his relationship.

We wandered through all the rooms. It was definitely bigger than it looked on the outside. He claimed five thousand square feet. I practically got lost in it. The backyard was equally amazing with a full deck and outdoor fireplace and kitchen. It was better decorated than the rest of the house with a plush outdoor couch, two recliners, and coffee table.

The doorbell rang then, and we retreated back into the living room, plopping down on the floor in front of the poof. He turned on *Avengers: Infinity War* as we ate and joked around.

That was the thing about Chase. Though I'd been into him *forever*, we also had always remained close friends. Pizza nights were a norm for us. He'd come home from school, we'd hang out, and it was never like we were going to hook up or anything. Our relationship hadn't been like that in a long time. He was so easy to be around, and it kept me occupied rather than dealing with all the stress in my life currently.

When we finished off the last slice, Chase took the box back into the kitchen and brought out two more beers.

"I can't. I still have to drive home," I told him as he settled in next to me.

"Or...you could stay," he said softly.

My head jerked up. "Excuse me?"

"I mean...you wouldn't have to drive."

I narrowed my eyes. "What do you mean? You only have one bed."

He looked at me with those big blue eyes. The ones that I'd always *wished* looked at me exactly how he was looking at me right now. That I'd always *wanted* him to feel for me. But besides our brief dalliance in high school, it had never been that. I'd loved him. I'd just never been enough.

"I think you know what I mean."

I jumped to my feet. "Did you ask me over here so that you could cheat on your girlfriend?"

"No," he said hastily.

"Chase Sinclair, you better explain yourself right the

fuck now. Or I'm walking out of that goddamn door," I said, pointing at it.

"We broke up."

My jaw dropped. "What?" I gasped. I still stood, wondering what to think about it all. "What happened?"

He shot me a look so earnest, it pained me. "Don't you know?"

"I honestly have no idea."

He got to his feet, towering over me the way he always had. "Annie, it's always been you."

"No," I breathed.

Because he couldn't be saying this. Not now. Not after *years* and *years* and *years* of hoping he'd finally see that I was the one. Of counting the years to thirty. So it didn't matter who I dated because Chase would always be there to pick me up later.

"You know it's true."

He stepped forward. I stepped back.

"I don't know that," I told him.

"Annie, I've always loved you."

"As friends."

"As more than friends," he insisted. "Always."

I shook my head. "Why are you saying this? Why are you ruining everything?"

He tried to take my hand, and I jumped back like I'd been shot.

"Annie..."

"I've waited my entire life for you, Chase. I casually dated. Never really found anyone. But now—*now* that I'm finally serious with someone—is when you bring all of this up?"

"I didn't know that you were going to be dating someone seriously!"

"And what about the ring?" I shouted at him. "You showed me the ring you were going to propose to Kennedy with!"

"I know. Then I saw you, and I realized I was wrong about everything. How could I marry someone else when my heart would always belong to you?"

I slapped his hand away as he tried to touch me. "No," I said again, tears coming to my eyes. "You don't mean any of that."

"I do. I always have. You're my forever girl."

"Don't call me that," I gasped.

It was what he'd called me when we made our pact. His forever girl. I'd cherished that thought for so long, and now, he was demolishing it.

"I don't understand why you're so mad. We made that pact. We said we'd end up together."

"That was a decade ago," I shouted at him. "We were eighteen and fucking stupid, Chase. We didn't know what would happen. We just couldn't let go yet, and you were leaving. You were always leaving me, and I needed reassurance that it wouldn't be forever."

"And it doesn't have to be," he said, raising his voice to meet my hysteria.

"This is only because of Jordan."

Chase wrinkled his nose. "I mean, I'm not thrilled that you're dating him, a Wright. But it's about you, Annie."

"No, see, you found out I was serious with someone. You saw us together at the Super Bowl party, and you decided you didn't like that I was happy with someone else other than you." I wrenched my purse off of the ground. "Well, too late, Chase. If you wanted to be with me, then you should have manned up and asked me before I fell in love with someone else, and not when you see your safety net closing."

"Annie!" he called as I stormed toward the door. He jogged after me, catching me by the elbow. "Please, I love you. You can't...you can't love him."

But I did. I just hadn't been able to admit it to myself until this moment. Wasn't Chase Sinclair just revelatory for my relationship?

"Good-bye, Chase."

Then I yanked the door and stepped out, leaving behind my best friend and the man I'd always thought I was going to marry.

30

ANNIE

*B*y the time I cooled off from my confrontation with Chase, Jordan was off work. I really, really needed to go over there and talk to him. The last few days, he'd been MIA. He still answered texts, but I hadn't seen him since his mom's revelation.

Can I come over?

I wanted to tell him what had happened. I wanted to talk to him about the rank situation. I just...I just needed him.

Kind of beat. Just going to crash.

My face dropped.

I could just snuggle you?

Just want to be alone tonight.

My heart constricted. I didn't want him to want to be alone. I wanted him to want to be held and comforted. Not that I had any clue what to do if he didn't want me there. I could just show up. I didn't want him to get mad, but I just didn't know what to do.

So, I let him sleep alone that night.

I slept in my empty bed and hoped that he'd come around tomorrow.

* * *

H e didn't come around the next day.
Or the day after that.

I saw him only briefly when I showed up at the office to check on him. And he was the same Jordan...except that he wasn't. There was something dark and heavy lingering around him.

He didn't want company. He wasn't good company. And he quickly ushered me back out of the office.

I knew he had to work twice as much with the winery friend-and-family event this weekend, and apparently, all the reps for the soccer complex had come in for meetings. He was working around the clock, and the stress must have been insane. But I'd never know because he was too busy to talk to me.

I was at my rope's end when I decided I needed an intervention to figure this out. It was outside of my wheelhouse. I needed to talk to someone who had been there.

With school in session, the parking lot in front of the Death by Chocolate was packed. I had to circle the block twice to find a spot and idle until the person backed out. I slung my bag over my shoulder and headed inside. It smelled like sugary goodness and looked like a Wonka creation, like I could eat everything in sight.

I stepped across the black-and-white tiled floor, past a group of undergrads lingering over their laptops at one of the French macaron–inspired tables and fruit-tart chairs.

Noise-canceling headphones dangled from their necks while they chatted and had their heads in their phones. It did nothing to detract from the minty-iced walls. I headed straight to the bar that was decorated as powdered-sugar countertops and lemon-bar cabinets. It was hard not to stare at all of the elaborate wedding cakes in glass boxes or the glass case of sweets. My stomach grumbled.

"Hey there!" Kimber said cheerfully, coming out of the back.

Kimber was Emery's older sister and the brains behind the establishment. She'd taken Sutton on part-time after Maverick died, and Sutton had found her passion in baking. They were a power team now.

"Hi, Kimber."

"What are you in for today?" she asked, wiping flour off her hands onto her apron. "Chocolate mousse? A chocolate torte? Chocolate cake with chocolate ganache?" She grinned ear to ear.

"Undecided," I told her. "Is Sutton back there with you?"

Kimber nodded. "Let me go get her while you think about dessert."

Sutton appeared a minute later, coated with a light layer of flour. Her smile brightened when she saw me. "Annie!"

"Hey, Sut."

She frowned. "What's going on? You look sad."

I sighed heavily. I wasn't sure if Helene had shared the information with the rest of the Wright family yet, but I was about to have to spill. "Jordan's mom has cancer again."

Sutton stared at me for a second without moving or blinking. When she'd found out three years ago, she'd dissolved into a puddle. It had been too soon after Maverick, and the uncertainty had wrecked her. I could see her fighting her instincts to save herself.

"That's...that's terrible," she finally breathed out.

"It is."

"How are the boys holding up?"

"Well, that's kind of the problem. Jordan has dropped off the face of the planet. I tried to see him at work, and he, like, quickly made me leave. I haven't seen him other than that since it happened."

"Oh no," she breathed. "He must be hurting so much."

"I know. I want to be there for him, but he doesn't seem to want me to do that."

Sutton sighed and put her shaking hands on the countertop. "That is a defensive mechanism. It isn't personal."

"I hope not. But this week has kind of been crazy, and I feel like I should be talking to him about it. I know he has a lot on his plate with the party this weekend and the soccer complex and his mom..."

"That is a lot," she agreed.

"But I thought our relationship was going really great, and now, I've been cut out. I'm not mad. I'm concerned. And I have things I need to tell him, but he won't see me."

"I'm glad you're concerned and not mad because he's going to need you once he finally lets his guard down."

Sutton was definitely speaking from experience. "What do you need to tell him anyway?"

I bit my lip and looked down. "Well, for one, I made my rank-choice selection."

"That's amazing," Sutton gushed, leaning forward over the counter. "Seattle?"

I swallowed and shook my head.

"No? But wasn't Seattle always the top pick? You said you loved it, and that Jordan would move with you."

I gave her a searching look. "How could I ask him to after he found that out about his mom?"

"Oh, Annie...you really love him, don't you?"

"Yeah," I whispered, swiping away a tear. "I guess I do because I chose Texas Tech as number one. So I could stay...and be here for him."

Sut clutched my hand. "That's a very generous and selfless thing to do. And you haven't told him?"

"No, I meant to, but I haven't seen him. And...I don't know. Something else happened."

"Oh boy," Sutton said, interpreting my apprehension.

"Chase declared his undying love for me."

Sutton's eyes rounded. "Fuck."

I laughed. "Yeah, pretty much. He only did it because I'm serious with Jordan."

"Isn't that what you'd been *trying* to do all this time anyway? Make him jealous enough to see what he was missing."

"Well, yeah, but it's different."

"So, now that it's worked...how do you feel?"

I winced. I'd always hoped it would work on Chase. Now though? "Terrible. I basically told him to fuck off.

That if he was only going to pick me because his safety net was closing, then it wasn't good enough."

Sutton broke into a smile. "That's amazing. Damn, I wish I could have seen that. What did his face look like?"

I chuckled, pushing my best friend. "Don't be mean."

"Fine," Sutton said with another laugh. "And you haven't told Jordan?"

"No," I said on an exhale. "He already doesn't like Chase, and he's dealing with so much. I planned to, but now, I haven't seen him, and I don't want to pile more on."

"I think that makes sense," Sutton said. She stepped away from the counter and pulled something out of the glass. She placed a double-chocolate cupcake on a small plate and slid it over to me. "I think you need this."

I groaned. "Is it that bad?"

"Chocolate makes everyone feel better."

"Thanks, Sut."

"Anytime. Just know that Jordan is going through something that you can't fix right now. As much as you want to. The best thing is to be there, ready to catch him. He'll come to you eventually about this, and it'll be fine. I'm sure of it. Grieving is hard, and it's different for everyone."

"I know. I remember," I said softly.

"I bet it'll all be better after this winery party. He's probably bombarded with work, and he doesn't want to think about anything else."

"You're right," I said, digging into the cupcake.

"I'm always right," Sutton said with a wink.

"Brat."

"Eat your cupcake. Try not to worry too much about your boyfriend. Everything will be fine in time."

Sutton returned to work while I finished my cupcake. I hoped that she was right. Sutton was the expert on all of this. I had to defer to her judgment. Even if my instincts were to barge into his house and demand for him to talk to me. I didn't want to push him away either. Love was so damn complicated.

PART V

COMPLICATED LOVE

31

ANNIE

*J*ennifer snapped my photograph, and I threw my hands up.

"Stop it!" I cried through a laugh.

"I wanted the honest reaction!" Jennifer said as we both stared up at the new exterior of the winery. "You really haven't been here since they started working on it?"

I shook my head. I really hadn't been here. Before the last week of Jordan being MIA, I'd been too busy at the hospital to come over. He'd mentioned that they were doing new construction work and gutting the interior. That Hollin and Julian were heading up most of the renovation work and hiring people. But I hadn't imagined this.

The barn had been reinforced and stained a lush brown. The drive, which had previously been gravel, had been paved a solid black, and there was a new parking lot with freshly painted white lines. All the walking paths had been cleared, and a coat of small rocks filled them all. They were lined with flowers and carefully tended bushes. And the pièce de résistance was the enormous sign erected at the entrance—*Wright Vineyard*.

"It's stunning," I told her. "I really love it."

"I knew you would. Julian had me come in earlier in the week and take photos for the website."

"I bet he did," I said with a wink.

Jennifer flushed. "It's not like that."

"It could be."

"He's dating someone."

I laughed. "I'm just messing with you."

"Anyway, he's trying to convince me to be the on-site wedding photographer."

"Oh my God! Would you want to do that?"

"Well, I'd love to still travel for elopements. They're my favorite. But I wouldn't mind something more stable. As much as I love to travel, it's hard being gone all the time."

"Well, I, for one, would love to have you home more."

Jennifer grinned. "Same. Plus, Hollin's sister, Nora, is graduating this semester and coming on as the wedding planner full-time. So, I'd like the people I'd work with, too."

"Did Nora plan the party?"

"Yeah, and wait until you see what she did inside. She's so talented."

"I can't wait to see it."

And my boyfriend.

I followed her across the parking lot and into the barn. My jaw fell open with shock. I'd been inside this barn more times than I could count when this place was West Texas Winery. It had been a rickety, ramshackle mess. But this was something else alto-gether. A fully-functional stage had been erected against the far wall for weddings or small concerts. The dirt floor had been replaced with smooth hardwood planks, polished and shiny. The rafters had been strung with crisscrossing lights that lit up the high-beamed ceiling. Two crystal chandeliers hung from the ceiling, bringing everything together. It was refined, sophisti-cated, and gorgeous.

"Nora did this?"

"She did!" Jennifer gushed.

"Hey y'all," Nora said, appearing then. "Heard my name."

Nora barely grazed five feet with bleached-blonde hair and a warm, welcoming smile. She was only twenty-one and the baby of our circle, so I hadn't had much interaction with her except when she showed up to our soccer games.

"This is so stunning!" I told her. "You did an amazing job."

She beamed. "Thanks, Annie. Just glad to get to do what I love. And to have both of my big brothers here!"

"Campbell's here?" Jennifer whispered. "I didn't see him come in."

Nora rolled her eyes. "He was carted in, in secret. He thinks he's hot shit or something."

"He kind of is," I admitted.

"Ugh! Not y'all, too."

I laughed. "I like Cosmere's music. Campbell went to a different high school. I didn't ever know him before he left. So, he just feels like a rockstar to me."

"Same," Jennifer added. "And their music is so, so good."

Nora sighed heavily. "Fine. I'll introduce you."

"Really?" I gushed.

"Rein in the excitement. His ego does *not* need to get any larger."

I laughed. "I think I can manage."

My eyes swept the room. There were a dozen people still putting up the final decorations for the room. And another dozen who were already here for the event, mostly Wrights in attendance to support their cousins. Emery with her pregnant belly standing with Heidi and Julia as they pointed out the decorations. Jensen and Morgan with their heads bowed. Landon, Austin, and Patrick were laughing near the dessert table. The event was friends and family only, and already, it was filling up.

"Have you seen my boyfriend?" I asked.

Nora nodded. "He's in the back with my brothers."

"Oh, well, good. Two birds with one stone."

Nora showed us the way through to backstage, which was much smaller than I'd thought it would be. It was more like one large room with a private suite that Nora explained was going to be used for brides, but right now, it had been commandeered by Campbell. She rolled her eyes a lot at how much of a diva she thought he was. I only saw the love she felt about it all.

Jordan, Julian, and Hollin stood together, discussing the event. Jennifer snapped a few pictures, which she declared to be men hard at work. She winked at me, and I slunk forward to interrupt.

"Hey," I said.

Jordan glanced over at me and something flickered in his face that I'd never seen before. I couldn't put my finger on it, but it almost looked like...dread?

I knew things had been weird between us since he'd found out about his mom, but I didn't know what this was all about. Was it just more grief? I wished that he'd just talk to me.

"Hey, what do you think?" Julian asked, stepping in when Jordan didn't say anything.

I swallowed back my fears. "It's all so incredible. I never in a million years would have imagined that this barn could look like this. It used to be a piece of junk that I thought needed to be torn down."

"We almost did," Hollin said with a laugh.

"It was touch and go for a minute," Julian admitted. "But Jor wanted to keep it. So, we kept it."

I smiled up at my boyfriend. "I'm glad you did."

"Yeah," he said with a tip of his head. "Excuse me. I have to go check on something."

Then Jordan turned on his heel and walked away. My eyes rounded and the guys tried not to look like they were shocked by his behavior. I gritted my teeth and dashed after him.

When we were far enough away from the rest of the group, I snagged him by the elbow. "Hey, you, wait a sec."

"I'll be right back," Jordan said.

"Jordan, come on."

He looked as if someone had kicked his puppy. I didn't know what the hell to do about it.

"I haven't heard from you all week."

"I've been busy. I'm busy right now."

"Okay. Can I come with you?"

"I'd rather you stay here. Shouldn't be long."

I huffed. "Jordan, what's going on?"

He closed his eyes as if he were in pain before meeting my gaze again. "Can we just talk about all of this is over?"

I bit my lip. "Can you just tell me what's wrong now?"

"After," he insisted. "I'll explain when this is over."

He pressed a kiss to my forehead and then strode away without allowing me a word in edge wise. I sighed heavily and shook my head. I tried to remember Sutton's words. That I couldn't help him fix anything. I just had to be here when he was ready. And clearly he wasn't ready yet.

With another sigh, I turned back to the group. Everyone was looking anywhere but at me, trying to pretend they weren't eavesdropping. Jennifer especially looked distraught. She took a step forward as if to comfort me, and I quickly plastered on a fake smile.

"Well, I think it looks spectacular," I said. "Y'all did a great job."

"And Nora did the interior work," Hollin said hastily, grabbing his little sister and roughing up her hair.

She slapped his hand away and worked at smoothing the French twist. "Don't be an ass."

"I usually leave that for Campbell."

And just then, the door to the bride's suite opened, and out walked Campbell Abbey.

Despite my frustration with Jordan, I still went into complete and total fangirl mode at the sight of the lead signer of Cosmere. When I'd said that I wouldn't help his ego, I'd really meant itI'd been following Cosmere since their big break two years ago. They had skyrocketed through the charts, hitting number one with "I See the Real You," the first single off of their second album. And then subsequent number ones with the next four songs. They'd been on a worldwide tour the last year. And I couldn't even *believe* he was here right now. It was surreal enough that he was from Lubbock.

I smacked Jennifer's hand. "That's Campbell."

Jennifer nodded vigorously. "Holy shit!"

We were idiots. Neither of us cared.

He wore ripped black jeans, a black V-neck T-shirt, and a black leather jacket. His dark hair was short on the sides and long and slightly curly on the top. He looked like he'd just walked off of a photo shoot.

But before either of us could say anything else stupid, Hollin started laughing. "What the fuck are you wearing?"

Campbell looked down at his clothes and then back up at his cowboy of an older brother. "Clothes?"

"You look ridiculous."

"Why thanks," Campbell said with the smile that made girls' panties melt all over the world. "We call this rockstar chic."

"Let me get my hat," Hollin said jokingly. "It'll really complete the do."

Campbell rolled his eyes at his brother and joined us. "Sure. Cowboy hat goes perfectly with this jacket."

"Oh," Julian said with a laugh. "So, Hollin is this much of a dick to everyone, huh?"

Campbell chuckled. "Pretty much his MO."

"Good to know," Julian said.

"Hey!" Hollin said.

I covered my laugh with my hand to try to keep from laughing. We stood around and chatted for a while longer until the noise from the other side of the stage became practically oppressive.

"I'll check on it," Nora said quickly. She scurried off with her clipboard and came back a minute later, eyes wide. "How many people did you invite again?"

"About a hundred," Hollin said.

"Why?" Julian asked.

"The place is already *packed*," Nora said.

"What?" Julian asked in confusion. "How?"

Campbell frowned and looked between them all. "Shall I guess?"

They all looked back at the casual rockstar in their midst.

"Oh," I whispered. "Someone leaked that Campbell was going to be here. It probably got back to Tech, and all the students showed up to see him perform."

Campbell shrugged helplessly as if this were his every day. Which...I suppose it was.

Nora bit her lip. "I guess I should have anticipated this. My jerk of a brother always ruining things." But she smiled when she said it.

Campbell just laughed easily. "It's fine. You hired security, right?"

Julian looked at Hollin. "We did. Right?"

"Um..."

"Oh shit," Campbell said.

The night was definitely going to be interesting.

"Maybe you should go out there before there's a riot," I said with a laugh.

Campbell nodded. "Good idea. Let me get my guitar."

While Campbell headed back into the suite, I left with Jennifer to check out what was happening. My eyes rounded in shock. It certainly was more than the hundred people we'd anticipated. I could see some familiar faces—Blaire, Piper, Sutton, the rest of the Wrights—in the crowd, but for the most part, it was a sea of unfamiliar people.

They'd all crowded the stage and taken up a chant. "Cosmere! Cosmere! Cosmere!"

"Well, I think the guys are going to have their hands full for the night, dealing with this," Jennifer said.

I nodded. "I think so, too."

Jennifer put her hand on my shoulder. "Is everything okay with you two?"

A soft sigh escaped me.

"I honestly don't know. Everything was going so well. Too well." I glanced over at her. "I should have known that if things looked too good to be true they probably are."

"No way. You and Jordan just make sense."

"I thought so too. But he hasn't talked to me all week. He's actively avoiding me. And then did you see the way he looked at me just now?"

Jennifer bit her lip. "Yeah. That was weird. What did he say?"

"Just that we'd talk after the party. That's not a good sign, right?"

"He just seemed stressed," Jennifer admitted. "Honestly, I don't think his mind was on anything but work."

"Probably. Or at least, hopefully, and now, with this..." I gestured to the rapidly growing crowd.

"He's probably twice as stressed."

"Just what he needs."

Jennifer cringed. "Just don't think about it until later. I know that's hard, but it'll be fine. I'm sure of it. Go hang out with the girls and enjoy the show. I know you like Cosmere as much as I do."

"I do." I hugged Jen. "Thanks for being so awesome."

"It's just who I am as a person."

I gasped and hip-checked her. "Was that a joke, Jen?"

She grinned. "You're rubbing off on me. Now, go."

With a shake of my head, I headed back out onto the main floor of the barn. After careening through a group of giddy undergrads discussing Campbell, I found Blaire, Piper, and Sutton standing just far enough away from the desperate gaggle of college kids.

"This is crazy," I said when I finally reached them.

"I'm not surprised," Piper said. Her eyes swept around the barn, scrutinizing the new interior. "It was bound to get out that Campbell was performing. They should have gotten security, had a guest list, et cetera. It's an amateur mistake."

Sutton chuckled at Piper. "Just because you hate Hollin doesn't mean that you have to hate the winery."

Piper softened. "I don't hate Hollin or the winery. I think it's stunning. They did excellent work. I honestly never would have thought this place was capable of looking this good. But...it's still the competition," she said with a wink.

Piper was easily the most competitive person I'd ever met. Sinclair Cellars was her baby. I could understand why she might be worried about a Wright opening a winery in this town. Their name was gold, and she didn't want to lose business, even as an established brand.

"So, what are they going to do?" Blaire asked. She had her arms crossed and was avoiding looking at the stage. "Are too many people here? Are they going to have to cancel the show?"

"No, the guys went to handle it, and Campbell is going to go on right away to avoid riots."

Blaire sighed heavily. "Great."

Man, I wanted to ask. I really wanted to ask. But I had my own problems. Might as well leave Blaire to her own since she clearly didn't want to talk about it.

Just then, Campbell stepped out onto the stage with an acoustic guitar strung around his neck. The crowd went *wild*. He shot them that same panty-melting smile and held his hand up as he approached the microphone.

"Hello, Lubbock!" he cried.

Everyone screamed and cheered and stomped their feet. The noise in this barn was louder than I'd ever heard it...even when it was a nightclub.

"Man, it's good to be home. I've missed you." Campbell tuned his guitar by hand while he said it, not quite looking out at the audience. When he was satisfied, he played up to the crowd again. "I wasn't expecting this big of a turnout, but it's Lubbock! We know how to turn out for our own, am I right?"

Another round of screams.

"Well, why don't I kick us off then?" His fingers moved

across the guitar as if he were caressing a woman's body, and the opening chords to their breakout hit filtered in through the speakers.

The crowd erupted over just those chords.

"This one goes out to every girl who's ever felt different," he said seductively, leaning into the microphone. "This is...'I See the Real You.'"

Blaire made a gagging sound. "I think I'm going to be sick," she said, ripping out of our group. "I'm going to just...go home."

"Blaire," I said with concern in my voice.

She shook her head. Her hand went to her stomach. "Seriously, I must have...eaten something that didn't agree with me."

Why did I doubt that?

"Okay. Be safe."

"I will," she said and then all but ran out of the room.

"She's been acting like this all day," Piper said with worry in her voice as she watched her best friend. "Actually, I'm going to go check on her. I'll be back."

Then Piper disappeared, too. Sutton and I exchanged a glance. We'd been friends long enough to be able to read each other's thoughts. Something had happened with Blaire and Campbell. I just didn't know what.

Campbell finished off the next song and went into his latest hit. I tried to let the stress of the evening go. I couldn't do anything about Jordan until he was ready. Even if it made me more anxious than I'd been in a while. I just wanted enjoy the music. I really did love Cosmere. But as Campbell moved into the next song, I felt a tap on my shoulder.

I turned around to find Chase Sinclair standing there with his hands stuffed into his pockets. "Hey, Annie."

God, I didn't have time for this. I didn't care that he looked...rough. Like he hadn't been sleeping well or eating. That wasn't my problem.

"I have nothing to say to you," I said, turning back around.

Sutton bit her lip as she glanced between us.

"Can I just apologize?" he asked.

"No, you cannot. You can go away."

"Annie," he breathed, moving between me and Sutton. "Come on. We've known each other our *entire* lives. You're my best friend. I can't lose you. Please just hear me out."

Sutton frowned. "Chase, maybe now isn't the time."

"I've been messaging and calling all week," he continued, ignoring her.

"Yeah, and you'd think that you'd get the hint that I wasn't responding."

Chase reached forward and turned me to face him. I broke out of his grip and tried to avoid the earnest gaze he was shooting my way, the one completely full of regret. He was hurting, and I hated when he was hurting. But he'd done this to himself.

"Annie, please..."

"I really..." I began, but then suddenly, Jordan appeared out of nowhere.

He pushed between us, shoving Chase backward.

"Jordan," I cried.

They were practically nose to nose as they stared each other down.

32

JORDAN

"*T*ime for you to leave, Sinclair," I spat.

Chase's eyes narrowed. "I don't think it is."

"Considering I own the place, I have every right to kick you out."

He glared at me. "This is unbelievable."

"Just stop it. Both of you," Annie said. Her hand wrapped around my bicep and pulled me back. "Chase, you should just go."

"Annie, come on!"

"No. You said what you came to say."

"So, what we have means nothing to you?"

She closed her eyes and breathed in deeply.

"And what exactly is between you two?" I growled.

"Nothing!" Annie said.

Chase just raised his eyebrows. "It's not nothing."

"Fuck," I growled as I stared between the two of them.

I'd spent the last week dealing with my mom's cancer announcement. Between that, the soccer complex, and this friends-and-family event, I'd been swamped. No time for anything except work and how fucked up everything else was in my life. I'd been worried about Annie heading off to Seattle and what I'd do now that my mom was sick again. I'd rushed into the decision to move with her, and now consequences were coming up. But I hadn't thought that Annie would find solace in someone else while I was figuring it all out.

Not until I'd seen Chase walk in that door and beeline straight for Annie. Not until Ashleigh had said that Chase had broken up with his girlfriend and he'd run right back to Annie. Then I hadn't been able to see think about anything clearly. I needed to talk to Annie after all this was over, but I couldn't stop myself from figuring out what the fuck had really happened. Ashleigh couldn't be right, could she?

So, I asked the question I didn't want the answer to, "Did you two hook up?"

Annie's eyes rounded wider. "What?" she gasped. "No! Why would you even think that?"

"So, you didn't go over to his house this week after he broke up with his girlfriend?"

She sputtered, "I did. But..."

"But what?" I snapped.

Chase chortled. "Oh, this is great."

"Shut the fuck up," I snarled at the same time as Annie did.

"Nothing happened," Annie told me. "I went over to have pizza with a friend. I didn't even *know* that he'd broken up with his girlfriend, and when I found out, I told him to go fuck himself and left."

"Which is why you never mentioned it."

She jolted back at the words. "Pray tell, when would I have told you?" she asked, anger seeping into her own words. "We haven't spoken in a week, Jordan. You've been avoiding me."

"I haven't been avoiding you. I've been busy," I reminded her. "Two businesses to run, remember? This has been hell week. And while I've been trying to deal with my own shit, you were going behind my back?"

"No! God, you are blowing this out of proportion. I didn't tell you because I never saw you, and then I fucking handled it. So, I didn't want to bother you with everything else going on and...your mom."

"Do not bring her into this," I said.

She held her hands up. Her eyes filling with her own brand of fury...laced in pain. "I'm not. I just...you've been acting all over the map since you found out."

"Don't," I snarled.

Annie winced, taking a step back. "Fine. Either you believe me or you don't. You haven't been around. I was the one who tried to talk to you earlier and you all but ran away, Jordan. These are the facts: I told Chase to go fuck himself. I told him that I didn't want what he was offering."

"How exactly did you get into a position where he could offer?"

She straightened then, as if my words had hit home. "Don't you *dare* try to victim-blame me. Chase is my best friend. I went to his house because he's a friend. It is *not* my fault that he blindsided me with this shit. And you need to fucking stop and think about how your words are hurting people that you care about."

"How do I know any of that is true?"

"Because you trust me!"

Chase chuckled behind us. "Jesus Christ, Annie, you're really dating this guy? What a douche!"

I stood there, chest heaving, wanting nothing more than to take out my fury on him. The cool, calm that I'd cultivated for the last three years dissolved. I'd spent hours in the gym or running to try to keep that side of me down, down, down. Buried so deep that none of my new friends and family would ever have to meet him. I'd gotten a punching bag to release energy. I'd started weight lifting, so I was too tired to feel the fury. I'd run and run and run until the anger was silenced. It had always felt like a dragon curling around my center, and if I didn't feed it, it would take over. My father was the same way. He'd taken it out on us. He'd taken it out on Mom. He'd taken it out on anyone unsuspecting of his writhing anger.

And I didn't want to be my dad, but fuck...it was all a goddamn mess. I was a mess.

My mom. Work. The party. Annie. Chase.

It was too much. Too much at once. I couldn't think around the atomic bomb settling in my chest. The feeling of watching from the inside as my life went up in a mushroom cloud of shit.

Then, it detonated.

My fist connected with Chase's fist. Annie shouted when it happened and pushed her way between us.

"What did you do?" she yelled at me.

"What the fuck?" Chase gasped, clutching his nose. I'd probably broken it.

"Jordan!" Annie cried out.

I came back to myself then. The red film cleared from my eyes. The anger ebbing just marginally to make me realize what I'd actually done. Who I'd become: my father.

I took a step back.

I didn't want to be anything like Owen Wright.

I leashed the dragon inside myself that wanted to shatter Chase Sinclair. But he wasn't really the problem, was he? The problem was that my life was falling apart and there was no way to put it all back together. I was in free fall, completely out of control. And the decision I'd had to make out of that free fall was destroying me.

Julian and Hollin rushed to my side. Julian knowing me well enough to jerk me back from Chase and snap at me. "Calm the fuck down!"

But I was already past that. I wasn't going to do worse. Chase had gotten what he'd deserved.

"I'm cool," I said, brushing Julian off of me.

Annie had dug a tissue out of her purse and was applying pressure to the blood running out of Chase's broken now. She looked back at me as if she'd never seen me before. It was a real look. She'd never seen this side of me. I'd hoped she never would.

"Fuck," I spat. I took a step toward her as if I could fix this. Even though I knew that I was about to make it so much worse.

"Don't," she said.

The rest of her response was lost as blue and red flashing lights lit up the inside of the barn and the signature *whoop, whoop* sounded outside of the winery.

33

ANNIE

"*W*hat now?" I gasped.

Sutton shook her head. "I don't know."

Chase was going to be fine. This was the moment that I'd always wanted in my life. *I* was the doctor in the house to check on Chase. Of course, I'd never expected it to be because my boyfriend had just punched him. In fact, I hadn't expected much of any of that to happen. Not a damn thing.

So much for waiting for him to come to me with his grief. Instead, it had exploded out of him.

This wasn't Jordan. This wasn't him at all. This was the pain and grief and everything else all bottled up into one perfectly, spectacularly terrible moment. It didn't make it hurt any less.

I closed my eyes to shield my heart. To try to hold back all the pain threatening to tear me apart. Because I loved Jordan...and I been planning to tell him tonight after the party. To tell him about staying in Lubbock for him. But now...

Well, now, everything was fucked.

And the police were here.

"I'm going to go find out what's going on," I told Sutton.

Ashleigh had stumbled over. Her eyes red and tears running down her cheeks as she gasped out her brother's name.

"Chase is fine," I told her. "Just stay here with him. He has a broken nose and will probably have a wicked black eye."

"We're going to press charges against that animal!" she shrieked.

"Ashleigh, breathe. It was one punch, and Chase is fine," I repeated. "No need to press charges."

"After what he just did?"

Chase shushed his sister. "Shut up, Ash."

And then he closed his eyes again and pressed his fingers to his broken nose. He winced. Yeah, that was going to hurt for a few days.

I left Chase with his sister and headed outside with Sutton. Campbell was still playing in the background as we stepped out into the cool night beyond and to the police officers standing around. Jordan, Julian, and Hollin were already dealing with them.

One of the officers spoke up as I approached. "You don't have to go home," he said with a thick country drawl. Then he tipped his head down and shot them a condescending look. "But you can't stay here."

"Sir," Jordan said, his voice stretched thin, "we have a

permit for the event tonight."

"You're overcapacity. I'm going to have to ask you to shut it all down," the man said, sticking his thumbs into his belt.

"Sir," Jordan tried again.

"Son, we can do this the easy way," he said dramatically, "or we can do it the hard way. Your choice."

Jordan clenched his jaw, and Julian stepped in. "We understand, sir. So sorry that you had to drive all the way out here for this. We'll take care of it."

"Good boy," the cop said.

I thought Jordan might assault a police officer with how tightly he was hanging by a thread. He must have thought better of it because he took a step back. Let Julian, with all of his charm and charisma, handle the police.

Hollin grumbled under his breath and tromped back to the entrance, ostensibly to send everyone home. He caught Nora at the entrance, and her eyes went wide. I lost what she said as they both scrambled through the door. A few minutes later, Campbell ceased playing, and a chorus of boos came from the crowd. Then a flood of disgruntled concertgoers came through the open barn doors.

The cops stood sentinel as the crowd filed through the parking lot and began the slow process of clearing the place out.

Julian was still working his magic with Jensen and Morgan both coming over to help smooth things over. The cops seemed to straighten up at the sight of them. Nothing like the power of the Wrights in this town.

Jordan finally turned to find me still huddled with Sutton off to the side.

Sutton saw him walk toward me, squeezed my arm, and made herself scarce. "Find me when you're done."

I nodded at her and met Jordan head-on. "Hey."

He ran a hand back through his hair. Only realizing afterward that his knuckles were broken and bloody. "You should go home."

My heart constricted, and I forced myself not to cry again. "After all that...that's all you're going to say to me?" I shook my head. "God, Jordan, nothing happened with Chase."

"I believe you."

"Then what...?"

"Annie, just go home."

"I don't get you. You don't talk to me for a week. You hole up and avoid me. Then when you claim we're finally going to talk, you assault my friend, and tell me to go home without an explanation?" I demanded. "This isn't you."

"This is exactly who I am."

"I know you, Jordan. Whether or not you want to believe it, I do. I know exactly who you are. And right now, you're hurting and taking it out on everything and everyone around you."

He gritted his teeth as if to keep himself from exploding all over again. "Go. Home."

I sniffled and shook my head. "Fine," I snapped. "I'll go to keep you from saying anything *else* you're going to regret."

"You think I regret a damn thing that happened in

there?" he demanded, pointing at the barn. "Chase had that coming to him."

"And me?" I shouted back at him. "Did I have that coming, too?"

Jordan looked away from me. "You said from the beginning that we were temporary."

I choked back a gasp. "And you don't think that's changed?" I asked, my voice strangled. "What about Seattle?"

"Seattle was a pipe dream!" he yelled.

I shrank back. "I thought it was real."

"Fuck, Annie. Day one, you said you were leaving, and I wanted to keep you, so I said I'd go. What else could I say?"

"You could have talked to me!" I insisted.

"And said what?" He laughed derisively. "You wanted Seattle. I wanted you. And now my mom has cancer. I can't leave Lubbock, Annie, and I can't keep you from following your dream."

"What if I just want you?"

Jordan shook his head. "No, that's not what you want. You'd regret it, and I'd never let you do it. If you want to get out of here, you'll go. We both knew from the start that you were leaving with or without me, and you still are."

Silence stretched between us.

Well, there it was.

I'd started this. I'd made us friends with benefits and told him to expect nothing more. Should I be surprised that he didn't see that I was in love with him? That I would have...*had* given up everything to stay here with him? This might have been grief talking, but it still hurt. It still hurt like he'd cut me open, looked at my insides, and somehow missed all the important parts.

"That's what you think of me?" I asked hoarsely.

"It's not what I think of you, Annie. It's just how it is. You and I were fun while it lasted, but you were the one who drew the line in the sand. You were the one who put a time limit on our affections. I'm just the one walking away so that you can follow your dreams."

I choked. He thought he was being *selfless*. He thought that by ghosting me and then breaking up with me, he was being *kind*. How dare he! How fucking dare he!

"You don't get to make that choice for me," I snarled as I wrestled the claddagh ring off of my finger. "You don't get to be an ass and think that you're doing the right thing in all of this. It isn't fair. I'm a whole person who can think and breathe and make my own goddamn choices."

I'd gotten attached to the ring, but I didn't want *his* version of *my* ring.

I flung the ring at him. It thudded softly against his chest. He furrowed his brows as if he didn't realize what I'd done, his hand landing on his chest where the ring had hit.

"And for your information, I already put in my rank choices for residency programs." I glared at him, trying to keep the tears at bay long enough to escape him before he could see me breaking. "I knew the minute that we found out about your mother's cancer diagnosis that you couldn't leave her, and I would never ask you. So I chose to stay in Lubbock and changed my rank choice to Tech."

Jordan's eyes rounded and he opened his mouth, a

small startled noise escaping him.

"You'd know that if you had talked to me at all in the last fucking week."

"Annie..."

"Save it," I snapped. "If this is what you think of me and...what you think of us..." I choked back on my tears and shook my head. I couldn't finish. "Good-bye Jordan."

Then, I turned on my heel and walked away.

Grief was an excuse for his behavior up to a point, but it wasn't enough to make up for how much he was hurting me. He could have talked to me. We could have worked through it together. Instead, he'd assumed that I'd leave him rather than staying here.

Part of that was on me. I *had* drawn the line in the sand and put a time limit on our love. But I'd thought that things were different since Seattle. I thought he knew what he meant to me. We'd just been on a different chapters of the same book. I'd seen the happily ever after waiting at the end of the tunnel and he'd only seen the inevitable destruction. Then he'd gone and destroyed it all himself.

"Annie," Sutton said, dashing to my side.

"How much did you hear?"

She bit her lip. "Everything." She took my hand. "I didn't think this would happen."

"Me either," I whispered.

"Annie...can you still change your rank?"

I shook my head furiously. There was no changing rank after the deadline. Everything was already set.

"I guess I'm stuck here...just like he said, with or without him."

34

JORDAN

I sat at a stool by the bar. An ice pack on my right hand, bourbon in my left, the bottle sitting in front of me, next to Annie's claddagh ring. The one I'd dug through the dirt to find after she threw it at me.

The winery was empty. All of the patrons had gone home. The party was over.

Jensen had been the representative of my cousins to come over and offer me help if I needed anything. I'd expected to see disappointment in his eyes. See that he finally saw me for who I really was, but it wasn't there. Just steady Jensen.

"We've all been there," he'd said as he shook my hand to go. "Trust me. I've pulled Austin out of much worse."

I still wasn't sure how I'd lucked out with them.

Then finally, even Nora had given up on cleaning and left for the night. She'd promised she'd be by in the morning, but I couldn't seem to care.

Hollin and Julian settled into the seats on either side

of me. Julian blew out a long breath. Hollin leaned his elbows against the bar and laced his fingers together in front of him.

"Well, that could have gone better," Hollin said.

Julian managed a choked laugh. "Understatement of the century."

I said nothing.

What was there to say? I was the reason things had gone horribly wrong, and I was supposed to be the sensible one.

But I hadn't been sensible about any of it. I'd thought that if I cut Annie out of my life for the last week, it would make it easier to break up with her tonight. It had seemed like the only sensible idea. I loved her. I wanted her to be mine. At the same time, I couldn't leave Lubbock. Not when my job was here and my mom had cancer again. I couldn't do that to her or Julian. Those two thoughts were incongruous.

Annie wanted to leave. I had to stay for my family. Thus, the only solution in my grieving, addled brain had been to let her go. Let her go live the life she had always wanted far away from here. It had hurt to think of a life without her, but I wouldn't be the reason she stayed.

Then she'd told me that she'd changed her rank choice to Lubbock anyway. She'd done it and I'd been too much of a fool to see that she wanted to stay here for me. Too much of a fool to see past my own grief.

What the fuck was wrong with me?

And how the fuck was I going to fix it? If I even could...

"I wonder who called the fucking police," Hollin

muttered.

"Don't know," Julian said with another sigh. "Cops said they got an anonymous tip. Could be anyone."

"What do you think, Jordan?" Hollin asked.

"I think I want to finish this bottle and forget tonight happened."

My mood was black.

Julian and Hollin exchanged a glance. Hollin reached for the drink in my hand the same second that Julian managed to snag the bottle.

"Well, that's enough of that," Julian said.

"What the fuck? Now you're taking the bourbon?"

Julian frowned. "I think you've had enough, and getting obliterated isn't going to change anything. Plus, I don't like to see you like this."

I knew why. It reminded him too much of Dad. This was the sort of thing Dad had done. Didn't matter how much I tried to run from his ghost, I was still his son. I still had his temper, his proclivity for alcohol, his general assholeness, and tonight, I hadn't been able to fool anyone.

Silence hung in the room. Hollin finished my drink in one giant gulp and then stepped around to the back of the bar to wash it up. He took the bottle from Julian and replaced it where it belonged. Then he poured me a water and tossed it across the bar to me.

"Drink up," he said, picking up a rag and wiping the bar down.

The tread of shoes against the hardwood floor made me lift my gaze from the goddamn water Hollin had given me. I'd been certain we were the only ones left. But there was Campbell. He'd stripped out of his leather jacket, revealing the jagged edges of his black T-shirt, and put on Chucks.

"Yo," he said with a tip of his head. "What a party. I expected to shut it down in LA but Lubbock?"

He chuckled and slid into Hollin's abandoned seat. He patted the bar twice. "Old-fashioned, my good man."

Hollin glared at his younger brother. "I'm not your bartender, asshole. Make your own."

Campbell chuckled and slid back out of the seat. He came around to the side with Hollin and made a perfect old-fashioned. Hollin looked at him as if he had grown a second head as he muddled the bitters and then added the orange rind to the glass.

"What?" Campbell asked, looking around at all of our surprised faces. "Cosmere had a solid couple years where no one gave a shit about us. I worked my fair share of odd jobs. Bartending being one of them. Anyone else?"

"We're good," Julian said.

"Your loss," Campbell said, taking his seat again and turning to face me. "Man, you *whaled* on that guy tonight. I could see it from the stage."

Hollin covered his face, and Julian went pale.

"Not the time, man," Hollin said. "Did you completely lose your filter in Hollywood?"

"Did I ever have a filter?" Campbell inquired.

"No," Hollin admitted.

"So, why did you punch him?"

"Because," I said, looking at this rockstar that I just realized I'd judged all wrong, "he was my girl's ex, and I thought they were hooking up."

"You thought?" Campbell asked. "But they weren't?"

I shrugged. "She said nothing happened. They've been friends forever, and I just lost it."

"Huh. He probably deserved it."

Julian and Hollin both nodded their agreement.

"He definitely did," I muttered.

I tapped the bar and stood up, passing the ice to Hollin and pocketing the ring.

"I think I'm going to call it a night," I told them. "Maybe when I wake up, this will all have just been some horrible nightmare."

"Are you good to drive?" Julian asked.

"You took the one drink I'd had all night."

"Just checking. Are you going to go home and drink?"

I tried not to glare at his concern. "No. I'm not Dad."

Julian winced. "I didn't say that."

He didn't have to. I could see it in his eyes. The scared little boy coming back out. I was supposed to be his protector. Not make him return to childhood trauma.

I managed a smile and clutched his shoulder. "I'll be fine. Just need to sleep it off."

"What happened with Annie?" Julian asked. He couldn't seem to hold it back.

I clenched my fists and then released them. "I screwed up. We're done."

"Fuck," Hollin said.

"You going to fix it?" Campbell inquired.

"I don't know if I can," I admitted and then walked out of the building.

I found my Tesla in the mostly empty parking lot, wedged between Julian's SUV and Hollin's giant pickup truck. It felt good to be behind the wheel. To actually have control of something. Because everything else in my life was slipping through my fingers.

I'd thought that Annie would be the exception to my relationship woes. That I wouldn't completely fuck it up and watch everything crumble in front of my eyes.

Nope. I'd been wrong.

I'd been driving for a few minutes before I realized that I really didn't want to go home. Back to my huge, empty house with Annie's things in it. With the wet bar standing there temptingly. I didn't need to make bad things worse.

So, I took the next turn without preamble, and in another minute, I pulled into my mom's driveway. She'd come to the party early since she wanted to see it all in its glory, but she'd left before the music started. She hadn't been feeling well. Since the party had been broken up, it was early evening and she would likely still be awake.

I knocked on the door, unannounced, and a minute later, my mom pulled it open. She was already in her nightgown.

"Jordan?" she said in surprise. "Everything all right? I thought the party would be going for a few more hours."

"I thought so, too."

She frowned at my choice of words. "Well, come inside and tell me about it."

I entered her house, happy for once for the cozy '70s-era home. It felt lived in. It felt like my mom, and that was exactly what I needed.

"Do you want a drink? Coffee? Tea?"

"I'm okay."

"Well, I'm going to have some tea. I'll make you a mug."

I nodded, falling down onto her overstuffed couch. It even smelled like home. Like I could curl up here on her sofa with tea and soup and feel better. Except I wasn't sick and everything that hurt, I'd done to myself.

My mom returned with tea and passed one to me. "Now, what happened with the party?"

"Someone leaked that Campbell was going to be there, and we hit overcapacity. Then I guess the cops were called, and they sent everyone home."

"Oh dear," my mom said. "What part of that explains your broken knuckles?"

Never could get anything past her. "I might have gotten into an altercation with Annie's ex-boyfriend."

My mom sighed, setting her tea aside. "How many times do I have to tell you that settling things with your fists helps nothing?"

"At least one more time, apparently," I said with a grimace that bordered on a smile.

"And how is Annie?"

"I think...we might have broken up."

"You think?"

I set down the tea and put my head in my hands. "I screwed up. I thought I was doing the right thing. She wanted to go away for her residency, and I didn't want her to give up on her dream. So, I made a total ass of myself and ended it."

"Oh Jordan..."

"I'm just like Dad. I fuck up *everything*."

My mom sighed softly and then came to sit next to

me. She put an arm around my shoulders and patted my knee. "Look at me."

With concerted effort, I turned to look at my mom.

"You are not *just* like your dad. And even if you were, that isn't a bad thing."

I laughed derisively. "How can you say that?"

"Because I fell in love with him and I married him."

"He was horrible to you!"

"Later in life, we had our differences, but I still refuse to believe that Owen is every part the villain that he has always been painted. He wasn't loved as much as his older brother, who got the bulk of Wright Construction. He was pushed to Canada, ostensibly to get him out of the picture. He didn't *know* what love was, and so he made a lot of wrong choices. It doesn't excuse the mistakes he made, but it gives a clearer picture as to who he is."

"But...he's awful. I have his hot-blooded anger and his quick-fuse temper and the addictive personality. Everything that is wrong with me is *him*."

"Also, nearly everything that is *good* in you is him, too," she reminded me.

"No," I said. "Everything good, I got from you."

"Your business sense comes from your father. Your protective nature comes from your father. Your ability to love so openly and quickly comes from your father."

"That's different."

She laughed. "You can't make your dad who you want him to be. He's multidimensional. He has layers. There's more to him than you give him credit for. And more to *you* than you give yourself credit for. What happened tonight was a mistake. But we don't live our life by our mistakes and failures. We learn from them. Owen did, and you will, too."

"Do you still love him?" I breathed. A question I'd never asked my mom.

"With my whole heart." She stared down at her hands. "But it didn't work out that way in the end. And sometimes, that's how it happens."

"I love you, Mom," I said, pulling her into a hug.

She squeezed me tight. "I love you, too." When she released me, she had that glint in her eye that I knew all too well. "But you'd better figure out how to make this up to Annie because I really like her."

"She's never going to talk to me again."

"I bet she will."

"I wouldn't if I were in her shoes."

"You were wrong. You know you were wrong. You just have to admit that and make it up to her."

"How could I possibly make this up to her?"

"Might I suggest the trifecta: flowers, chocolate, and *a lot* of groveling."

I laughed because there was nothing else to do. "Do you think that will work?"

"I think that she loves you, and if you're sincere, she'll listen."

"She doesn't love me," I whispered.

"I wouldn't be so sure," my mom said. "The important thing right now is, how do you feel about her?"

"I love her," I said without hesitation.

"Then you know what you have to do."

And I did. I knew exactly what I needed to do.

35

ANNIE

I didn't hear the banging on the front door or the subsequent doorbell. I'd cried myself to sleep the night before, and I hadn't planned to surface the rest of the day. Jennifer had a photoshoot in the morning and evening. So, I'd expected to have the entire house to myself to wallow. Now that the floodgates had opened, there was nothing left to do.

Until a five-year-old jumped on me in bed and started giggling. "Aunt Annie!"

I peeked out from under the cover to find my niece, Aly. "Aly Cat, what are you doing here?"

"Daddy said that you were sad and we needed to bring you doughnuts."

I laughed. "That sounds like your dad."

"I want the chocolate ones!" Aly cried.

She hopped off my bed, and I could see that she was in a full ballet ensemble—tights, leotard, and tutu. Her own mop of red curls pulled up in a bun. This kid lived and breathed ballet.

"With sprinkles?" I asked her.

"Yes! Sprinkles are my favorite."

"All right. I guess I'll get up then."

Aly ran out the door. "Daddy, I got her up, and she wasn't even mad!"

I snorted as I tugged on black sweats and a red Tech sweatshirt. At least Isaac knew to bribe his kid to wake me up instead of doing it himself. I'd hit him too many times, growing up, for him to attempt it on his own.

"Doughnuts?" I asked cautiously as I stepped into the living room to find Isaac and Peyton standing there.

"Rise and Shine," he said, indicating our favorite doughnut shop.

"You know a way to a girl's heart." I hugged his fiancée. "Hey Peyton. I didn't know you were in from New York."

Peyton smiled as I scooped up one of the lone chocolate doughnuts covered with sprinkles left after Aly ate just the chocolate tops off of three others. Crazy kid.

"Last-minute plans," Peyton said. "It's good to see you."

"Aunt Annie," Aly said. She was skipping and doing dance leaps around my living room. She had more energy in one pinkie than I'd had any other morning of my life. "Daddy said that if you got your shoes on, we could walk to the playground."

I arched an eyebrow at Isaac. "Bribery?"

"It works."

Peyton chuckled.

"Let me finish my doughnut," I told Aly.

"Okay. Are you finished now?"

I took another bite and shook my head.

"What about now? I like going down the slides."

"I know you do," I told her with a laugh. Nothing like Aly to raise my terrible, terrible mood.

"You're finished!" she cheered as I ate the last of the doughnut. "Now, can we go?"

"Patience, Aly."

She screwed up her face at her dad like she'd heard that word one too many times and knew it didn't apply to her.

I went back in search of socks and tugged on tennis shoes and a beanie. "All right. Now, we can go *if* we can stop at J&B on the way for coffee."

"Done," Isaac said.

It was brisk for early March. That last haunting cold that clung to Lubbock for dear life. With our luck, it'd still snow one more time before spring officially broke through.

I got Peyton and me both large black coffees. I held the cup tight to warm up my hands as we walked to the next block, where there was a park and playground. Aly ran the rest of the way to the playground and immediately befriended another girl who was there with her mom. The mom tipped her head at us.

"I'm going to watch Aly," Peyton said pointedly. "Give y'all time to talk."

Peyton disappeared, her lean dancer legs cutting quick across the space to stand next to the other mom.

"Oh great," I murmured into my coffee. "Big-brother talk."

"So..." Isaac said.

"How much did you hear?"

Because there was only one reason he was here this morning. If Peyton was in town, I expected to see him long enough to watch Aly before they disappeared to do grown-up things. Long-distance was hard. Another reason I hadn't wanted to do it.

"It can't possibly be as bad as I heard," Isaac said.

"Oh, it's probably worse."

"I was told that Jordan punched Chase, you and Jordan got into a huge argument, the police were called, and then you had a very public breakup."

I took a fortifying sip of my blistering hot coffee. "Actually, that's pretty much right."

"Jesus, Annie."

"Tell me about it."

"Jordan's my boss, or I'd definitely beat him up for you."

I laughed softly. "You'd lose. I saw how he hit Chase. You'd *definitely* lose."

"So, what are you going to do?"

"I really don't know," I whispered into my coffee. "I was hoping to not have to think about it."

"That usually solves everything."

I snorted. "It's just...it's complicated. I'm mad at him. Furious, honestly. He was out of control, and he said some horrible things that I'm ninety-five percent sure he's going to deeply regret, but it doesn't change that he said them."

"No, it doesn't."

"But also...his mom's cancer is back."

"Oh God, Annie, I had no idea."

"No, she hasn't told anyone else, and he's hurting. It's not an excuse, but he was on the end of his rope before it all went down."

"Well, I guess you have to decide if you want to make it work or start over in Seattle."

I crumpled in on myself at those words.

"What?" he asked.

"I...I changed my rank choice to Tech, so I could stay in town after I found out about his mom."

"And he was *still* an asshole?" he asked with wide eyes.

"Well, I hadn't told him."

"Annie..."

"It was supposed to be a surprise. A happy surprise. Then he blew up on me, thinking I was going to choose Seattle over him and...fuck. I kind of spilled the beans in the heat of the moment, and now, we're both just mad and sad and everything is terrible."

"Are you going to talk him?"

"Well, I really don't want to."

"I think you should talk to him."

I sighed. "It's too fresh. I can't imagine we'd do anything but yell at each other again."

"Maybe, but eventually, you will have to discuss this." I nodded at him. Then his eyes tracked his daughter. "Aly!" he yelled. "Don't climb up the slide, honey."

Peyton waved him away and directed Aly to climb up the stairs instead.

Isaac turned his attention back to me. "Look, I went through the worst shit possible. I lost Abby." Aly's mom had died in childbirth. "I never thought I'd find love again. Then Peyton came back into my life. So, even if it doesn't work out with Jordan after you two talk, there's someone out there for you. Whatever you decide, it's going to be okay."

I smiled wanly at my brother. "Thanks, Isaac."

I wasn't sure I believed him, but I appreciated him being here. Right now, I didn't know what I wanted besides being left alone. Everything felt too bright, too close, too much. And I didn't want to have to make a decision about Jordan while I still felt like I'd been run over.

And I didn't *have* to make that decision yet.

After Isaac, Peyton, and Aly left, Jennifer came back. She forced me to pet Avocado and Bacon, claiming that pets help with oxytocin. Then we vegged, watched *Schitt's Creek*, and ate pizza until she had to leave again for a senior shoot. I moved on to ice cream straight from the container and was happily into season two, rewatching David and Moira attempt to fold in the cheese, when I heard another knock at the front door.

I tilted my head up and groaned, "What now?" Then I called out loudly, "Come in!"

And in walked Ashleigh Sinclair.

I nearly groaned again. "What are you doing here?"

"I came to check on you," Ashleigh said.

She was in a sparkly pink sequined dress that came to her knees with matte black heels. Her gorgeous blonde hair was expertly coiffed and her makeup flawless. She didn't go anywhere without her hair and makeup done, but this was a lot, even for her.

"Why did you really come?"

Ashleigh sighed. "Can't I just check on you?"

"In that?"

"Fine. I did want to check on you, but I also want you to come to Chase's welcome-home party."

"No," I said and turned back to the TV.

"Annie, come on. It's important."

"Nope. Not going. Sorry, Ashleigh, but Chase and I are not on speaking terms. He crossed a line."

"Is this about him inviting you over to his place when he broke up with Kennedy?"

"He told you about that?" I asked in surprise.

"Yes, well, he was freaking out. He was worried that he'd ruined your almost three decade friendship over a mistake. He loves you, and he would never risk losing you, Annie."

"That's the problem. He wants more than I can offer."

Ashleigh sauntered farther into my house, grabbed the remote, and turned off the TV. "He's sorry. I know that he came to the party last night to apologize." She arched an eyebrow. "And look where that got him—a black eye."

"What do you want me to say? That I just forgive him for expecting me to roll over when he was ready. I don't owe him anything."

Ashleigh crossed her arms. "I'm not saying you owe him. I'm saying that you're friends. You don't just suddenly stop being his best friend."

"You do when the other person crosses the line."

She huffed. "You've both had feelings for each other

for years. *Years*, Annie. If you hadn't been with Jordan would you have been as mad as you are?"

I frowned. No. Of course, I wouldn't have. I'd always thought Chase was endgame. Then I'd blown up on him when he'd confessed feelings that I'd always wanted from him.

"Exactly," she snapped.

"Look, if he couldn't even come here on his own and had to send someone else to convince me to come, then maybe he isn't really sorry," I said with a shrug.

"Chase has *no* idea that I'm here," she told me. "He doesn't think that you'll forgive him, but I know that you can't stay mad at him forever. You've known each other too long. Please, Annie." Her blue eyes were wide and sincere. "Please."

I lolled my head back. "I really don't want to go."

"Friends don't let each other down."

I sighed heavily, feeling myself giving in. If Ashleigh was lying, I was going to kill. "I'm going as *just* friends."

Ashleigh jumped up and down, clapping her hands. "Excellent. Get up and get dressed. I'll do something with your hair."

"Am I going to regret this?"

"No! It's going to be so much fun."

Oh, I was definitely going to regret this.

36

ANNIE

he party was already in full swing when Ashleigh and I finally showed. It had taken longer to get my hair into the lush waves that Ashleigh wanted, and then I'd let her go to town with my makeup, too. The forest-green slip dress I'd chosen was something I'd worn for a med school banquet. I'd paired it with my new pair of black heels and left the house after Ashleigh applauded my clothing choice.

Now, we were here in the mansion of a house I'd practically grown up in, and I felt entirely out of place. I'd spent more time here than at my own house, but those days were long gone.

"I'm going to go save Julian," Ashleigh said, squeezing my arm. "Have fun!"

I watched her go with trepidation. I'd forgotten that Julian would be here. I sure hoped this didn't get back to his brother. The last thing I needed was for Jordan to think that Chase and I were getting together. Fuck.

I headed toward the kitchen to track down a drink and nearly ran smack dab into Chase. He caught my arm.

"Annie?" he all but gasped.

I could tell that someone, ostensibly Ashleigh, had applied makeup to his battered face to try to make him more presentable. And she must have had high-end cosmetics because it'd mostly worked. It looked more like he hadn't slept in a few days than that he had a black eye. His nose had been reset cleanly, and only a small cut was still visible.

"Hey, Chase."

"What are you doing here? I didn't think that you'd…" He trailed off, gesturing around him.

"Ashleigh," I said by way of explanation.

He shook his head. "My sister. She can do anything she puts her mind to."

"Yep."

"I'm really glad that you came, but you didn't have to. I know that I shouldn't have dumped all of that on you when you came to my house the other. I'm sorry. I really am."

"I know," I admitted with a sigh. "You were an ass."

"Yeah, I was."

"Let's just not be that stupid again, okay?"

"That sounds like a deal."

"We've been friends since we were babies. As long as we're on the same page, I don't think that we should stop now."

"But just friends?" he asked softly.

I nodded. "Just friends."

"All right." He looked disappointed, but he let it go.

"Well, let's get you a drink. I'm so glad you're here. My parents are going to freak."

Chase snagged a glass of champagne and passed it to me. Then I followed him into the living room. His mom, Charlotte, put a hand to her chest when she saw me.

"Annie, darling!" she gushed, pulling me into a hug. "You look stunning. We're so glad that you're here."

"It's good to see you."

"Oh, Annie," Arnold Sinclair said when he saw me. "What a treat!"

I grinned up at him. "Glad to be here."

"These two used to run around this house for hours when they were young," Arnold said to the couple in front of him.

"How cute," the woman said.

"Annie, this is Bart and Angelica Lawson. They own a very successful law firm here in town and have offered guidance to Chase for his new venture."

"Nice to meet you," I told them. Though their name rang a bell. "Are you Katelyn's parents?"

"Why, yes!" Angelica cried. "She's our little ballerina. She's running around here somewhere."

"Right." I remembered then that Peyton had had an issue with all of them this Christmas season. That they seemed like perfectly nice people, but were actually entitled assholes. Not that I intended to bring any of that up. "I'm going to grab a bite. Lovely party. Excuse me.."

I hastily brushed past them, feeling overwhelmed by the pleasantries. I'd been enjoying a perfectly wonderful night of ice cream and television. Now, I was here, making small talk. Kill me.

When I made it to the buffet table set up along a long, open wall in the living room, I picked up a ripe strawberry and nibbled on it as I decided on my next move. I'd made up with Chase, and then promptly left him behind with his parents. I could feel his eyes on me, but I turned my back instead. This was such a bad idea.

"Fancy meeting you here."

I jumped at the sound of Julian's voice and turned to meet him. "Hey."

He was dressed up in a fitted navy blue suit with a white button-up and pink tie. They all fit him, as if they'd been hand-tailored to his specifications. He did seem to love fashion way more than his brother.

"I didn't expect for you to show."

"I didn't anticipate coming."

Julian reached for a cucumber-and-cream-cheese sandwich. "Are you...here with Chase?"

"No!" I blurted hastily. Then I took a breath. "No, I'm not here with Chase. Ashleigh actually made me come because we've been friends so long. So, I'm just here as a friend."

"I see."

I reached out and grasped his suit sleeve. "Please, don't tell your brother I was here, especially not here with Chase."

His gaze softened. "I'm not going to tell him. I really don't want to think about how Jordan would react to you being here with Chase after last night."

"Me either," I said with a shudder.

"Are you going to talk to him?"

I arched an eyebrow. "Should I?"

He blew out a breath. "I wouldn't blame you if you didn't."

"But..."

"But he was a better person when he was with you, happier. I don't know...maybe that doesn't mean anything to you after what he did and said, but he really cares for you. I've never seen him like this before."

"It doesn't excuse what he said."

"No, it doesn't," Julian agreed. "But he *is* going through a lot right now. He might look like the strong one, Annie. He puts on the *big-brother protector* bit really well, but the only reason it comes out is because he needed someone to protect him, too, and there was no one there to do it. And now, he doesn't know how to ask for that help."

I swallowed hard at his words. We didn't talk about his dad much, but there was enough emotional trauma there for him to have put up these boundaries. And then to not know how to navigate those problems on his own without violence. I'd seen it happen myself last night.

"Yeah. Maybe," I whispered.

He grinned that charismatic Julian smile. "Either way, I'm glad you're not here with Chase. That would be awkward."

I laughed. "It would be, wouldn't it?"

Ashleigh appeared then. "Come on, baby. They're about to make the toast."

My eyes finally found Chase's in the crowd. He beckoned me over. I smiled at Julian and then headed to Chase's side. It was strange to be there as he draped a casual arm around my shoulders. This was the life that

I'd always thought I would be living. And now, it was a specter of reality.

Chase's father said a few words that I barely heard. I raised my fresh glass of champagne into the air and celebrated my closest friend coming home.

As soon as it was over, I slipped out of his grip and found the stairs to take me away from this. Coming here had been a mistake. I couldn't breathe. I was still too fucked up from yesterday, and trying to pretend with people I knew, let alone strangers, was just too much.

No one was on the second floor, which housed an extra guest bedroom, Arnold's at-home office, and Charlotte's workout room. It was the office that I meandered to because it had the best view of the pool.

Of course, Arnold always kept it locked, but Chase and I had played up here too many times, growing up, for me not to know how to jiggle the lock to get it open. It was an old thing, and he probably should have had it replaced a long time ago.

I hit the lock just right, and, *voilà*, an empty space for me to wallow.

I stepped into the darkened interior, carefully closing the door behind me. Even in the dark, I could see the bookshelf-lined walls, stacked full with legal and real estate material. There was a shelf or two for classics and the like that Chase and I had scoured once upon a time. The legal stuff had been too boring. Arnold's enormous oak desk took up the majority of the back of the room with his massive chair. I'd sat in it a few times and always felt like I was being swallowed.

With a sip of my champagne, I passed the brooding

desk and pushed open the glass balcony doors. The cold hit me like a two-by-four. I shivered against the unwelcome onslaught and immediately yanked the doors closed. So much for that idea.

I could see partygoers poolside through the glass. A few looked up at the sound of the door opening and closing, but I was far enough back that I didn't think that anyone could see me.

A teenage couple kissed on a chaise. Probably the wayward Katelyn. What else was there to do at a grown-ups' party?

My idea was ruined by the cold. So, I stepped away from the balcony and its voyeur appeal and back to the desk. I tugged out the mammoth chair and sank into the plush leather. I didn't feel any bigger or more of an adult in the thing. Perhaps it only worked on big, strong men.

I rolled my eyes and set my champagne down on a stack of papers. His desk was shockingly messy. For someone who did so much business, I'd never understood how he was so unorganized. But maybe there was a method to the madness.

I flicked on a small desk light, just enough glow to see by, but not enough to alert anyone to my presence. I kicked my feet up onto the desk, leaning back in the big chair and tilting my head back. This night wasn't what I'd thought it would be. I was glad that Chase and I were back on even footing. He still wanted more from me than I could give him, but he valued our friendship enough not to push. I hoped.

With a melancholy sigh, I reached back out for my champagne.

"Fuck," I gasped as the nearly empty glass toppled over, spilling its contents.

I jumped to my feet and floundered around for something to clean the mess with, but there was nothing. No towels or anything but my silk dress. And I just wasn't ruining that for Arnold Sinclair's paperwork.

I lifted the first few pages away from the wet and tried to flutter them back and forth so that they'd dry out. It really wasn't *that* much alcohol, but enough for my presence to be known.

I arranged the wet paperwork out on the floor, hoping it would all dry out in the meantime. Which was when I actually *looked* at what was in front of me.

"What the hell?"

I dropped to my knees before the row of pages I'd splayed out on the floor to dry. The first was a map. A map I recognized because I'd seen it on Jordan's dining room table while he worked. It was the map of Wright Vineyard.

The next was permit paperwork. I remembered Jordan complaining about it weeks ago. Somehow, it had expired, and a new one had had to be filed. Now, it was here...in Arnold Sinclair's study.

Another page showed signed paperwork for an offer to buy a property. I squinted at the address, which had been mostly obscured by the champagne spill, but I had a pretty good idea where it belonged. The Sinclairs had made the counteroffer on the winery.

I rocked backward at the revelation. The mystery of the ghost of the winery was solved. The Sinclairs were the saboteurs.

37

ANNIE

Ten minutes later, the door creaked open to the office.

I jolted at the sudden interruption.

"I knew I'd find you in here," Chase said.

He stopped with the door half-closed when he saw me on the ground, surrounded by paperwork.

"Uh, what are you doing?"

I jumped to my feet. "Did you know?"

"Know what?" he asked.

"Was it you?"

"Annie, I have no idea what you're talking about." He stepped deeper into the room. "What's all this paperwork? Were you going through my dad's things?"

"I spilled champagne on them on accident. I was airing them out."

A half-truth. It had been the original purpose of putting them on the floor. The real reason was so that I could take photographs of all the evidence with my phone.

301

"Was that why you were on the floor?"

"Chase, tell me if you knew."

"Perhaps you should elaborate."

I shook my head. I'd gotten all the information I needed, and if Chase was involved, then I needed to get out of there. Being stuck upstairs with him was not high on my priority list.

"I'm going," I said, pushing past him toward the door.

He grabbed my shoulder. His eyes full of alarm. "What's the rush? What's going on? Just talk to me, Annie."

"You sabotaged the winery," I snapped at him.

Confusion remained on his face. "I'm sorry, what?"

"The winery!" I said, my anger getting the better of me. "You and your family tried to ruin the new winery venture by the Wrights."

"I don't even know what you're talking about. Someone tried to sabotage the winery?"

"Just go look at the paperwork," I said, throwing my hand toward the papers on the floor.

"Okay," he said uncertainly. "Don't leave yet."

He stepped over to the paperwork and read through everything that I'd found. His confusion turned to dismay. Then he shook his head and looked back up at me. "I had nothing to do with any of this. I had no idea, Annie. I was in Houston for most of when this went down, judging by the dates."

Which made sense, of course, but I couldn't shake the feeling that he'd been playing me all along.

"And you just happened to come home in the middle of this?" I demanded.

He shrugged. "I guess. I don't do any work with my father's real estate ventures. It's Ashleigh who handles this kind of thing for him."

I froze there in the doorway to the office as the words hit me.

Ashleigh.

"Say that again."

He picked up a paper off of the ground and brought it over to me. "Ashleigh handles this kind of thing. My dad doesn't involve himself with small, technical work."

"But it's all signed by him."

"No," he said, handing me the paperwork. "See."

I stared down at the paper. The signature there that said *Arnold Sinclair*. "I don't see."

"That's her forge. She got really good at it in high school. I could recognize it anywhere."

I stumbled back a step at the news. "Forged."

Now, *that* was damning.

The rest of it had been legal. Despite how frustrating it had been—the second offer, the permit, the health inspection—all of that had been perfectly legal. But if Arnold Sinclair hadn't actually been doing *any* of this... and Ashleigh had been forging his name ... well, that was criminal.

"Why...why would she do this?" I asked him. My shock registered on my face.

He shrugged helplessly. "I don't know. Why does my sister do anything?"

That I definitely didn't have an answer to.

But *Ashleigh* of all people?

She was dating Julian. They'd been together for two years. She had to want him to succeed. It was illogical.

Fuck. Julian!

I dashed out of the office without a word to Chase. He called my name as I sprinted down the stairs at a pace that would have normally been terrifying in four-inch heels, but adrenaline propelled me forward. My eyes darted around the living room, but there was no sign of Julian.

I texted him.

Where are you?

Out by the pool. Why?

Don't move.

I braced against the cold as I darted toward the back exit. Chase caught up with me as I raced outside.

"Annie, what are you doing?" he asked.

"Righting a wrong."

"You're going to freeze."

He stripped out of his jacket and offered it to me. I deliberated and then decided to take it. It was too cold not to.

"Fine," I said, pulling it around my shoulders.

I found Julian standing with Ashleigh next to an outdoor heater. With a deep breath, I sent him the pictures I'd taken and then approached. He was peering down at his phone when I stopped in front of him.

His brow was furrowed as he read.

"Annie!" Ashleigh gushed. "Where have you and Chase been?"

She asked it in that cutesy voice of hers. And of course, it probably did look bad that we'd disappeared at his party, and I showed back up in his jacket, but I was so beyond caring.

"Why did you do it?" I asked her. I still clutched her forged signature in my hand.

"Do what?" she asked, batting her eyelashes.

"What is this that you sent me, Annie?" Julian said. He glanced up at me. His eyes were wide. He knew exactly what I'd sent him.

"I stumbled across that in the Sinclair's study."

Julian's face paled. "Really?"

"What is it, baby?" Ashleigh asked.

She leaned against him to try to see his phone, but he turned it away from her.

Oh yeah, he knew now.

"Why did you do it?" I repeated to Ashleigh.

"I still don't understand."

"Wait...how is Ashleigh involved?" Julian asked.

"Ashleigh handles her father's affairs, don't you?" I held up the piece of paper. "And that's the signature you forged, isn't it?"

Ashleigh blustered, "Annie, I have *no* idea what you're talking about."

But she didn't say it the way that Chase had with any sincerity. She said it like she'd been caught and was trying to figure out a way to get out of this.

Julian blinked. "*You* tried to sabotage the winery?"

"No!" Ashleigh cried.

"All those times that I complained to you about how hard it was to get anything done at the winery. When I told you that I wanted to know who was doing this to us. I even suggested it was a ghost, and you latched on to that so quickly," he said, as if putting all the pieces together. "You wanted it to be a ghost. That way, it wasn't you all along."

Ashleigh looked like a cornered dog. I didn't know if she was going to roll over or bite.

"It was *Daddy*!" she said, tears bursting from her eyes, as if on cue. "That's his signature. He wanted to do it."

Chase jumped in. "Ashleigh, we both know that's not Dad's signature."

"Why would you do this?" Julian asked. He looked half like he wanted to comfort her and half-horrified.

"I didn't. I swear!" she gushed.

Julian shook his head. "Tell me the truth."

He looked ready to shake her.

She wiped her eyes. Thank God for waterproof mascara. A hiccup and then, "I...I just wanted you to work for Daddy."

Julian's face was a mask of shock. "You...what?"

"You didn't want to work for Wright," she told him, reaching out for his hand. "You told me that so many times. You weren't valued there. You weren't your brother. I wanted you to have the winery when it was your idea! Then you brought your brother on, and suddenly, it wasn't even *your* winery anymore. It was his. You were pushed to the side. I wanted you to have your own thing. Where you weren't connected to your brother."

"Where I was connected to *you*," he said hollowly. "Beholden to you."

"No, never!" she cried, reaching for him again.

He stepped back. "No, I think I understand perfectly, Ashleigh."

Real tears fell this time when she suddenly saw what was happening. "Please, Julian. Please, I love you."

"You took the venture I loved and cared about, the venture I *invited* my brother to be a part of, and then you tried to destroy it."

"That's not what happened!"

But it was.

"And you did it for selfish reasons. Because you're selfish." Julian shook his head and took another step back. "We're done."

"No," Ashleigh gasped, falling to her knees before him and clutching him. "Julian, no, please. Please don't say that. I love you. I only had your own interests at heart."

It was painful to watch. Because she had deluded herself enough to believe the words coming out of her mouth.

Julian tugged back, releasing her grip on him. "I think you believe that, but it's not true."

Then he turned his back on her and walked out of the party. Chase knelt down next to his sister, but I didn't have an ounce of pity for her. Not after the lengths she'd gone to try to hurt people I cared about.

I followed Julian out of the party and touched his arm. "Hey. Are you going to be okay?"

He looked up at the stars and shrugged. "I don't know. Two years. Two years with her and then..." He splayed out his hands.

"I'm sorry. I didn't want to lay this in your lap, but..."

"No, I'm glad you did. I need to tell Jordan and Hollin."

I nodded. "I understand. That's a good idea."

"How are you getting home?" he asked.

"Uh..."

"I'll drive you," he said, pointing out his SUV down the block.

"I can catch an Uber. It's fine."

"Just get in, Annie. Jordan would kill me if you didn't get home safe."

"Are you...are you going to tell him I was here?" I asked as we walked over to his car.

Julian blew out a breath. "You don't want him to know that you figured this out?"

"I just...I'm not ready to deal with him."

Julian nodded, the weight of his latest breakup heavy on him. "I understand that. I can't imagine talking to Ashleigh anytime soon." He opened the passenger door for me. "Guess we'll both have to deal."

And wasn't that the damn truth?

38

JORDAN

"Jordan!" a voice called from the front door.

I pushed away from my desk in my office and strode into the living room, surprised to find my brother had let himself in. "Hey, what's going on?"

"Why didn't you answer your goddamn phone?"

I touched my pockets, realizing I didn't have the thing on me. I didn't even know where it was. I'd been distracting myself with work. It was easier than trying to learn to relax.

"I don't have it on me. What's wrong?"

"Well, I already talked to Hollin, but we have a problem."

I sighed and headed into the kitchen. I pulled out two beers and dropped one on the counter for him. "Not sure I can have any more problems."

Julian didn't complain. He took the beer and chugged the entire thing. I narrowed my eyes at my brother. He liked to drink, but I'd never seen him chug before.

He dropped the empty beer down. "Can I have another?"

Now, I was concerned. I grabbed another one for him. "Fuck."

"Yeah."

He took another fortifying drink and then sank into a seat at the island. "Ashleigh and I broke up."

This didn't seem like a problem to me, but Julian had dated her for two years. It had to hurt.

"What happened? I thought you were happy."

Julian pushed his phone across the table to me. I picked it up and saw it was open to an image folder. I clicked on the first one, which was a map of our winery. Pretty normal. I flipped to the next picture—the permit. The next—the offer. And then I saw what he'd clearly meant for me to see. Arnold Sinclair's signature on these pages.

Something went cold inside me. "What the fuck is all this, Julian?"

"Exactly what it looks like. The place is haunted by the Sinclairs."

"Why would Arnold Sinclair give a fuck about our winery?"

"Oh, he doesn't. Those are forged signatures." Julian took another long drink. "Ashleigh forged the signatures."

I was silent. My mind whirring through all the possibilities of why his girlfriend would want to ruin the winery. But I came up with nothing.

"Is she out of her mind?" I asked.

"She wanted me to work for her family. She thought

you were keeping me down or some other bullshit excuse that she'd invented. She wanted me to be beholden to her, and so she did this shit."

"Fuck, fuck, fuck," I ground out. "Man, this is..."

"Terrible," Julian agreed.

"Manipulative and conniving."

"Yep."

"How'd you find all of this out?" I asked, passing his phone back.

Julian opened his mouth and then closed it. He looked away, as if he didn't want to answer that or he didn't have a good enough answer.

"Julian?"

"Fuck, I'm not supposed to tell you."

"What? Why?"

Julian sighed as if he knew it'd come to this. "Annie found them. Though I wasn't supposed to say that."

"Annie?" I asked slowly, drawing her name out in disbelief. "Wait, was she at the Sinclair party tonight?"

He nodded. "Not with Chase," he added hastily.

"Uh-huh."

"Ashleigh brought her."

"So she'd end up with Chase."

"Just shut up," Julian growled. "That's not what happened, and if you'd get your head out of your ass, you'd realize that she just saved our fucking asses here. Now, we can go after the Sinclairs and get them to stop this shit. Because I'm ninety percent sure that she leaked the show with Campbell and called the police."

It wasn't often that Julian raised his voice. Let alone to me. But I could see that he was sincere. What mattered

K.A. LINDE

was the winery situation. I could process what Annie had been doing there later. Julian needed me, much like I'd needed him the night before.

"You're right," I said evenly. "She probably did both of those things." I paused as something else came to me.

"What?" Julian asked.

"Ashleigh was the one who told me that Annie had gone over to Chase's. She told me at the party. That's right before we fought."

Julian sighed heavily. "Fuck."

"She really is sabotaging everything."

"Yeah," he said hollowly.

"I'll get in contact with our attorney tomorrow. Have a cease-and-desist sent to the Sinclairs and threaten them with a lawsuit for falsified paperwork."

Julian deflated at the words. As if he'd been waiting for the moment where I would take control and he wouldn't have to worry about it anymore.

He dropped his head onto the counter. "What the fuck is wrong with me? How could I date someone for two years that does this shit?"

"This has nothing to do with you."

"You never liked her," Julian said.

"That doesn't matter."

"Everyone hated her."

"You didn't," I reminded him. "Why...did you like her?"

He shrugged, looking back up at me. I wanted to build a wall around my little brother and make it so no one could ever hurt him again. But there was nothing I could do about this, and I just had to watch him suffer. At least I would get to use my attorney against the scheming bitch.

"She was different with me," Julian said, as if that were an explanation. "Just realizing that wasn't enough."

"I'm sorry, man. This weekend sucks."

"Understatement." He finished off the second beer. "What are you going to do about Annie?"

"She didn't even want you to tell me she went to the party. Do you think I have much of a chance?"

"I think she's hurting, but yes, unlike me and Ashleigh, you have a chance."

"Then I'm going to win her back."

Julian's smile brightened the room. "Damn right you are."

*J*ordan didn't contact me over the weekend. A part of me was happy to have the time to myself before I went back to the hospital Monday morning. I was thankful for long shifts, so I could forget about this messed up weekend.

The other part of me...had been hoping he'd reach out. I didn't want to talk to him, but I wanted him to want to talk to me. Which sounded ridiculous, but there was no way *I* was making the first move. I'd thrown that ring at him. Ball was in his court.

Cézanne was in the lounge when I dropped my stuff off in the morning. "What are you doing here?"

"I moved over to a pediatric ER for an extra week. I thought it would help me in family practice," she said as she finished off a coffee. "I heard you had an eventful weekend."

"Blah," I said. "I don't want to talk about it."

"Well, let me tell you about *my* weekend," she gushed.

I sat down to finish my own coffee. "By all means."

"I might or might not have hooked up with Gerome."

My eyes widened. "*Gerome*, Gerome? From the soccer team?"

"The one. We met at a family reunion. Our families don't really get along, and we're not related, but it's like his cousin and my cousin got married. That kind of thing. A cousin of a cousin married his cousin of a cousin of a cousin." She waved her hand. "We kind of got into it, and then one thing led to another."

"Oh my God! That's amazing. I can't believe this."

"Me either, honestly. I always thought he was just like his family, and he always thought I was just like mine. Turns out...nope."

I squealed with Cézanne over her new boy, excited that at least *someone* had gotten some this weekend.

Then a man walked into the lounge.

"Uh, I have a delivery for Annie Donoghue."

"That's me," I said in confusion.

He held up a giant vase of a dozen red roses. "Here you go. Enjoy!"

I took them from him, and then he walked away.

"Shit, girl. Look at that!" Cézanne said.

I set them down on the counter and took the card out with a trembling hand.

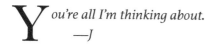

Y*ou're all I'm thinking about.*
    —J

. . .

Cézanne read over my shoulder and did a little dance. "Oh boy, he's in deep."

My eyes were wide as I stared at the stunning blooms. They smelled amazing. They weren't enough, but maybe they were a start. A sign that he was still thinking about me after what had happened. What girl could turn down flowers anyway?

"You going to forgive him yet?"

I set the card down with a sly smile. "Not yet."

* * *

Tuesday was hectic.

I felt dead on my feet by the time lunch rolled around. How had Tuesday turned into such a Monday? I trekked into the cafeteria to find Cézanne. She waved me over.

"You're late," she accused.

I shook my head and yawned. "It's been crazy."

"Someone delivered pad thai from Thai Pepper for you," she said. "I claimed it."

I blinked. "Pad thai?"

"Yep." Cézanne shot me the look. "No note though."

I bit my lip in excitement.

I didn't have to guess who had gotten it for me.

Neither did she.

* * *

"**W**hat do you think he's going to send today?" Cézanne asked the next morning.

I rolled my eyes at her. "Nothing."

"Psh, two days in a row, and he hasn't called or texted? Boy has a plan. You'll get something."

"I don't think so. If he wanted to make it up to me, he'd come here and apologize."

"Would he? Or would he send you another dozen roses?"

"Shush," I said, hitting her with my mask as I left the lounge.

Wednesday, unlike Tuesday, was dead in the ER. I never thought that was a real thing. It was always swamped. Not that the doctors let me slack or anything. I was thoroughly busy with the dreaded paperwork.

By the time I was off some blear-eyed twelve hours later, the sun was fully down, and all I wanted to do was crawl into bed and wait for tomorrow. Sutton had texted earlier to see when I was going to be home, which meant she probably wanted to hang out. I'd told her when I got off, but I really didn't want to do anything.

I strode out with Cézanne at my side.

"I guess I was wrong."

"How often do you say that?" I asked her.

She shrugged. "Often enough. But I really thought he'd do something."

A woman jumped out of an idling Uber Eats car when we started down the drive. "Annie Donoghue?"

I furrowed my brows. "Uh, yes?"

"These are for you." The woman passed me a white box with the Death by Chocolate logo on the top.

Cézanne smirked. "Never mind. I wasn't wrong."

I opened the lid and found a dozen chocolate-fudge cupcakes with chocolate icing. My favorite.

"Are you going to eat all of those?" she asked.

"Have one," I offered.

She cackled. "And here we both thought that he wasn't going to do anything."

"I can't believe he's doing this. I really can't." I pulled out a cupcake and bit into it as we walked to our cars. It was as chocolatey delicious as I remembered. "God, these are good."

"I can believe it," Cézanne said. "And I'm so glad that I get to enjoy the spoils."

I laughed and rolled my eyes at her. "You're ridiculous."

Carefully balancing the box of cupcakes on the hood of my car, I unlocked the door and then got inside with the dessert. My insides flipped at another day of presents. It wasn't the same as him apologizing, but maybe this was right. Maybe a good grovel showed that he cared more than his words would. Especially after all the vitriol we'd spewed at each other.

I immediately sent a text to Sutton with a picture of the cupcake box.

Traitor. You could have warned me.

She sent back a picture of her winking.

Hopeless romantic.

* * *

Maybe Cézanne was right. Maybe he would send something else today.

"What do you think he'll do today?" Jennifer asked excitedly from her seat on the sofa.

"I have no idea."

"But you think he will do something?"

"Well, yesterday, I doubted him and then..."

"Cupcakes."

"Exactly," I agreed. "So...I don't know."

Then the doorbell rang.

I jumped. I put down one of yesterday's cupcakes that I'd been having for breakfast and hurried to the door. I couldn't even believe this was happening to me. I'd never had a guy do anything like this. Once it was done, it was done. Yet, here he was, making an effort to apologize. Not with base words, but with actions.

I peered through the door and found a guy on a bicycle. I pulled the door open slightly. "Can I help you?"

"I have a delivery for Annie Donoghue."

"That's me," I said, jittery and excited by the prospect.

He passed over a large cup with the letter *J&B* scrawled across it. Plus, a little brown bag. I took them both from him and turned back to find Jennifer had jumped off the couch and was running to see.

"What is it? What is it? What is it?"

I took a small sip of the drink. Fuck, it was exactly how I took it. "Coffee."

"And?" She gestured to the bag.

I opened it and found two breakfast burrito from my favorite food truck. I pulled out the first, and my name

K.A. LINDE

was scrawled on it. I set that one down and looked at the other with a laugh.

"What?" she asked.

I passed it to her. "It has your name on it."

She melted. "He sent *me* breakfast, too?"

"Appears so. Guess he didn't want you to go hungry."

"Can he be my boyfriend, too?" Jennifer asked with a laugh.

I rolled my eyes. "You're silly. I'm going into the hospital. Enjoy the burrito."

"Can't wait to find out about tomorrow!"

A small smile graced my features. Despite myself, I couldn't wait either.

* * *

Friday was my day off.

I was supposed to be studying for my boards. Not wondering if Jordan was going to send me another surprise. And if he was...what it could possibly be.

Cézanne sent me a text in the middle of the day.

Anything yet?

Nope.

It'll be there.

Then, thirty minutes later, Sutton messaged.

Have you heard from Jordan?

I haven't.

Gah, I can't wait to see what he has planned.

Maybe nothing.

I don't believe that.

I didn't either. Not anymore.

An hour later, Jennifer was in my messages.

What romantic thing happened to you today?

Nothing. Just studying.

Tell me when it happens!

What if nothing happens?

But because everyone was messaging me, I couldn't get anything done. Eventually, I gave up and took a shower. I'd just finished and was toweling off my hair when the doorbell rang.

"God," I grumbled, throwing on sweats and a T-shirt as I rushed for the door. "I'm coming."

I yanked the door open and came face-to-face with a flower delivery service from my favorite boutique, The Fig & Flower.

"Annie?" the woman asked.

"Yes," I said, looking at the roses in her hand.

"I have quite a surprise for you."

"You do?"

"I do," she said with a big, genuine smile.

Then I saw that there were other people behind her. Three other people in flower-shop aprons, carrying their own bouquets of flowers.

"Can I come in?"

I blindly opened the door and watched them all parade into my house, putting flowers on seemingly every surface. A few dozen on the dining room table, a few in the kitchen, the coffee table, around the television, and the side table. The house was so consumed by flowers that it felt as if my house had been transformed into a flower shop. My mouth hung open at the sheer quantity of the display.

Then the helpers disappeared, and the woman stepped up to me. "One more thing, dear." She handed me a single red rose and an envelope. "You must have someone in your life who loves you very much."

I could barely speak around the knot in my throat. "Thank you."

"My pleasure. Truly."

She walked out, and I sank into a chair at the table. I dropped the rose and the note on the table and stared around the room in shock. I couldn't even fathom how much this must have cost him. That he'd even thought to do it.

I should open the note. I wanted to. But my hands were shaking too hard.

Instead, I got my phone out and took a video of the room with all the flowers before zeroing in on the note. Then I sent the whole thing to a group chat with Cézanne, Jennifer, and Sutton.

The texts came in instantaneously.

Jennifer: !!!!!!!!!!!!!!!!

Cézanne: Now that's how it's done! What's in the card?

Sutton: OH. MY. GOD! He went all out. Look at all those flowers.

Jennifer: Note?

Sutton: Open it! Open it!

Cézanne: You're KILLING us, Annie. Literally killing us.

Sutton: We're dead.

Jennifer: DEAD!

I laughed at my friends and their enthusiasm. They were the best. And it gave me the courage to break the seal on the envelope with my name on it and pull out the letter.

M *eet me at the barn tonight at 7 o'clock.*
    —J

I took a picture of the note and sent it to my friends.
    Sutton: OMG! Are you going to go?
Cézanne: You have to go.
Jennifer: You absolutely do.
Sutton: Annie! What are you going to do?!?
I bit my lip. All week, he'd sent me things and not shown his face. He gave me the space I needed to deal with what had happened last weekend. And he'd done it with poise and so much romantic groveling. It'd be a lie to say he didn't care. That he hadn't been trying to prove he wanted to make up.

I was glad to have that week, that space. I'd anticipated the deliveries and thought about him all week. Last week had been a nightmare, a real colossal failure. But it didn't change how I felt about Jordan. It didn't change that I was still going to be in Lubbock this fall. And I didn't forgive him just because he sent a few flowers or anything, but his reasoning, though misguided, had been in my best interest. He'd thought he was leaving me so that I didn't have to choose. And he didn't know that I'd already chosen.

It was stupid and wrong, but also selfless. Stupidly selfless.

He hadn't wanted to hurt me and in trying not to hurt me, he'd made everything worse. But that didn't mean I had to leave it like that. Maybe I, at least, owed him a conversation.

I texted back to my friends.

Okay...okay...I think I'm going.

40

ANNIE

*M*y hand rested on the handle to the barn door.

I wasn't the type of person to hesitate, but still, I hesitated. Last weekend had been terrible. I was a firm believer in the idea that when someone showed you who they were, you believed them. Was I going back on that after finding out who Jordan really was? *Was* that even who he really was?

My hand clenched the cold metal doorknob. I could walk away. I could turn around right now and walk away from all of this. And yet, I hadn't moved.

Because I didn't want to walk away.

I'd been a fool about Jordan Wright once before. I'd hardened my heart against him, avoided him, and done everything in my power to not think about his too-handsome face or those broad shoulders or the way he'd made me feel inexplicably complete. And it hadn't worked. It just hadn't worked. I'd fallen for him even harder and faster than the last time, and I didn't want it to fucking end.

Sometimes, relationships needed work. I couldn't run away every time it got hard. I couldn't assume he was a bad person off of one interaction. Not after the last couple months of perfection. Didn't he deserve a chance to prove me wrong?

So, I took a deep breath and yanked on the door, prepared to hear him out.

I gasped softly at the interior of the barn. I'd seen it all done up for the event last weekend, but it was nothing compared to what it looked like now. Jordan must have had Nora stage the place. There was no other explanation. Soft white drapery made the twinkle lights appear to be constellations across a night sky. Flowers bloomed in bouquets around the room, interspersed with every size candle imaginable. The room glowed with flickering candlelight, and at its center was Jordan Wright.

My breath caught at the sight of him in a sharp suit and tie, standing with his hands in his pockets, waiting for me.

"Hey," I said as I came to stand before him. My eyes continued to scan the room, unsure if I should settle entirely on him. "This is elaborate."

He smiled. Such a Jordan smile. Soft on the edges with his eyes lighting up. "I thought you might need elaborate."

"You could have started with *I'm sorry*."

He finished the last step between us. "I'm sorry."

"You're right. Probably not enough."

"Probably not," he agreed with a small laugh. "Worth a try though."

"Suppose so."

I fiddled with my fingers, distinctly feeling the absence of my ring. I was so used to twirling it when I was nervous.

"Do you know why I bought the winery?" he finally asked.

I blinked at the change in subject. It wasn't what I'd expected. "Because Hollin and Julian cajoled you into it."

"Well, that's the reason I got involved, but not the reason I eventually said yes."

I shrugged. "No, you never mentioned."

He held his arms out, gesturing to the barn around him. "When I looked at this barn, I saw a dirt-filled piece of junk that we'd sink way too much money into to ever make it profitable. It was a bad investment, and I didn't want to do it. But when we came over to look at the place, something hit me at the sight of it." He sighed. "This was our first date. You brought me to this ridiculous bar and tried to get me to line dance. I hadn't laughed that much in years. I was smitten. And I wasn't ready to let those memories be demolished. I wanted to keep them. So, every time I walked inside, I saw you in cowboy boots with that effervescent smile on your face."

I swallowed hard at his words. "What do you see now?"

"You throwing this ring at me," he said, holding the claddagh ring up to the light. "And how much I completely fucked it up."

"Yeah, you did."

"There's not an excuse for how I reacted last week. I cut you out of my life while I tried to deal with my mom's news. Then I overreacted to everything and treated you horribly. I'm so sorry for all of that. I was worried about my mom and her dealing with cancer *again* that I couldn't process anything. I thought I was making the right decision by letting you go. I couldn't even see that I was making the decision *for* you and not *with* you."

I swallowed. "Yeah, I thought we were a team."

"I know. I'm sorry about that. I had a long talk with my mom about it. She was actually the one who suggested the groveling."

I chuckled. "She's a smart woman."

"She is. She really is. For so long, I've thought that I was a mirror image of my father. That I hurt the people closest to me, and I had no control over the fury that burned through me. But my mom made me realize that I'm not just like my dad. That I get to choose who I am. And I choose to never be that person ever again."

"Sounds like a good start."

"And I want you to know that Seattle..." He shook his head, taking a step forward and reaching for my hand. I thought I'd pull away, but God, his hand felt so right in mine. "Seattle was never a pipe dream. I shouldn't have said that. It was what I really wanted."

"Me too," I whispered.

"I know this won't make up for how I reacted last weekend, but I might have a solution."

I tilted my head. "A solution to what?"

"Seattle."

"Oh. There's no solution to that, Jordan. Once ranks are in, that's that."

"I know that that is normally how it works," he assured me. "But I decided to see if there was a way around it. So, I spent the last week on the phone with Cush figuring out who to speak to about the position. You earned it on your own merit, I just pulled the strings to make it happen."

My body froze in place. My brain couldn't catch up to the words that he was saying. I blinked and blinked again. This couldn't be real. It just...it wasn't possible.

"What are you saying?"

"Seattle is going to offer you a place in their residency program," he told me. "And I want to go with you, Annie."

My hands were shaking. "How...how is that possible? I just...I can't believe it, Jordan."

"You only chose Lubbock because of me. I'll be damned if you stay here and regret it." He took my hands in his. "I want you to have everything, Annie. Everything and more."

"But...what about your mom?" I gasped.

"I spoke to her and Julian. We discussed me leaving and they both agreed that this was different than last time. I was going to stay in Vancouver for no real reason except complacency. If I wanted to be with you, then leaving made sense."

"But your job..."

"I'd already discussed it with Morgan."

My eyes widened. "You had?"

He nodded. "Long before I knew about this. She said I

could work in a Seattle office and commute on and off to Vancouver. I would do anything to make it work."

Tears formed in my eyes. Damn it! I'd sworn that I wouldn't cry. But somehow, that stupid comment had hit me so hard in the feels. Because I had wanted Seattle and I wanted to make it work so bad, too. I'd wanted what he'd had there that weekend so bad.

And now...here he was, offering to me on a silver platter.

Everything I'd ever wanted.

The residency. A cross-country move. The man of my dreams.

Except...was it what I wanted? Was it really?

"No," I said softly.

Jordan's brow furrowed. "No? You don't want me to go?"

I laughed softly. "No. I think you were right last weekend."

He looked cautious. "About what?"

"As much as I hadn't wanted to hear it, Seattle was a pipe dream."

"It can be real."

I shook my head. This felt right. This felt more right than anything else. I'd wanted Seattle for no real reason except that I'd convinced myself that I wanted to get the hell out of Lubbock. But did I really want to go? When I stopped to think about it, it didn't even feel real. My best friends were here. My parents and Isaac and Aly were here. Isaac and Peyton's wedding was happening soon. And Jordan...Jordan was here with his family, too. If I wanted something with him, would he hate that I'd taken him away? As much as he thought I'd hate him for taking away Seattle? How could I leave when I had everything right here?

"I could," I said carefully. "I can't even believe that you managed to circumvent the ranking system. Is there anything a Wright can't do?" He laughed, a real smile hitting his features. "But we'd just decided on Seattle because I'd always said I wanted to leave. At the end of the day, if I'd wanted to leave, wouldn't I have done it a lot sooner? I love Lubbock. Everyone I love is here. So, when the choice came, it was so easy to change my order, Jordan. Too easy. I did it as soon as we found out about your mom. It was almost like I never really wanted to go in the first place."

"Fuck," he breathed. "That same night?"

"Yes. I'd been planning to surprise you the night of the party. To tell you that we didn't have to move to Seattle. We could stay here with your mom and be happy. But then..."

"Then I went and fucked it up."

"Yes, you did." I laughed as he pulled me into a hug. "You fucked everything up."

"I'm so sorry. I'm sorry for everything I said and did that day." He tilted my face up to look at him. "I thought I was making it better by fixing the Seattle situation."

"You were," I said. "I'm not sure I would have known you were serious before then. That you really wanted this."

"Of course, I want this to work. I'd do anything for you, Annie. I'm in love with you."

"You're...in love with me?" I whispered.

He nodded, drawing me a little closer and brushing a strand of my red hair off of my face. "Unequivocally."

And I saw it for the truth. Jordan Wright loved me. He'd gone above and beyond to fix my future...our future. I said that I'd hear him out, listen to what he had to say. This didn't sound like a man still in a temper. This sounded like the man who took care of me and adored all of my eccentricities and loved me...unequivocally.

And my own feelings were so clear in that moment.

So real and so raw.

Jordan Wright was the only person who had made me feel complete. If I didn't hide from myself, I knew that he was the only person I wanted. The only person that I could imagine spending my life with. I'd run from him long enough. No more excuses.

"You don't have to say anything," he said carefully. "But this week has been torture without you."

I laughed softly. "You could have come in person instead of sending gifts."

"What would have been the fun in that?" he asked. "I think I won your friends over before you."

I rolled my eyes. "Was that planned?"

"It wasn't. Just a bonus. My only concern was you." He cupped my jaw. "I love you, Annie. I love you and I missed you and I want to be with you. What do you want?"

I smacked his arm as I tried to keep from crying. "I want to be with you, Jordan. Of course, I do. I just...I don't want what happened Saturday to be my life."

"Never," he insisted. "I can't promise that I won't get

mad again, but I would never risk losing you. I'm not going to shut you out. You get all of me."

"I like that," I admitted.

"Can you forgive me?"

"If you keep sending cupcakes," I joked.

He laughed, bringing his lips down, almost hesitantly onto mine. "All the cupcakes you want."

"I'm holding you to that, Wright."

"Everything I am is yours." The kiss deepened as he drew my mouth open, brushing his tongue against mine.

"I love you," I whispered against his mouth.

"I love you, too." He kissed me again, harder, full of promise.

And when he pulled back, he removed my ring from his coat pocket and held it out to me.

"Can I get back to guarding your heart?"

The tears came for real this time, and I nodded emphatically as he slid the ring into place on my hand. Where I never intended to remove it again.

EPILOGUE

$\mathcal{T}$he grand opening for Wright Vineyard was finally here. Everyone had been working day and night to get it up to tip-top shape. The new harvest of grapes wouldn't be in yet, but the barn, cellars, and grounds were officially ready. Tours would be happening. Cosmere had one free weekend to come to Lubbock to perform. And the town was buzzing about the new venture.

Not to mention, Jordan's attorney had made it perfectly clear to the Sinclairs what would happen if they did anything to mess with this opening. So, it was unlikely that the ghost of the vineyard would rear its head.

The front entrance was teeming with people for the exclusive Cosmere show. Apparently, people had started lining up hours ago. It was madness. I guessed the last show getting broken up by the police had really made everyone want to come.

They'd actually hired security this time. I flashed my

staff lanyard and bypassed the line and went into the barn. The barn had gone fully minimalist to account for all the people. Jordan had gotten expanded capacity approved for the concert. Another precaution against the Sinclairs.

"Hey, Nora!" I called as I jogged up to her. "Seen my boyfriend?"

She graduated two weeks ago and had fully nose-dived into the vineyard. I could already see her touch everywhere.

"I think he's backstage."

"Thanks."

"Hey," she said, tapping my tank top. "Do you see that?"

I glanced over to where she nodded her head to find Jennifer with her camera around her neck and Julian standing in front of her. They were both laughing at whatever he was saying.

"Oh," I said softly with a wide smile.

"Yeah. He went right over to her when she showed up."

"*Really*?"

"Will report back on the adorable flirting."

"Definitely. Let me know. I thought Jennifer was on her *ninety days no guys* kick."

Nora shrugged. "She mentioned that to me after that abominable date last week. All about how she was—how did she put it?—focusing on loving herself first."

"Yeah. That's what she said to me, too. How long do you think she'll hold out if Julian pursues this?"

"A week," Nora said with a laugh.

"I'll take that bet," I said, winking at her as I disappeared to find Jordan.

I was happy for Jennifer.

This spring, she'd gone through a string of bad dates. Like *really* bad dates. She'd put herself out there, and it had backfired wildly. I didn't know if she'd go for Julian again, but I couldn't wait to find out.

I bypassed security to get backstage and found the entirety of Cosmere lounging around a long table. I tried to suppress my fangirling. Campbell was a totally normal guy. Why wouldn't the rest of them be the same?

"Annie!" Campbell said, jumping up from his seat and dragging me over to the rest of the band. He'd been back a few times since the last show. He claimed Lubbock brought him inspiration, and he was writing like he hadn't in years.

"Annie, this is the band. Yorke on guitar." He pointed to a tall, broad guy with hair pulled into a man bun and a full beard. "Vivian on bass."

"Viv," she corrected him. "Just call me Viv."

Viv had electric-purple hair cut into a sharp bob. She was a stunner.

"This is Santi," Campbell said, pointing to the drummer in a destroyed black T-shirt and a pair of drumsticks. "And Michael on keys."

Michael had short black curls and honey eyes that the girls went wild for. Not speaking from experience...

"Nice to meet you all," I said a little breathlessly. "I was looking for Jordan."

"Oh, he just stepped out."

I nodded at them all again, trying to ignore the

fangirling, and headed to the back entrance. Just as I got to it, Jordan opened the door.

"Annie."

"Hey, I was looking for you."

He tugged me tight against him and pressed his lips against mine. "I missed you."

"You too."

Jordan was true to his word. There had been no repeat of what had happened. Not even a sign of his fury. It wasn't completely gone, of course. Nothing could just disappear, but we were working on it together. He'd come a long way.

"I do have someone that I want you to meet though."

"You do?" I asked in surprise.

He hadn't mentioned that anyone else was coming to the opening.

"Yeah. It was unexpected for me. Julian doesn't even know yet."

I arched my eyebrows. "Who—"

But my question was cut off by the man who stepped into the back entrance of the winery with all the presence of a Wright. He looked so much like Jordan and Julian that there was no denying that this was their father.

"Oh my God," I whispered.

"Annie, this is my dad."

Owen Wright stuck his hand out. "Annie, I've heard so much about you. It's truly a pleasure to finally meet you."

I'd heard *a lot* about Owen over the years. That he was a terrible father, tried to steal the company from Morgan, and generally ruined his sons' lives. But since Jordan and I had gotten back together, I'd also heard all the good stories about Owen. The ones that he'd tried not to remember in all of his anger at his dad. I'd known that they were trying for some sort of reconciliation. I just hadn't expected...well, this.

"It's nice to meet you, too," I said as I shook his hand.

"I think I have you to thank for this," Owen said.

"Me?"

"Yes, I think you're the cause for this all-new Jordan. I'm proud of how far he's come and happy that he's found someone so incredible in his life."

I flushed. "I'm just glad that he's happy."

"And I am." Jordan slipped a hand around my waist.

"Well, we should do dinner while I'm in town," Owen said. "Maybe Julian and his girlfriend could come, too."

Jordan winced. "Julian isn't seeing anyone right now. But the three of us would be great."

"Agreed," Owen said. "I'm going to go find him before this concert gets started and I miss the chance."

Jordan looked conflicted about it but eventually let him go. His dad disappeared from backstage to find Julian.

"This is a huge step, Jordan."

"Yeah. We're really doing better. Julian still doesn't want to talk to him though. So...I don't know how that conversation is going to go."

"It's going to be fine," I assured him. "The show is about to start anyway. So, they won't have long to talk."

"It won't take long for my dad to screw it up. Maybe I should..."

"Let Julian deal with his own problems. You can't protect him from everything."

"I know," he said finally. "Still hard."

I pressed another kiss to his lips, and he pulled me back out of the barn. Cosmere was set to go on any minute. I could hear that they'd let in the massive crowd from outside. I giggled as Jordan pushed me into the side of the barn.

"Hooking up behind the barn. So original."

He laughed and buried his head into my neck, as his hands roamed under my tank top.

"Hey," he said, leaning his forehead against mine.

"Hey," I breathed.

"I love you."

"I love you, too."

"What do you think of this?"

"Of what? Us?"

"Sure."

I ran my hand down his chest and tugged him closer by his belt. "I like us."

He kissed me again. "What do you think about moving in?"

My eyes rounded. "To the *barn*?"

He laughed and kissed me again firmer. "Move in with me, Annie."

"Well, I need to talk to Jen. She'd have to find a new roommate or get a new place."

"Is that a yes?"

"I'll think about it."

He kissed me again. "Move in with me."

I giggled. "Yes, yes, yes. Of course, I want to move in with you."

"Good. That's what I wanted to hear."

"Pushy," I said as a joke.

He winked at me and then pulled my hand up to his lips. He pressed a kiss to the claddagh ring he'd gotten me, which I still to this day never took off.

"Going to have to get used to that, love." He looked down at the ring. "And maybe get you another ring."

My eyes rounded. "Jordan! One thing at a time."

He chuckled as he pulled me back to him while the first notes of Cosmere's hit song "I See the Real You" started up. He wrapped an arm around me, and we started slow-dancing to the upbeat music.

"Fine. One thing at a time. But I want everything with you, Annie. I want you in my house, in my bed, wearing my ring, with my name."

"You want me to be a Wright?"

"With benefits."

"Of course," I said with a laugh. "I might find this acceptable."

"Good. Annie Wright has a nice ring to it."

"It sure does." I shivered at the words. "Should we go back inside?"

He just held me closer. "I think I'll stay out here and enjoy this dance with my future wife."

I snuggled closer to him, still unable to believe that after all that we'd gone through, we were right here, in this moment. This unimaginable moment of utter perfection.

Jordan Wright was mine, and I was his.

Benefits and all.

THE END

ACKNOWLEDGMENTS

It was such a joy to be able to return to the world of the Wrights. So I would like to thank the readers, who have come year after year to meet this family set in the dusty, Texas town I live in. I never thought it would have as much magic as it brought to me, and I can't thank you enough for letting me continue to do what I love for a living. You're the best! And I can't WAIT for you to meet Julian & Jennifer!

ABOUT THE AUTHOR

K.A. Linde is the *USA Today* bestselling author of more than thirty novels. She has a Masters degree in political science from the University of Georgia, was the head campaign worker for the 2012 presidential campaign at the University of North Carolina at Chapel Hill, and served as the head coach of the Duke University dance team.

She loves reading fantasy novels, binge-watching Supernatural, traveling to far off destinations, baking insane desserts, and dancing in her spare time.

She currently lives in Lubbock, Texas, with her husband and two super-adorable puppies.

Visit her online: www.kalinde.com

Or Facebook, Instagram, Twitter, & Tiktok:
@authorkalinde

For exclusive content, free books, and giveaways every month. www.kalinde.com/subscribe

CPSIA information can be obtained
at www.ICGtesting.com
Printed in the USA
LVHW111407010721
691676LV00011B/169